### "Red Diver, Green Diver, I want you both home. Now."

Rourke's voice blared urgently. "Negative on that come home order, sir. We've got a problem. Green Diver's air hose is tangled."

Sunday scowled. "Why is it every accident has to turn into a full-scale disaster? Status report, Red Diver."

Static sizzled like bacon in a frying pan for over five seconds, then another ten seconds. Finally Rourke came on again, shakier than before. "Topside, this is Red Diver. Green Diver is more fouled up than ever. What do I do?"

"Stay put. Help is on the way." Sunday jammed the mike onto the jack and whirled. He surveyed the other trainees. "I need a volunteer."

"I'll go, sir," Carl said.

Refusing to acknowledge him, Sunday took a step toward the others. "Isn't there one of you with the guts to do the job? One lousy volunteer is all I'm asking."

Brasher moved, donning his helmet. "We're wasting time, sir. Give me the extra line and hose."

Chief Sunday was practically beside himself. He brought the gear himself and shoved it at Carl. He asked almost plantively, "Why *you*? They hate your guts."

Smoothly securing his brass helmet, Carl slowed just enough to say, "I's what a Navy diver does, sir."

# MEN OF HONOR

A Novel by David Robbins

Based on the
Motion Picture Screenplay
by Scott Marshall Smith

AN ONYX BOOK

ONYX
Published by New American Library, a division of
Penguin Putnam Inc., 375 Hudson Street,
New York, New York 10014, U.S.A.
Penguin Books Ltd, 27 Wrights Lane,
London W8 5TZ, England
Penguin Books Australia Ltd, Ringwood,
Victoria, Australia
Penguin Books Canada Ltd, 10 Alcorn Avenue,
Toronto, Ontario, Canada M4V 3B2
Penguin Books (N.Z.) Ltd, 182–190 Wairau Road,
Auckland 10, New Zealand

Penguin Books Ltd, Registered Offices:
Harmondsworth, Middlesex, England

First published by Onyx, an imprint of New American Library,
a division of Penguin Putnam Inc.

First Printing, October 2000
10  9  8  7  6  5  4  3  2  1

# Foreword
## by Carl Brashear

Not in my wildest dreams did I ever think I would be the subject of a major Hollywood film. I grew up on a farm in the rural section of Kentucky, three miles from Sonora. Each morning after I finished chopping wood, milking cows, and feeding the livestock, I walked three miles to a one-room segregated schoolhouse. I did not like living and working on the farm, but it was just the way most colored people lived in that community those days. High school wasn't encouraged. The nearest high school for colored people was in Elizabethtown, fourteen miles away.

While most of my childhood friends found jobs in the area, I wanted more. In 1948 I left the farm to join the United States Navy. I was seventeen years old, educated only through the seventh grade, with little work experience except at a gas station. I hoped the Navy would offer me more opportunities and a brighter future.

I had no idea what job I would do for my country. Following basic training, the Navy classified me as a steward. In those days, most colored sailors were given this assignment, which involved cooking and serving meals to the officers, plus maintaining the officers' living quarters. I accepted this stereotyped position assigned to me. I had no other choice.

Initially the whole new experience of being a sailor

frightened me. Going from the farm to serving meals to high-ranking officers made me nervous. Regardless of my assignment, I just wanted to do a good job. It took a few months, but I soon began to adjust to military life and befriend some of the other people in my command.

I soon realized that in order to transfer from the steward branch to the seaman branch and advance in the Navy, I needed more education. I enrolled in the United States Armed Forces Institute, which helped me through all the basic math, physics, and other courses that I needed to complete the General Education Development tests and gain a high school equivalency certificate. I took additional military correspondence courses and gained on-the-job training in order to pass the fleetwide advancement examination with a high score. Then I had a chance to transfer from the steward branch into the seaman branch.

The first time I saw a man dive, I knew I wanted to be a diver. But the first time I put in a request to be a diver, the Navy did not approve it. As a seaman, I took all of the naval courses such as seamanship, rigging, damage control, fire fighting, boat handling, navigation, and painting. All these courses put me on the fast track toward rating as a boatswain's mate and allowed me entrance into the deep-sea diving school in Bayonne, New Jersey.

But once in Bayonne, I soon learned that coloreds were not readily accepted into the diving program. On two occasions, I found a note on my bunk that read, *We will drown you today, nigger*. The training officer told me that I couldn't handle a curriculum that dealt with diving, physics, diving medicine, and underwater salvage and recovery. The school's training program was designed to place each student under physical and psychological pressure, but I was faced with additional pressure due to the color of my skin. I studied alone. I didn't get the extra instruction given to the other students. Despite these setbacks, I knew that it was important to remain calm. A diver cannot be easily shaken under pressure. I stayed focused on my goal by having pride in myself, being determined, and having a can-do spirit and a positive attitude. In 1953, I successfully completed the program.

Following my graduation, I continued my path of advancement in rating as a boatswain's mate and, my specialty, as a deep-sea diver. My assignments as a deep-sea diver included salvage and rescue, submarine rescue, temporary additional duty as a petty officer in charge of a high-powered crash and rescue boat, and as aquatic escort to President Eisenhower's yacht, the *Barbara Ann*.

On March 25, 1966, while assigned to overseas duty on the USS *Hoist ARS 40,* I lost the lower portion of my left leg during a salvage operation. A pipe came loose, flew across the deck, and struck my leg below the knee. The accident happened at five o'clock in the evening, but I didn't make it to the hospital until eleven o'clock that night. They brought me in thinking I was dead. When I finally arrived at the Portsmouth Naval Hospital in Virginia two months later in May, I had developed gangrene. A team of doctors reviewed my situation and predicted that they could cut off and then reattach my leg, but that it would then be four inches shorter. They also said that I could be walking in a brace within thirty-six months. I did not concur. I told them I wanted my leg amputated. They thought I was crazy.

I realized that I could not perform my duties as a chief petty officer and a deep-sea diver in a brace, and that I would have a better chance of continuing my job with a prosthesis. Despite all that had happened to me, I remained focused and confident about returning to full duty. It had never been done before, but I felt that God was going to help me to accomplish the task.

However, the naval officers and doctors were of another opinion. They reasoned that with an artificial leg, I wouldn't be able to support a 290-pound deep-sea diving outfit while swimming underwater using SCUBA; they disbelieved that I could run two miles for physical fitness or that I could keep my balance on a ship in rough seas. They said I did not meet the physical requirements set forth in the Navy Regulations, ETC. The Navy began to make preparations for my dismissal on a medical discharge.

I simply could not accept their decision. I had not yet attained the goals I had set for myself. In my efforts to prove that I could still do my job, I had to defy my superiors, my doctors, and all those people who said I could not continue to perform my duties as a chief petty officer and as a deep-sea diver.

Soon after I was fitted with a prosthesis, I became determined to secretly leave my hospital room and engage in strenuous diving evolution, physical exercises, and other training maneuvers that sometimes caused my stump to bleed inside the prosthesis, causing severe pain in my leg. I often had to soak my raw stump in a bucket of hot salt water to ease the pain and stop the bleeding.

After fourteen months of struggle and fighting to prove myself, I was finally able to convince the Naval Bureau of Medicine and Surgery and the Bureau of Naval Personnel that I was capable of returning to full active duty. I was restored to full duty in March 1968, the first person in naval history to ever gain this status as an amputee.

Let me say right now that I thank God for all the people in the medical profession because they fixed me. But you see, it was left up to me to do the rest and continue on my journey toward achieving my goals.

Today, people ask me how I did it. I tell them it was through faith in God, by being determined, and by retaining a positive attitude and a can-do spirit. In spite of my adversities and misfortune, the word "can't" was erased from my little vocabulary.

The accomplishment brought me recognition through magazine and newspaper articles, as well as local and national radio and television programs. Following an appearance in 1979 on the television show *Comeback,* a number of individuals and networks tried to put a movie based on my life into development. These efforts were unsuccessful until 1995, when a member of Bill Cosby's production company approached me. The representative arranged for me to meet screenwriter Scott Marshall Smith. As a result of our meeting, a screenplay was written.

Hollywood director George Tillman, Jr. and producer Bob Teitel expressed interest in my story. When I met these two young men, I felt a confidence that I had not felt before. I knew that my story would make it to the big screen. After all these years, it was finally going to happen. During that first meeting, we discussed facts about my life, highlights of my naval career, filming locations, the use of necessary props and equipment, and even who would portray me. Cuba Gooding Jr. was our first choice.

Cuba and I developed a fantastic working relationship. I visited the set on many occasions and made myself available to Cuba for consultation to support his fine work. There were many scenes that I found disturbing because Cuba's portrayal of me was very real. Watching him act, I was instantly transported to the day I came in late to start plowing the fields with my father, and seeing my father's hands bleed from the hard work. I relived the day that I showed up at the deep-sea diving school, where they thought that I was there just to be a cook. The amputation scene was especially disturbing to watch as it was filmed, as was the scene that showed me having to complete twelve steps on my artificial leg wearing a 290-pound deep-sea diving outfit. From our close work together, I can say that I grew to love Cuba like a son. I am very pleased with Cuba Gooding Jr.'s outstanding and powerful performance. Co-star and veteran actor Robert De Niro was also inspiring to watch. It was such a joy to watch these two Academy Award®-winners working together.

It is impossible for this film to include all of the difficult salvage and recovery operations I conducted, or all of the dangerous rescue missions in which I took part. In addition, the film does not include a number of other challenging situations that I encountered during my naval career as a result of being a black man in a white-dominated profession as a deep-sea diver. However, the film does portray very honestly the spirit and courage it took to advance through the Navy to become the first black American deep-sea diver, and the first amputee to attain the rate of master chief petty officer and master diver.

Some people in the Navy may have used my race against me, but I never used my race against myself. I have always viewed the color of my skin as a source of pride, strength, and inspiration. I believe that in America, anyone can achieve what they want if they work hard, and have faith in themselves and in others, regardless of race, color, or creed.

For the past thirty-four years I have worn my prosthesis proudly, without using a crutch or cane. I do not regret any of my actions and look upon my misfortune more as a nuisance and an inconvenience rather than a disability. I appreciate all the assistance and cooperation the Navy provided in support of this film. I applaud

George Tillman, Jr. for his skillful directing of this movie, and the detailed knowledge he shared with all who were involved with the project.

I am hopeful that the people who read this book and see this film will be inspired to overcome life's difficulties and disabilities by maintaining a positive attitude and can-do spirit. This has been my motto in life, as evidenced in all of those official medical records that refer to me as "that damn stubborn chief petty officer."

*CMBrashear*

Carl Brashear (left) with director George Tillman, Jr.

# Introduction
## by George Tillman, Jr.
## Director of *Men of Honor*

It was in January of 1996 when the script came across my desk. I can remember the day. I had just finished viewing my first cut of *Soul Food*—a two-hour and forty-five-minute editor's cut—and I felt that it was going to be a great movie. I wanted to make another film right away, but I didn't want to sit in front of a computer for another year writing that next story.

This is when my producer, Robert Teitel, came to me and told me about this fabulous script he had just read. It was then called *Navy Diver,* and it was exactly the story I was looking for. Brilliantly written by Scott Marshall Smith (who, incidentally, is from my hometown of Milwaukee, Wisconsin), the script detailed the incredible journey of Carl Brashear to become the United States Navy's first African-American master diver.

I had never heard of Carl Brashear or his achievements. I never knew what the job of a Navy diver was, but I found Carl Brashear's story to be a human story that was inspirational, heartwarming, and important. The script had a strong African-American hero, an interesting view into the world of Navy divers, and engaging characters. Ultimately, the script had something to say.

Bringing the story to the screen would be an incredible challenge. It would be a period piece, covering three decades. In addition, it would require three major underwater scenes, two major action scenes on a boat, and great attention to detail to ensure that the scenes involving naval diving procedure and military etiquette were authentic. And we had to make the film for under thirty-eight million dollars. Could it be done?

As a director coming off a seven-million-dollar debut, I faced a tremendous task. I had never directed underwater sequences, tackled visual effects, or even shot on top of water before—hell, I couldn't even swim. But after I flew to Norfolk, Virginia, one cold winter in November of 1997 to meet Carl Brashear, I was convinced his story had to be told.

If Carl Brashear could endure racism, graduate from diving school with only a seventh-grade education, lose a leg, and still prevail to become a master diver and the first amputee to be given full active duty status in the history of the United States Navy, then I could take on the challenge of making this film.

Inspired by Carl Brashear, I had to become like him. For the young generation, white or black, he's living proof that you can follow your dreams and succeed with determination, no matter what your obstacles are. Carl Brashear made a significant achievement. Though the general public may not yet be familiar with Carl's accomplishments, *Men of Honor* shows that Carl's remarkable triumphs are not to be taken for granted.

It took Carl nineteen years to get his story onscreen. I'm privileged that he chose me and it was a pleasure to have him on the set every day working as an adviser to Cuba Gooding Jr., Robert De Niro, Bob Teitel, myself, and our amazing cast of *Men of Honor*. It was an incredible challenge and an awesome experience for me as a director.

And thanks to Carl, I can swim now.

*George L. Tillman Jr.*

## The Diver's Creed

*The Navy diver is not a fighting man.*
*He is a salvage expert.*
*If it's lost underwater, he finds it.*
*If it's sunk, he brings it up.*
*If it's in the way, he moves it.*

*If he's lucky, he dies young two hundred feet beneath*
*   the waves,*
*Because that is the closest he will ever come to being*
*   a hero.*

*No one in their right mind would ever want the job.*
*Or so they say.*

# PROLOGUE

The hiss of surf lapping the shore was the first sound Billy Sunday heard. The next was the low groan that escaped his lips. He hurt all over. His head, his chest, his hands, hell, even his eyeballs. It felt as if he had collided with a battleship. His head throbbed so bad he could hardly think, and his mouth tasted as if he had sucked on a dead fish. He couldn't remember what day it was, or what year.

*No, wait!* Sunday thought as renewed life seeped into his limbs. The year was 1966. He knew that much. He opened his eyes and discovered he was lying facedown in sand. Forcing his arms to work, he rolled over and looked down at himself. His Navy uniform was a mess, all torn and ragged and bloody. He didn't need to touch his face to know he was bruised and battered, or that it had been days since he last shaved.

Sunday squinted up into the harsh glare of the morning sun. The next second a dark silhouette reared overhead. Blinking, he saw it was a man in a gaudy shirt and bright yellow shorts. A tourist, he guessed.

The man's comment confirmed it. "Nine hundred and forty-eight bucks to bring my kids to North Carolina for some fun on the beach and what do we find? You. Not a good way to start the day, I'd say."

Sunday's gaze shifted to a boy of ten or so who was

staring down at him in undisguised horror. The boy's father glowered and the youngster promptly retreated a safe distance.

"North Carolina?" Sunday said. The last he knew, he had been in Florida. Suppressing the torment, he slowly sat up. An urge to cough came over him, and when he did, fresh blood dribbled over his chin. As sluggish as a snail, he wiped it off.

The vacationer frowned. "I saw you and your three Marine buddies drive in last night. You had quite a party. The noise kept waking us up."

"I don't make friends with Marines," Sunday said curtly. At least, not when he was sober. He tried to stand but couldn't. Sighing, the man pulled him upright—none too gently—and Sunday grimaced as more agony racked his body. They started toward the motel, the vacationer supporting him.

"It's none of my business, mister, but don't you think you're a little old to be drinking all night and picking fights with Marines?"

Sunday was limping, his left leg on fire. "Old? I'm only fifty-one." As they took another step, more of what the man had just said registered. "I picked the fight? Are you sure?"

The vacationer nodded. "You insulted their mothers, for starters. Rather colorfully, I might add. But they didn't seem to appreciate it. They appreciated it even less when you told them the Marine Corps wasn't fit to wipe the Navy's ass."

"I told them that?" Sunday chuckled. "Did I win the fight?"

The man shook his head. "I peeked out my window and saw part of it. You put up a good battle but the odds were stacked against you. And you were so soused, I doubt you could see straight."

"Then maybe I am too old," Sunday said, and was going to grin until he gazed past his benefactor and beheld two husky shore patrolmen approaching at a brisk clip. "Damn. You're right, friend. This isn't a good way to start the day."

An hour later Sunday was seated in a chair at a train station, his wrists manacled, the shore patrolmen on either side, their uniforms crisp and clean, their young faces scrubbed and shaved. Compared to them he resembled a drunken derelict. Ignoring the boy scouts, Sunday focused on the coin-operated TV. An emergency news broadcast had come on, and Walter Cronkite was speaking in grave tones.

". . . thirty-six hours ago an American B-52 bomber crashed into the Mediterranean Sea. Moments before impact the bomber's crew jettisoned a fifty-megaton nuclear warhead. The bomb is capable of leveling a city, and it now lies somewhere at the bottom. At this hour, the greatest naval search in human history is under way . . ."

The camera showed a large convoy of U.S. Navy vessels combing the Mediterranean. Among them was the Navy's lead recovery ship, the USS *Hoist*. A diving platform was being craned out over the seething water and perched on it were a pair of Navy deep-sea divers.

Sunday's interest intensified and he leaned toward the screen.

One of the shore patrolmen noticed. Ropeleski was his name, an arrogant pup who had a habit of smirking whenever he looked at Sunday. "What do you think? Should you be out there with them?"

"Why not?" Sunday absently responded. "I'm the best goddamned diver in the U.S. Navy."

"Hell, you ain't in the Navy, old man," Ropeleski responded. "You're nothing but a damn deserter."

"AWOL!" Sunday gruffly declared. "I was AWOL.

There's a difference. Twenty years ago a man would go on a bender like mine and they'd pin a medal on his chest and take him downtown for a blow job and—" He abruptly stopped. On the TV screen a black Navy diver had appeared and was adjusting his gear. "Ornery son of a bitch," Sunday muttered.

"A friend of yours?" Ropeleski asked.

Sunday chose not to answer. He stared at the screen, remembering.

Ropeleski leaned down and put a hand on Sunday's shoulder. "Don't tell me you're sweet on niggers, old man?"

Cold fury welled up within Sunday but he held it in check. He grinned at the idiot, and Ropeleski laughed. Sunday joined him, hoping to lull them into making a blunder.

The other shore patrolman figured he was just as witty as his friend. "The chief, here, is a damn nigger lover? Say it ain't so!"

Still laughing, Sunday gestured. "What was that, friend?" he asked, pretending he hadn't heard.

The simpleton took the bait and bent over him. "Don't your ears work? I just said that you're a damn—"

Exploding into motion, Sunday slammed his head against the second shore patrolman's jaw and the man folded on the spot, out cold. Ropeleski blinked in astonishment, rooted in his tracks like a great dumb ox as Sunday whirled and deftly looped the manacles around the dumbfounded bigot's wrist.

The chain bit deep into Ropeleski's flesh, so deep he let out with a startled shriek.

"All right, asshole!" Sunday barked. "I've had enough of your bullshit. Now you're going to start addressing me as Master Chief or I'll snap your goddamn wrist! Do you read me?"

Ropeleski was imitating a statue, afraid his wrist would be mangled if he so much as twitched. "But you're not a master chief no more!" he squeaked.

Sunday gave the manacles a wrench. "Trifling me, motherfucker?"

"Master Chief!" Ropeleski bleated. "Sorry, Master Chief!"

Sunday barely heard him. He was staring at the TV again, at the black Navy diver. "Carl," he said softly, with immense fondness, and memories surged within him.

# CHAPTER ONE

*Sonora, Kentucky. 1943.*

Twelve-year-old Carl Brashear raced down the dirt road, his bare feet slapping the ground in swift cadence. Were it not for the fact that his mother had paid good money for his school clothes, he would gladly have stripped off his shirt and tossed it aside, too. Spring was literally in the air, and Carl was filled with a zest for life, for fun.

The man behind him, however, wasn't.

"Carl!" Out of a thicket bordering the road barreled the heavyset schoolmaster, his pale face flushed from exertion, his cheap suit sprinkled with bits of vegetation and dust. "Boy, you come back here!" he thundered, shaking his fists in impotent rage. "You can't leave until I say you can leave? Do you hear me?"

Carl heard, but he chose to keep running. A glorious blue sky was overhead, and the lush woods were alive with the warbling of songbirds and the chattering of squirrels. The day was made to order for exploring and excitement, not for reciting the multiplication table by rote or learning about the Boston Tea Party.

The schoolmaster was still in pursuit, huffing and puffing like a steam engine almost out of steam. "Darn you, Carl!" he cried. "If you keep skipping school, you won't ever amount to anything in life! Is that what you want?"

The appeal fell on deaf ears. A narrow path appeared on the right and Carl bolted into it, laughing with glee. High maples and oaks dappled him with shadow as he raced over fifty yards, around a bend to the grassy bank of a broad pond. To the west a pair of ducks took wing, quacking in protest at having their privacy invaded. A turtle plopped off a log and sank from sight, a water snake slid in among some reeds.

Without hesitation Carl dived in, sucking air deep into his lungs a heartbeat before he knifed the water. Strong, even strokes brought him to the bottom, to the rusted hulk of a sunken car he had visited many times before. A crumpled door hung ajar. Careful not to snag his clothes, Carl eased past it and hunkered inside.

Craning his neck, Carl peered upward and soon saw the distorted image of the irate schoolmaster float into view at the pond's edge. Grotesquely bloated like some hideous monster, the image stormed back and forth, gesturing angrily.

Carl patiently held his breath. Daily practice enabled him to stay under for minutes on end, far longer than any of his friends. He waited as the schoolmaster continued to pace and swear. Finally, the harried man wheeled and stalked off, defeated once more.

To be safe, Carl waited another thirty seconds, then he cautiously slipped from the junker and slowly rose until just his eyes and nose broke the surface. He glanced right and left, wary of a trick, but the coast was clear. The rest of the day was his to do with as he pleased. Grinning, he flipped onto his back and gently floated, his arms out from his sides. In the trees a robin chirped, and above him fluffy clouds sailed lazily by.

This was the life.

Later that night, in the cramped, stuffy attic room Carl shared with his brothers, he lay on his bed beside the window and listened to one of his younger brothers, Willy, snore loud enough to be heard in Louisville.

The candle on the sill flickered as Carl reached past it to tweak the volume on the small, homemade, battery-powered radio. The announcer was relating the latest clash between U.S. and Japanese forces on an island Carl had never heard of. Casualties were high on both sides, but thanks to the pummeling of Japanese positions by Navy guns, U.S. forces had been victorious.

Carl's eyelids were heavy yet he refused to sleep. For the umpteenth time he stared in fixed fascination at the old *Life* magazine he had found one day by the side of the highway. On the back cover was a Navy recruiting ad. In it, a young white sailor clung for dear life to the rail of a pitching destroyer in turbulent, storm-tossed waters, and above the seaman in bold letters was the caption: *Adventure and heroism await you in the U.S. Navy.*

"Adventure and heroism," Carl whispered, his eyes aglow with the promise. The words resounded like the musical peals of a church bell, stirring him with glorious images of a life on board a great ship, sailing oceans and seas so vast they made the pond seem paltry. "Adventure and heroism," he repeated, lowering his cheek to the pillow.

Sleep claimed him. Carl dreamed of being on a Navy vessel in the thick of Pacific combat. The ship took a hit from an enemy Zero. Fearlessly, he dived into shark-infested waters to save friends who had been blown overboard by the explosion. His dream ended with an admiral pinning a medal the size of an apple on his chest.

Warmth on Carl's face returned him to the real world. A new day was dawning. The radio was still on, and a different announcer was reporting on a different battle on a different island. Yawning, Carl rose on his elbows and gazed out the window. In the dim light a tall, square-jawed man was driving a mule-drawn plow across a field, guiding the animals with skill born of long experience.

His father always got an early start. Sharecroppers didn't keep banker's hours.

The shuffling scrape of shoes on the floorboards drew Carl's attention to the arrival of his older brother, who stumbled over to his own bed. As usual, his brother reeked of alcohol and wore a spiteful scowl.

For a reason Carl had never been able to fathom, he always seemed to be mad at the world. "Daddy's been lookin' for you, Red Tail," Carl said. "He's pissed you skipped out on workin'."

Red Tail shrugged out of his shabby coat and dropped it on the bed. "Yeah, well, if he catches you foolin' around with his radio, he'll whup your smart ass."

"I'd like to see him try," Carl said defensively. His father had always been a little too quick to anger and a lot too quick to punish. For their own good, he'd always claimed.

Chuckling, Red Tail plunked down. "What, you think you can take him? Ever hear of being too big for your britches?"

Carl stared back out the window. His father was plowing another furrow in long, brisk strides.

"I can't believe he's mad at me," Red Tail remarked. "I plowed right along with him for three straight days, until I was about ready to drop. But that wasn't good enough." He paused. "Nothin' I do is ever good enough."

Same here, Carl wanted to say, but he didn't.

"Look at him out there," Red Tail said. "Bustin' his back from sunrise until midnight, and for what? Being a sharecropper stinks. To hell with Doc Maddox. Let the old buzzard plow his own damn fields."

"Dad doesn't do it for Maddox," Carl said.

"Then who? The governor of Kentucky?" Red Tail snorted in amusement. "You don't have no idea what you're talkin' about."

From the doorway came a quiet voice laced with patient love. "Yes, he does."

Carl and Red Tail both turned. Their mother was in her heavy nightgown, her dignified features quirked upward in a kindly, knowing smile. "I'll have breakfast ready in a bit," she announced. "One of you go tell your father."

"I will," Carl volunteered, and she departed. Grabbing his clothes from off the floor, he began to dress.

Red Tail sank back onto his bed and covered his eyes with a forearm. "Be my guest, little brother. All he'll do is rag on me."

Donning his shirt, Carl skipped downstairs and hurried out through the kitchen.

His mother was at the stove. She bestowed another caring smile as he passed. "Tell Mac I said not to be stubborn. It isn't healthy to work all day without eating."

"Yes, ma'am."

The cool morning air made Carl shiver. Hustling to the field, he jogged to overtake the plow. The curved steel blades were shearing into the rich earth like hot knives into butter. His father saw him coming but didn't slacken the pace.

"What are you doing out here, son? You should be gettin' ready for school."

"Mom is fixin' breakfast," Carl said. "She wants you to go eat."

"Tell Ella I can't. I promised Doc Maddox I'd be done by Friday evening, and by God, I will if it kills me."

"It just might," Carl said. The years of backbreaking toil had taken a fearsome toll. His father was old before his time, yet still as sturdy as the old oak by the pond. "Daddy, you're actin' like—"

"Like it's my own farm?" his father finished for him. "No, son. I know better. No matter how hard I work, I ain't ever going to own this land."

Carl stayed abreast of the plow as they came to the end of the field and his father turned the mule, starting yet another furrow. "There's something you should know. I heard Mama and you talkin' the other night. You're going to lose the farm if this wheat ain't in on time. Doc Maddox is going to bring in another family where the kids work, too."

At last the elder Brashear stopped. "His threats don't matter. School is more important, and my kids are going whether they like it or not. So get, before you're late. And don't skip out again or you'll regret it."

Carl didn't move. He stared at his father's callused hands, at dozens of old scars from cuts the reins had made, and at fresh cuts from the toil over the past several days. It spurred him to a decision. "I ain't going to school today. I'm helpin' you with this field."

Pride flickered across his father's face, but Mac smothered it. "Forget it. You've never plowed before. Besides, didn't you hear me? School counts more. So scat." Firming his grip, Mac went to move on. "Don't fret none over me, son. I always come through. By tomorrow night I'll have the plowing done."

Carl nodded at the land yet to be tilled, acre after sprawling acre. "Daddy, by tomorrow it will be too late. *Today* is Friday. You've been workin' so hard, you lost track of how long you've been at it."

"What?" Mac gaped in dismay. "That can't be!" As the terrible truth sank in, defeat crept over him and his shoulders slumped. "I reckon that's it, then." He aged another five years right before Carl's eyes. "Make me a promise, son."

"Sir?"

"Don't end up like me."

Never in his life had Carl seen his father so utterly sad. He wanted to reach out, to hug him, but the dull thud of approaching hooves intruded. Red Tail, dressed in work clothes, was leading two mules with plow rigs in tow. His older brother and his father looked at one another, and his father shut his eyes as if in anguish even though he was smiling.

"Well, are we fixin' to stand around talkin' all day, or do we get this damn field done?" Red Tail asked.

Mac straightened and clucked to his mule. "Get along there, Sarah!" he goaded, sounding snuffly, like he did when he had a cold and his sinuses were congested. "Get along, I say!"

Red Tail tossed a set of reins at Carl's feet. "What are you lookin' at? I couldn't sleep, anyhow."

Carl watched his brother begin to plow, then he snatched up the reins and gave them a tentative shake. When the mule didn't react, he slapped the reins hard and the animal brayed and surged forward like a thoroughbred out of a starting gate. Carl was nearly dragged off his feet. He had to run to keep up. Recovering, he fought to keep the plow from tipping, and by some miracle he managed it.

Soon the morning chill was gone. The temperature climbed. Carl toiled on under a blazing sun, his young sinews strained to their limit, his throat parched. He thought of the pond, his private haven, and of the Navy, and as he worked, he daydreamed.

*1948.*

Years passed, and in the same field under the same burning sun Carl Brashear toiled as usual. But Carl had changed. In place of a gangly youth strode a broad-shouldered young man whose shirtless torso rippled with steely muscle. He was handling a team of mules as expertly as his father ever could, with a casual ease that was deceptive. As he raised a forearm to wipe sweat from his brow, he spied his mother at the edge of the field. She had on her best dress, the one she saved for church and socials, the one with the pretty red ribbons.

"Come on, Carl!" Ella beckoned. "You'll miss the bus to boot camp if you don't get a move on!"

Carl brought the plow to a stop near her and let the rig drop. "I'm not quite done," he said. He had promised he would finish before he left.

"Your brother can do the rest." Ella grabbed his arm and practically pushed him toward the house. "Get dressed, quick. There's no time to spare."

Carl didn't argue. It was a big day for him, the biggest of his life, and he couldn't afford to be late. He put on his best clothes and the shoes his mother had scrimped to buy, and together they set out to hike the two miles to the rural bus stop.

Long before they reached it, rain began to fall. By the time they got there Carl was soaked, but he was too excited to let it spoil his mood. A bus had already arrived and was noisily idling, smoke spewing from its exhaust, its door wide open. Close by stood a tin-roofed shed plastered with Navy recruiting posters, some weathered with age, some sparkling new.

Waiting to board were two lines of recruits, segregated by color, the whites in front of the blacks. The Navy recruiter who had signed them up was moving among the inductees, distributing a brand-new copy of the Blue Jackets manual to each man.

Carl eagerly accepted his and flipped the pages. "Listen, Mom! That recruiter fella was right. Berlin, Athens,

Guam—the Navy has a base just about anyplace you can name!" He flipped to another section. "Look at all these jobs! Shipfitting, radarman, communications, gunnery school. There are dozens! I just wish I knew what I want to be."

Ella reached up and tenderly smoothed the lapel of his coat. Blinking back a tear, she said, "Knowing you, it'll be something big, something special."

Carl grinned, but it faded when he saw who was standing off in the rain. "Dad?" His father appeared to be holding something, carving on it with a jackknife.

"Did you really expect him to stay away?" Ella asked.

"The man hasn't said one word to me since I talked to the recruiter," Carl reminded her. "He treats me as if I don't exist."

"He's scared for you, is all. Powerful scared."

"He is?" Carl said uncertainly. If his father was concerned, he had a peculiar way of showing it. Carl was going to ask her to elaborate but the Navy recruiter picked that moment to return, all smiles and sugary sincerity.

"Coloreds now! On you go!"

The line slowly moved toward the open door. Carl gave his mother a warm embrace, pecked her on the cheek, and fell into step with the rest. Almost immediately a shadow materialized at his elbow.

"The recruiter says my first leave will be in September," Carl said without turning.

"I wouldn't believe everything that man tells you," Mac stated. "He's like one of those car salesmen. He'll tell you whatever it takes to get you to do what he wants."

An awkward silence descended. Carl had so much he yearned to say but he couldn't find the right words. "Anyway, I'll come back to help you mow the hay—"

"Don't you dare!" his father growled. "Don't ever come back!"

Stung to his core, Carl stopped cold.

"I mean it, son. You get in there and fight. Don't take empty promises. Bust the old rules if you have to. And when it gets hard—and it *will* get God-awful hard—don't quit. Ever. Do yourself proud. Do your mother and me proud." Mac put his hand on Carl's arm. "Don't come back for a good long while. You have your own life to lead now. Just remember to take care. Don't let anything happen to you, hear? Ella couldn't take it."

Carl was too stunned to speak. His mother had been right, as she always was. "I'll take care," he said.

"One more thing," Mac said. Opening his long coat, he slipped his old radio into Carl's palm. "Charge it when you get where you're going."

Choked with emotion, Carl gazed from the radio to his father and back again. The line was moving and he had to move with it, so Carl couldn't tell if the moisture that suddenly sprouted on his father's cheeks were tears or raindrops.

The recruit behind him gave his arm a nudge. "Hey, what's that supposed to mean?" He jabbed a thumb at the radio.

Puzzled, Carl held it up. Four large letters had been freshly carved into the wooden base: *A-S-N-F*. He shrugged, having no idea. The door loomed before him and he lifted a leg to step up.

"In you go, boy!" the Navy recruiter said, grabbing Carl's free hand and pumping it. "You've got a big future ahead in the United States Navy!"

*Three months later.*

Carl Brashear had died and gone to hell. They called it the USS *Hoist* but Carl knew better.

The Navy had betrayed him. He had hankered to learn electronics, or to become a communications specialist, or a sonarman, or any of more than a dozen jobs that promised rewarding careers. Instead, the Navy made him a cook and assigned him to the hellhole otherwise known as the USS *Hoist*'s galley.

Carl always thought the burning heat of a hot summer's day out in the fields had been the worst he would ever endure, but he had been wrong. The galley was an inferno; the grills and ovens roasted him alive. Perspiration poured off him in drenching sheets, and the hat he wore did little to stop the stinging sweat from getting into his eyes every time he blinked. His uniform was caked to his body, the apron he wore only added to the discomfort, and he couldn't get the smell of food out of his clothes no matter how many times he washed them.

Now, slaving away over a grill covered with dozens of hamburgers, Carl flipped one to keep it from becoming too well done and muttered, "That lying, no-good, sack of manure recruiter."

"How's that, boy?" asked Chief Floyd, who had come up behind him unnoticed. The old black chief of stewards was a heavyset, friendly, likable guy who didn't put on airs as a lot of the noncoms and officers were wont to do.

Carl told him about the pimply-faced recruiter back in Kentucky, and the last words the man had said to him as he boarded the bus in the pouring rain. " 'You've got a big future ahead in the United States Navy'—my ass!"

Chief Floyd's eyes crinkled. "Let me get this straight. I want to be sure I understand." He paused. "You *believed* him?"

"Sure I did," Carl said, flipping another burger. "I figured a man who wore a Navy uniform wouldn't lie to me."

The chief burst into hearty gales of laughter, laughter

he couldn't control, laughter that brought tears to his cheeks. Two young black cooks, Junie and Coke, had overheard, and they started cackling, too.

Embarrassed, Carl flipped a hamburger so roughly, it broke in half. "I don't think it's so damn funny," he grumbled.

Chief Floyd checked his mirth enough to say, "Son, a black man in the U.S. Navy has three choices. He can be a cook, an officer's valet, or he can get the fuck out of the Navy. Some big future!" He roared with glee again, then said, "No one with half a brain ever believes a recruiter. They're trained liars."

Carl remembered his father had tried to warn him of the exact same thing. Grinding his teeth, he gave the broken burger a smack with the spatula, flattening it like a pancake. For the next hour he simmered, as hot inside as it was in the galley, performing his duties mechanically. He was so mad, he wanted to reach out and throttle each of the sailors who filed through at mealtime. They were white, so they got to do whatever they wanted. He was black, so he had no choice in the matter. It wasn't right.

When the meal was over and the galley cleaned spotless, the exhausted cooks filed out onto the deck. They were always allotted break time, and Carl loved to lean on the rail and gaze out over the limitless azure ocean. Not today, though. He stared with unseeing eyes, roiling inside like a boiler ready to blow its stack.

Coke had moistened a towel. Sinking down, he leaned back and placed it over his head. "When I get me some shore leave, the first thing I'm going to do is fill a bathtub with ice and sit in it for a week."

"You'd freeze to death," Junie said.

"But I'd die happy," Coke responded, grinning. "I've about forgotten what being cold feels like."

Whoops and shouts from the rear of the *Hoist* caused all of them to gaze aft. The majority of white sailors on board were beating the heat by diving off the rear deck into the sea. It was a daily ritual, but a ritual only whites were permitted to take part in.

Carl straightened, his jaw muscles twitching. It, too, wasn't right. As he had a habit of doing, he came to a sudden decision and announced, "I reckon I'm going to go take a swim."

Coke raised the towel to peek at him. "Nigger, are you crazy? Tuesday is colored swim call. You know that. And today ain't Tuesday."

"But I'm hot today," Carl said.

"It's Friday," Coke pointed out, as if that alone were sufficient reason for all of them to welter while the whites cooled off.

Carl thought of another Friday, years ago, on the farm, and he started toward the rear deck.

"Don't, Carl," Junie pleaded. "Those crackers see that nappy head coming, they'll—"

"What? Make me wash more dishes?" Carl stalked on along the rail, past a group of chiefs lounging at ease. To a man, they tensed as he walked by, their conversations dying. Carl didn't care. Up ahead the white sailors were nudging one another and pointing. But Carl didn't care about them, either. As he came to the spot where they were jumping off, a beefy slab of flab grabbed his arm.

"Hold on there, boy. What do you think you're doing?"

Without comment, Carl jerked loose and launched himself over the side. He dived neatly, cleanly, as he always had at the pond. The sensations that washed over him as he plunged under the water were exquisite. A feeling of being where he belonged, of being in his element.

Rising to the surface, Carl swam toward a distant buoy, content to take his time. Above him harsh yells had broken out. He glanced over his shoulder and saw Lieutenant Hanks at the rail, a search and rescue swimmer beside him.

"Fetch him back!" the lieutenant ordered, and the Navy lifeguard dived in and started in pursuit.

Carl smiled grimly. So they thought they could haul him back against his will, did they? Well, they had another thing coming. He redoubled his effort, swimming swiftly, streaking for the buoy like a two-legged porpoise.

The lifeguard slashed through the water in pursuit. Cheers went up, the whites boosting the lifeguard, the blacks from the galley screaming hysterically for Carl. Even the chiefs got into the act, among them Chief Floyd, who screamed as loud as anyone for Carl to go, go, go!

Only one onlooker was silent. Chief Billy Sunday's eyes narrowed as he watched the race. His chiseled face gave no clue to what he was thinking. As the other chiefs shouted and jumped up and down in wild exuberance, Sunday calmly scraped a match to life and lit a pipe.

Out on the ocean, Carl was almost to the buoy. The lifeguard had proven to be a magnificent swimmer and had narrowed the gap to twenty yards, but in a few more strokes Carl touched the buoy and stopped. Treading water to catch his breath, he gazed back toward the *Hoist*. Everyone had fallen silent and most were gaping in astonishment.

The lifeguard stopped five yards away. Shaking water from his face, he smiled and said begrudgingly, "You beat me, fella. I was going flat-out and I still couldn't catch you."

Back on the *Hoist,* Chief Billy Sunday puffed on his pipe a few times, then shifted and gazed toward the upper deck. The commotion had drawn the vessel's commander, Captain Pullman, from the bridge.

Carl was in heaven. Rolling onto his back, he floated and stared up at the sky, just as he always liked to do at the pond back home. He was content to float there the rest of the day but the lifeguard paddled closer.

"Listen, I'm sorry, but I'm under orders to take you back. The longer you stay out here, the worse it'll be."

Reluctantly, Carl angled toward the ship. They swam back together, Carl savoring every moment. The cool breeze, the tangy salt water, the wide open expanse of ocean—all of it invigorated him. Willing hands helped pull them on deck, and as Carl unfurled he found himself nose to nose with an irate Lieutenant Hanks.

"Did you enjoy yourself out there, Brashear?" the officer asked sarcastically.

"Yes, sir," Carl admitted.

"Good for you. I hope you enjoy the brig just as much."

# CHAPTER TWO

The loud metallic clang of the cell door slamming shut had no effect on Carl, which surprised him. Being thrown into the brig was the worst thing that could happen to a sailor, next to a dishonorable discharge. He turned, still dripping wet, and saw something that *did* affect him.

Captain Arthur Pullman came down the companionway and motioned for the two sailors who had brought Carl there to leave. Lighting a cigarette, he studied Carl, squinting through the smoke. "Anything to say for yourself?"

Carl hesitated. For the captain to become personally involved, he must be in a lot more trouble than he had imagined. He tried to make light of his transgression by saying, "Well, sir, it was hot on that deck. And I just happened to notice we had a big damn ocean, and figured it had room for me and all the white folks you could throw in it."

"Do you think this is funny?"

"No, sir. I don't," Carl said, but his tone gave him away. He thought it was more than funny. It was stupid. So very stupid of them to make so much fuss over a trifle. All because blacks weren't allowed to swim on Fridays.

"How fast do you think you swam out to that buoy?" Captain Pullman inquired.

Carl wondered what that had to do with anything. "In under a minute, I suppose, sir."

"Forty-eight seconds, to be exact. I timed you on my watch." Captain Pullman paused. "Do you like being in the Navy?"

*Here it comes,* Carl thought. The other shoe was going to drop. He would be kicked out, his whole career ruined, all because he let his temper get the better of him. "Sir, I've been wanting to wear a Navy uniform since I was twelve years old."

"I'm sorry to hear that. Effective immediately, you're relieved of your duties pending dismissal. Unless"—Pullman studied him more intently than ever—"unless you want to apologize."

Carl stared down at the floor, a wave of defeat washing over him. If he refused, he would be kicked out of the service. He would let his father down, and disappoint his mother. Worse, the dream he had harbored for years would be shattered. All he had to do, though, was say he was sorry and his transgression would be forgiven. All he had to do was apologize for doing what the white sailors had been doing. All he had to do was kiss the Navy's unjust ass and he could walk out of the brig as if nothing had happened.

His face hardening, Carl looked at the officer and didn't say a word.

"Your response is noted," Captain Pullman said, and started to turn.

Carl's heart fell. His silly pride had just cost him everything he ever wanted out of life.

Unexpectedly, the captain stopped. "Ever hear of the search and rescue swimmers? You know, a sailor falls overboard and they—"

"—dive in and save him," Carl said. "Like the one the

lieutenant sent after me. Yes, sir. For that duty a man has to be a deck seaman."

A hint of a grin etched Pullman. "You just became one. Effective immediately, I'm transferring you to their unit. You're the fastest damn swimmer on this ship, and you've got the balls to back it up."

"Thank you, sir!" Carl blurted, amazed at his stroke of incredible fortune. "I'll pack up and report to the deck compartment berthing in one hour."

Captain Pullman was walking away. Without bothering to look back, he responded, "You'll do no such thing. You're just there to swim. Nothing else. Stay with the stewards."

Carl beamed. That was okay by him. Where he berthed wasn't anywhere near as important as the fact that he never had to cook another damn hamburger as long as he lived. "I don't believe it!" he marveled aloud. "I've just made seaman!"

Half an hour later, after changing into a dry uniform, Carl sat down in the stewards' quarters to write a letter to his folks. It was the third he had written since he left. One had been to tell them how hard boot camp was. The second, to tell them how much he hated being a cook. This time he wrote with zeal and passion: *The captain did right by me and I'll never forget it. Search and rescue is a big step up. It's a real job, and it can lead to better things. I'm still not sure what I really want to do, but whatever it is, I'll make both of you proud of me.*

Carl stopped. His radio was playing Blind Willie's "Cold, Cold Ground," and Junie was singing along and swaying to the music. Coke was over in front of the mirror admiring himself while pomading his hair.

Junie winked at Carl, then said playfully, "I don't see why you go to all that bother, Coke. It's a lost cause."

"Says you," Coke responded, indignant at the slur. "I'll have you know the ladies can't keep their hands off me. I have a woman in every port."

"All two of 'em?" Junie said, and some of the other stewards chortled.

"Yeah, yeah, have your fun," Coke said, stroking his hair as if he were petting a cat. "I can't help it if I'm a natural-born heartbreaker."

"A natural-born bullshitter is more like it." Junie held his own.

Carl applied his pen to paper: *Anyway, Dad, the mail chopper is due any minute now, so I'd better get this topside. Give Mom a big hug for me. Tell Red Tail I never thought any woman would be crazy enough to marry him. And let Willy and Jace know I'll be sending them a surprise pretty soon.* His younger brothers had been helping out in the fields, and Carl intended to send them each a pair of sturdy leather gloves to protect their hands. Finished with the letter, he signed his name with a flourish.

"You hear that?" Coke asked, tilting his head.

A faint rhythmic throbbing resounded down the companionway.

"The chopper!" Carl exclaimed. He quickly fished a few dollars from his pocket, folded the letter over the money, and slid both into the envelope. Rising, he scooted out, licking the envelope on the fly. He couldn't be late or the chopper would leave without it.

The Navy supply helicopter edged in low over the USS *Hoist* and hovered fifty feet above her deck. At a nod from the pilot, the copilot started craning down the supplies to a knot of waiting sailors. The pair had gone through the drill a hundred times, and they had the routine down pat.

Stifling a bored yawn, the pilot scanned the vessel,

thankful he had chosen Aviation. The mere idea of being cooped up in a cramped ship for week and months on end was unbearable. He loved the freedom that came with flying, as well as the privileges.

A tiny beep intruded on the pilot's reverie. A light on the control panel was pulsing like the beat of a red heart. "Shit," he said under his breath, and flipped a series of switches. The light stayed on.

Pressing a button on his headset, the pilot urgently reported, "*Hoist,* this is Bearcat 727. Be advised we have a tail rotor chip light. I will break off and try to clear your stern."

Taking a deep breath, the pilot gingerly pulled back on the control stick. The instant he did, the helicopter went into a dizzying spin. The control stick jerked in his hands, and it was all he could do to hold on. The ship, the ocean, and the sky whirled in a sickening dance.

"Mayday! Mayday!" the pilot bawled. "We're going in!" He heard the copilot scream, and he would have done the same except he had clenched his teeth and was heaving on the stick with all his might.

Carl Brashear strode onto the deck and into a tremendous blast of wind that ripped the envelope from his hand and set it swirling away. About to go after it, Carl looked up as the supply chopper roared right over his head. He whirled, tracking its descent as the craft whipped around and around like a child's top gone berserk. Through the canopy he could see the pilot fighting in vain to keep the whirlybird aloft.

The helicopter slammed into the ocean. Almost immediately a gigantic fireball erupted, the force of the blast knocking sailors back from the rail. Carl flinched as sizzling heat and blinding light engulfed him. Shielding his eyes, he beheld a pool of fire where the chopper had just been. The burning fuel spread rapidly, sending a column of thick smoke skyward.

Above Carl, the public address system crackled to life. From a speaker Captain Pullman's voice sternly rasped, "Splash a diver now! I want those men brought up alive! Do you hear me? Alive!"

The fire was dying as swiftly as it had formed, leaving a black, oily smear like a bull's-eye on the dark blue surface.

Sailors started running every which way, scrambling to their duty posts. Carl was riveted in place, as much by horror at the tragedy he had witnessed as he was by indecision. He didn't know what he should do, where he should go.

When some sailors pounded by, headed for the diving station, Carl went with them. Others were already there. A dive tender was operating a large winch, lowering a heavy metal platform toward the sea. On the platform, his back to Carl, stood a man in a deep-sea diving suit, donning a burnished metal helmet.

"Move it, people! Move it!" Captain Pullman blared.

Mere seconds before the platform reached the water, the man in the diving suit secured the helmet and motioned to the dive tender. At water level, the platform's descent ceased. The diver promptly went over the side, vanishing in a cauldron of churning bubbles and froth.

A fearful silence gripped the onlookers, a dread of anticipation settling over them as others crowded to the side, anxiously awaiting the outcome.

Carl moved nearer, the better to see over those in front. Hanks spotted him and jabbed a thumb at the sailors manning the ropes.

"Sailor! Get on a steadying line."

Unsure what the officer meant, Carl looked around in confusion.

"Grab a rope and be ready to pull it!" Hanks snapped.

Nodding in comprehension, Carl dashed to help. He filled a gap between two other men near the front of the line, wrapped his hands around the rope, and braced for what was to come. The wait was an eternity. Most of the sailors fidgeted nervously, a few whispering among themselves.

Lieutenant Hanks paced back and forth, muttering over and over, "Where the hell is he? Where the hell is he?"

Captain Pullman came from the bridge and stood on the upper deck, his hands on his hips, his worry transparent.

Suddenly the diver reappeared with a burden draped over a shoulder. Slowly, with consummate care, he rolled a body onto the platform, then clambered up out of the water.

"Pull, damn you!" Lieutenant Hanks shrieked. "Pull as if your lives depended on it!"

In a frenzy of flailing arms, the men complied, raising the platform faster than the winch ever could. Every second was crucial.

Carl did his part, the rope sliding through his hands so fast it gave him friction burns.

"Move, move, move!" Hanks hollered.

Within moments the glistening metal platform hove up level with the deck. Water cascaded from the helmet and shoulders of the man in the diving suit. At his feet lay sprawled the limp form of the chopper pilot. As soon as the platform stopped, Carl and another sailor bounded up to help swing the pilot's inert body onto the ship.

"Out of the way!" A medic shouldered them aside and knelt. He felt for a pulse, frowned, then tried to revive the pilot anyway. A minute later he looked toward Captain Pullman on the upper deck and sorrowfully shook his head.

A pair of tenders removed the diver's helmet and Carl got his first good look at who the man was. He recalled seeing him several times before, but he didn't know the man's name.

"If only I'd been a couple of minutes faster, this poor bastard would be alive right now," the rescuer said.

Captain Pullman cleared his throat. "You did your best, Chief Sunday." The captain nodded toward Hanks. "Lieutenant, finish the detail. Report to me afterward." Rotating on his heel, he headed inside.

"Aye, aye, sir."

Carl never had liked the junior officer much, and he suspected the feeling was mutual. It had been Hanks who sicced the search and rescue swimmer on him, and it was Hanks who had sent him to the brig.

"All right, you heard him," the lieutenant said. Sliding sunglasses from a pocket, he put them on. "Chief Sunday, shed the gear. We'll send a fresh diver down."

"I can do it," Sunday said.

"Did I ask you?" Hanks countered. "It was a direct order." He glanced at a younger sailor, a man Carl had seen in Sunday's company. "Caughlin, you'll do the honors. Suit up and go on down to get the rest of the dead meat."

A ripple of disgust passed through the men at the lieutenant's harsh words.

Stretcher bearers arrived to carry the pilot below. Thankfully, they covered the flier's ghastly countenance with a blanket before lifting him.

Chief Sunday, scowling ferociously at Hanks, shed the Mark Five diving rig and handed it to Caughlin. "Be careful down there. The chopper is on its side and there's a lot of broken, twisted metal. Don't let it rip your suit or foul your line."

"Don't worry, Mother. I know what to do," Caughlin quipped.

It took a while for the younger diver to prepare. The

heavy platform was winched onto the deck, and he stepped onto it.

Carl could tell the pair were good friends. He watched as Sunday stepped off the platform and two sailors pushed it over the heavy sea rail. A dive tender began to winch the platform down while another tender carefully played out Caughlin's air hose. Caughlin steadied himself and smiled up through the helmet at Sunday.

Without warning, the platform abruptly plummeted eight to ten feet and drew up short with a piercing shriek from the winch.

"What the hell?" Lieutenant Hanks exclaimed.

Carl wasn't an expert on winches but even he knew something was dreadfully wrong. Wisps of smoke were curling from the large roller around which the cable was wrapped.

Chief Sunday started toward the dive tender. "The bearings are giving out! Bring him up! Bring the platform up!"

Before the tender could act, the winch gave another earsplitting screech and the roller spun madly, playing out the cable with frightening speed. The platform dropped like a boulder, careening out of control. It canted at a steep angle, nearly pitching Caughlin off, and slammed against the side of the ship, slicing the younger diver's air hose clean in half. After another second, the platform lurched even more violently, throwing Caughlin clear. Upended, trailing the useless tube of hose, he tumbled end over end and crashed into the waves with an enormous splash. In the blink of an eye he had disappeared, swallowed by the sea.

Pandemonium reigned.

Sailors yelled and cursed. The tenders were trying in vain to steady the platform. Lieutenant Hanks darted to the rail, and blanched.

"I want a rescue team on deck, ASAP!"

"We can't afford to wait for another diver to suit up!" Sunday shouted. Shouldering past panicked sailors to the equipment that lined the diving station, he snatched up a face mask with a short hose attached.

Carl had seen divers use similar masks. Jack Browns, they were called, although why he couldn't say. He did know Jack Browns were used for shallow work, not for going deep as the chief was about to do in order to save Caughlin.

Sunday shrugged into the mask. He tested the air flow, then swiftly cinched a weight belt around his waist.

Lieutenant Hanks had been observing the preparations with increasing irritation. "What the hell do you think you're doing?"

"I'm going to bounce dive," Sunday replied. "I'll hook him on a rescue line so we can yank him out."

"Bounce dive?" Hanks repeated.

"Go down and come back up before the nitrogen builds up in my system," Sunday said while moving toward the end of the platform. "I've done it once before—"

"I know what a bounce dive is, and it's too dangerous," Lieutenant Hanks said.

Sunday was almost ready to jump. "I've got a man dying down there."

"Stand fast, Chief Sunday!" Lieutenant Hanks commanded. "The U.S. Navy doesn't exist merely to showcase your particular brand of Saturday matinee heroics." He glanced down at the dark depths of the ocean. "I've already got one diver dying and I'm not about to lose another. We'll have a couple of fresh men suit up and retrieve the body. It's the best we can do."

"Caughlin will be dead long before they get to him."

Carl had the impression the junior officer was expecting a "sir," but it never came. Instead, Sunday grabbed the end of a rescue rope.

Lieutenant Hanks looked fit to throw a temper tantrum. "Listen closely, Oakie, because this is a direct order. You are to stay out of the water. Do you hear me?"

Sunday crisply saluted. "Yes, sir," he dutifully said. Then, to the astonishment of those present, he went over the side, the rescue rope wrapped tight around his left hand, and bailed into the drink, diving feet first.

Carl was as amazed as everyone else. Defying a direct order was unthinkable. The Navy brass were prone to tolerate lax behavior by enlisted personnel, but never open disregard.

The lieutenant gripped the rail so hard, his knuckles were pale. Livid at the insult, he fumed, "God damn that insubordinate bastard! I'll see that he pays! If he makes it up alive, he'll wish he'd listened!"

Carl's dislike of Hanks reached new heights. The hothead was more concerned about going by the book than saving a sailor's life. But that was always the way with junior officers. To impress their superiors, and earn promotions that much faster, they were fanatical about following regulations. Some were notorious for handing out punishments for every little infraction. They were the bane of Navy life, and enlisted men learned early on to toe the line or suffer the consequences.

"Do you think Chief Sunday can save that fella?" a seaman whispered to a friend.

"If anyone can, it's him," was the answer. "Sunday is a tough S.O.B. Hell, all those divers are."

"And crazy, too, to put theirs necks on the line day in and day out. The Navy couldn't pay me enough to do what they do."

"Me, either," the first man said. "It takes more gumption than I'll ever have. But someone has to do the job. And I'm glad there are guys like Sunday willing to risk their butts to save ours. I respect them for that."

"Don't get me wrong," the other said. "I respect them, too. I just wouldn't want to *be* one."

Carl joined the rest of the seamen as they stared into the briny brink, waiting for the divers to reappear. And while he waited, he pondered.

The naval hospital was much too quiet for Billy Sunday's tastes. "Just like a damn morgue," he muttered aloud. He longed to get out of the oxygen bed and back on his feet, but he had to endure another two weeks of bed rest before he would be cleared for active duty.

Of more immediate importance to Sunday was the X-ray being examined by his attending physician.

Dr. Dinkins was a mousy fellow with an Adam's apple that bounced whenever he swallowed, and it bobbed now as he intently leaned toward the light box. Dr. Dinkins winced as if he were the one in pain, then he removed the X-ray from the clamp and slowly turned toward the bed.

"Master Chief Sunday, I'm afraid I have some rather bad news. You have sustained a serious air embolism—"

"Embolism!" Sunday declared much louder than he intended. He couldn't help himself. He knew what an embolism was, and the effect it could have on his career.

Nearby patients had started at the outburst, and Dr. Dinkins recoiled half a step. "Please keep your voice down," he whispered. "There's no sense in disturbing everyone." Coughing, he said with genuine sympathy, "Both lobes of your lungs have been severely scarred."

Much to the doctor's annoyance, Sunday took his cob pipe from the nightstand and opened the drawer to look for matches. "That last bounce dive was a lulu. We can't cheat the laws of nature forever, can we, Doc?" He tried to be lighthearted. There was still a chance, albeit very slim, that his career could be salvaged, but the physician's next statement brought his whole world crashing down.

"I'm afraid the condition is totally inoperable."

Sunday refused to accept the prognosis. "Ain't that a bitch?" he bellowed, hiding the anxiety that seared him like red-hot coals. "So what happens the next time I go diving and start taking on bottom pressure?"

"Any increased pressure at all will kill you, Chief Sunday. Instantly," Dr. Dinkins said with cold professionalism.

"Kill me? God damn. You had me going. For a minute there I thought this was serious."

Dinkins wasn't amused. "It is. And if you would be so kind as to keep your voice down, it would—"

"Keep it down?" Sunday interrupted. "Hell, no, Doc! Truth is, I feel like singing." And with that, Sunday shoved the white sheet aside, dropped his pipe back on the stand, and slid out of bed in his gown. He cast his eyes about looking for his clothes but they were nowhere to be found.

"What do you think you're doing?" Dr. Dinkins asked testily. "You're not fit enough yet to be up and about."

"I've been lying here too long as it is," Sunday said, an acute sense of desperation goading him unsteadily toward the exit. He wanted out of there. He *needed* out of there.

Dr. Dinkins trailed him. "Where are you going?"

"To get a drink. To celebrate," Sunday said bitterly. "What else?" He was gaining strength with every stride.

"Come back here." The physician motioned at a nurse, who spun and scooped up a phone. "I haven't discharged you yet."

Sunday paused. Before he went, he had to know for

absolute certain. He had to hear the words themselves. "To hear you talk, I can't go diving anymore."

"You can't, Chief," Dinkins said with finality. "Not ever."

There it was. And why? "Because one lousy atmosphere of bottom pressure, and pop! My lung blows up like a blood melon with a worm inside!"

"Please, Chief Sunday. You're scaring the other patients."

Sunday needed to scream, to curse, to rant, to vent his rage at the injustice of it all. "They're scared? What about me?" Sunday noticed a metal cart close by and snapped his fingers. "Wait! I've got an idea. I'll be looking to make a career move. Maybe you can use me around here. I could always change the bedpans." In a burst of fury he sent the cart flying, spilling the bedpans on it.

Patients and staff throughout the Enlisted Men's Ward stopped whatever they were doing to gape. A woman visitor cringed in fear, a man on crutches backed away.

"Damn, damn, damn!" Sunday cursed loudly, as upset at himself as the rest of the hospital staff were. He charged toward the door again, paying no mind to a husky orderly who surged through it.

"Here, now. We can't have you acting up like this."

As the man reached for his shoulders, Sunday delivered a chop to the orderly's gut that folded the man in half. Dizziness suddenly gripped Sunday but he fought it off and took a few more steps. Three more orderlies arrived, barring his path, and he took a swing but missed. The trio piled on, overwhelming him by sheer force of numbers.

"Try not to hurt him!" Dr. Dinkins cried.

The orderlies didn't try very hard.

Sunday was punched, kicked, gouged. He gave as good

as he got, though, landing solid blows right and left, yet in the end they were too much for him. As they half carried, half dragged him back toward his bed, Sunday slumped in despair. Not from being manhandled, but from the knowledge that from then on, nothing would ever be the same.

The life Sunday loved had come to an end. Diving was everything to him, and had been since his first snorkeling experience as a teenager opened up a whole new world, a watery realm of mystery and excitement that made the monotony of everyday life bearable. As a youth in Oklahoma, he'd spent his summers exploring the bottoms of every lake within driving distance. The deeper they were, the better he liked it. Later, he'd enlisted in the Navy for the express purpose of becoming a deep-sea diver. It was all he ever wanted out of life.

And now a fluke of fate had stripped his dream away.

Sunday was barely aware of being placed into bed and of the doctor examining him.

"You've sustained a few bruises but otherwise you're fine," Dr. Dinkins said. "I trust there won't be a repeat of your outburst? If there is, I will prescribe sedatives to keep you docile."

An urge to pop the doctor in the nose washed over Sunday but he resisted the temptation.

"Really, now, Chief. You're being rather childish. It's not as if this is the end of the world, you know."

"Maybe not your world, Doc," Sunday said glumly. "But it sure as hell is the end of mine."

Carl couldn't quite say what motivated him to attend the disciplinary hearing. He hardly knew Billy Sunday. But when he heard the scuttlebutt, he made it a point to go. To his surprise, the room was packed. Evidently

Sunday had a lot of friends, and not just in the ranks, either. Half a dozen officers were in the front row.

The hearing was already under way. Carl quietly slipped into a chair at the very back of the room. Chief Sunday sat by himself before a long table at the head of the chamber. On the other side of the table were Captain Pullman and the other officers selected for the hearing board. One of them was none other than Lieutenant Hanks, whose smug, superior smirk did not bode well for the chief.

Captain Pullman selected a sheet from a folder and read formally, "Chief William Sunday, for an act of heroism above and beyond the call of duty, you are hereby awarded the Navy and Marine Corps Lifesaving Medal. Wear it proudly, with distinction."

Sunday grinned. Several of the enlisted men whooped and cheered, falling silent instantly when Captain Pullman raised a hand.

"However, given your current physical condition and the far graver issue of your recent misconduct . . ."

Carl saw a number of seamen glance toward a doctor and several orderlies. The latter were black and blue, and one had a nasty welt on his forehead. What they had to do with the hearing was beyond him.

Captain Pullman continued, ". . . you are to be medically disqualified from diving. You will also be fined half a month's pay for three months running, and you will be reassigned to a training position. The orders will be cut shortly." Pullman leaned forward. "A word to the wise, Chief. Learn to embrace a newfound respect for authority. You can't go through life snubbing your nose at those who only have your best interests at heart."

Lieutenant Hanks grinned wickedly. Carl could see the chief's profile, and the pure hatred that flashed between them was obvious.

Chief Sunday slowly stood. Without comment, he saluted Captain Pullman and looked at each of the other officers in turn. All except for Hanks, whose self-satisfied smile was now replaced by a fierce scowl.

Pivoting on his heel, his shoulders squared, Sunday marched from the hearing room. In his wake flowed those who had been there to give him moral support, solemnly filing out as if they were part of a funeral procession.

Carl, though, didn't budge. He had been giving a lot of thought to Chief Sunday and the incidents with the copter and Caughlin, and he had made up his mind about a critical decision in his own life. Soon the hearing room was empty save for Captain Pullman, who had turned to a window and was shaking a cigarette from a pack. Rising, Carl silently walked to the table.

About to strike a match, Captain Pullman glanced around. "Seaman? What can I do for you?"

"Sir, that's what I want to be," Carl announced.

Pullman finished lighting up, snuffed out the flame, and took a long drag. "You want to be a Navy master diver?"

"Yes, sir."

"Not all that long ago you were a cook."

"Sir, the man I just saw—" Carl began to express his sentiments. In all his life, only one other man had ever impressed him as much as Billy Sunday. That had been his own father.

"The man you just saw is a master chief, the highest rank an enlisted man can attain in the U.S. Navy. Many good people spend their whole careers trying to achieve it, and fail."

"It's not just the rank, sir," Carl said.

"Ah. Well, as much as I admire Billy Sunday, he's not

exactly an ideal role model. He likes to raise a little too much hell now and again."

"He likes to save lives, too."

Captain Pullman did a double take. "I see. Well, your initiative is commendable, but they don't take colored divers. I'm sorry, Brashear, but it's as simple as that."

Carl was unwilling to give up. "What if you gave your personal endorsement, sir? Wouldn't that have some weight?"

"My personal—?" Pullman said, and grinned crookedly. "Hell, I just made you deck seaman, and now you want me to buck the system on your account? What makes you think I owe you that much?"

"Sir, the way I figure it, I owe you," Carl confessed.

Captain Pullman took another, longer drag on his cigarette. "The other day in the brig when I mentioned you have balls, I had no real idea." Sighing, he stood and gathered up Sunday's file. "All right, Seaman. I should have my head examined, but I'll honor your request. I'll endorse you as a candidate for diving school."

Carl started to smile.

"Before you break out the champagne, keep one thing in mind."

"What's that, sir?"

"You don't have a snowball's chance in hell of being accepted."

# CHAPTER THREE

A Greyhound bus grinded to a stop beside a wrought-iron gate. Above it a large sign proclaimed: BAYONNE NAVAL BASE. Beside the gate stood a guard shack manned by two shore patrolmen.

The bus door clanked open and down the steps came Carl, his uniform clean and ironed, his cap at a rakish angle, his shoes polished to perfection. Swinging his duffel up onto his wide shoulders, he moved toward the shack. From his shirt pocket he took his orders and gave them to one of the guards.

The man scanned the papers with careful scrutiny, then said, "Wait there. They'll send someone to pick you up."

Setting down the duffel, Carl stretched, relieving a kink in his spine. He had been on the bus for over ten hours. Beyond the gate, buildings lined an asphalt road and base personnel were bustling about their daily duties. The sun was only an hour high in the sky but the heat and humidity were already stifling. Bugs droned incessantly, and off in a stand of trees a bluebird was warbling.

The bluebird of happiness, Carl reflected wryly. After two years he was finally having his fondest desire fulfilled.

Five minutes later a Buick convertible wheeled toward the gate, its radio blaring country music. Behind the wheel was a familiar face. Chief Billy Sunday brought the vehicle to a screeching halt in a spray of dust, gave Carl the once-over, and whistled softly. "Will you look at this?" he said more to himself than to Carl or the guards. "Mister Navy! His bell-bottoms are bleached, his shoes are all shined up, and his hair is newly cut. Yes, sir. All we need now is an organ grinder." Sunday grinned. "Welcome to Bayonne, New Jersey. A pimple on God's ass."

Carl snapped a salute. "Seaman Brashear reporting for duty."

Sunday pulled out his ever-present pipe. "You don't say."

"Chief, we've never met, but I served with you on the *Hoist*. I saw your last dive. It wasn't fair what they—"

"Then you saw my best dive," Sunday broke in. His interest had perked. "USS *Hoist,* huh? I expect I remember you now." He snickered. "What's for breakfast, Cookie?"

Carl didn't take offense. "I wouldn't know, Chief. I'm reporting for diving school."

"That's right," Sunday said. "Rumor has it you wrote over a hundred damn letters requesting admission. You've got some grit, don't you?"

"Yes, sir."

Sunday squinted up into the harsh glare of the sun. "It's going to be a hot one today." He worked the gearshift. "Give it up, son. Take the next bus out. It's for your own good." With a nonchalant wave, he executed a tight U-turn and drove back onto the base, raising more dust as he squealed out.

Carl was dumbfounded. The man he admired so highly had just given him the brush-off. He saw the guards laughing, and he was about to move into the shade when his stubborn streak asserted itself. Still at attention, he stood there, waiting for the chief to return. He would wait all day if need be. After all he had gone through to get there, he wasn't giving up, no matter what.

The sun crawled ponderously higher, creeping across the blue vault of sky like a snail across a log. By mid-morning the temperature was well up in the nineties. By noon it had pushed past one hundred.

Carl was a statue, his arms at his sides, his jaw firmly set. Sweat layered him from head to toe, and his uniform itched like crazy. His throat became as dry as a desert. But he had endured worse heat plowing on the farm, and again in the galley.

Everyone ignored him. Vehicles and people on foot came and went, most barely giving him a second glance. A jeep whined up to the gate, the pair of officers inside joking and laughing, neither paying him no more mind than they would a stray dog.

Other trainees reported in and were admitted with ease. One looked toward Carl and made as if to walk over but a word from a guard sent him through the gate.

The afternoon was the worst. Carl's lips became dry and swollen, his vision blurred from the burning perspiration. His legs ached abominably, every muscle protesting. Several times he swayed from fatigue but he always recovered and straightened himself.

Toward sunset a group of rowdy sailors in a jeep sped off for a night on the town. Several pointed and cackled.

The day was almost over. A rosy crown framed the western horizon. Soon the sun would sink, relinquishing the heavens to blossoming stars and bringing with it a vastly welcome chill. But it was too little, too late. Carl was close to passing out. He felt as if his brain had been fried on a grill and his blood transformed into molten lava. His chin dropped to his chest.

The blare of country music snapped Carl out of his

exhausted reverie. The Buick was coasting to a stop next to him, Chief Sunday regarding him quizzically.

"Damn, Cookie. Look at your fine uniform! You stood out here all damn day?" When Carl nodded, Sunday shook his head in amazement. "Had anything to drink?"

"No, Chief," Carl croaked.

"Hell, you're liable to get sunstroke pulling a fool stunt like this." Sunday crooked a finger. "Climb in, Cookie. What say we cruise into town and get us a few cold ones?"

As much as Carl would like to, he responded, "I can't do that, Chief. I haven't reported for duty yet."

"You don't want to, either," Sunday said. "You only think you do." He drummed his fingers on the steering wheel. "Ever been to New York City? Greatest god-damned city in the world. How would you like to go there?" Sunday didn't give Carl a chance to answer. "Tell you what. We'll go have a tall one, on me. Then I'll buy you a ticket to New York or whatever burg you came from. How would that be?"

"My orders are to report for training."

"You don't want to go home? I thought all colored boys always want to get back home to their mammas."

Carl had taken enough. "Sir, I'm a Navy man. Where I come from there aren't any oceans. Just dirt farms and ornery mules. And no self-respecting Navy man makes his living driving mules. Sir."

The comment sobered Sunday. Raising his hands from the steering wheel, he looked at his palms.

In the gathering twilight Carl saw old scars just like those his father had, and the ones on his own hands. Scars from mule-skinning. The implication shocked him, and it seemed to shock Sunday to a degree, too.

"Do you know what the Chinese say, Cookie?"

"Can't say as I do, sir, no."

"Be careful what you ask for. You just might get it."
The chief twisted toward the guard shack. "Let him in."

One of the shore patrolmen opened his mouth as if to
argue but Sunday shot him a glare that could peel paint.

"Thank you, Chief," Carl said.

"Save it, Cookie. You have no idea what you're in for.
If you did, you'd turn around and run like hell." Sunday
tromped on the accelerator and sped off.

Shouldering the duffel bag, Carl proudly walked on
through the gate. Almost immediately he saw that the
buildings were dilapidated wooden structures well past
their prime. Everywhere he looked, everything had the
same run-down appearance. Of all the bases he had seen
or heard of, Bayonne qualified as the worst. A high
barbed-wire fence separated it from industrial slums
every bit as deteriorated and antiquated.

A banging noise resounded, the clamor of metal on
metal, and someone began shouting. Around the next
turn stood a half-naked swabbie who had on nothing but
underwear and was pounding on a pot with a large
spoon. "I stole a pie!" he hollered. "I stole a pie!"

Ahead were some sailors, all of them white. The scowls
they bestowed on Carl were not promising. Hitching at
his belt, Carl moved among them. Suddenly something
hit his shoe with a gooey *splat*. On the shiny tip of Carl's
polished shoes was a running yellow gob of chewing
tobacco.

The hulking mass of muscle who was responsible made
no attempt to conceal it. Carl had seen him report in
earlier, and recalled the man's name was Rourke. Now
Rourke spat again into the dust next to Carl's other shoe.

Coming as it did after a day of pure torture, Carl almost snapped. He lowered the duffel to free his hands
for punching. Just then the glint of sunlight drew his gaze
to the top of a dilapidated wooden blimp tower. A squat,

uniformed officer had trained binoculars on the group. On *him* specifically.

From out of the knot of seaman sidled a barrel-chested, flaxen-haired kid who smiled nervously and said, "H-h-hi. Name's S-S-Snowhill."

"Pleased to meet you," Carl said, glad to finally find a friendly face.

Snowhill nodded guardedly at the officer on the tower. "D-d-don't s-st-stare at him. M-m-makes him m-m-mad."

But Carl couldn't stop staring as a pair of sailors deposited a fat bulldog in a ten-gallon bucket at the base of the tower and yanked on a pulley line to raise the dog up into the squat officer's outstretched arms. "Who is he?"

"C-commanding officer. B-b-but everyone c-calls him M-M-Mister Pappy. W-war hero. They were going to make him an a-admiral or something up in D.C. before they found out he's g-got more screws loose than a S-S-Studebaker. So they sent him here." Snowhill lowered his voice. "B-better salute him or you'll sp-spend your first n-night in the b-brig."

Sound advice, Carl reckoned, and saluted Mister Pappy.

Lowering his binoculars, the officer receded into the shadows.

"C-c'mon," Snowhill stuttered. "I'll sh-show you to the b–barracks."

"I'd be grateful," Carl said, slinging the duffel over his shoulder once more. As he walked off, he could feel Rourke's hate-filled gaze bore into his back.

The building was as broken down as the rest. The door creaked as it opened, and a musty smell clung to the walls. Carl entered first, Snowhill slipping in behind him. The only unused bed was at the far end of the room, and between Carl and his goal was a gauntlet of hard, hostile faces. As he began to move quietly down the center, the front door creaked again.

"Gentlemen!" Chief Billy Sunday merrily declared. "In 1948 President Harry S. Truman had the courage and forward thinking enlightenment to desegregate the United States military. In keeping with the spirit of the President's mandate, I don't want to hear anyone around here use the word 'nigger.' Hear me?"

In unison, the trainees chorused, "Aye, aye, sir!"

"Good. Now I want all of you to welcome the Bayonne Diving School's first colored trainee, Boatswain's Mate Second Class Carl Brashear."

Carl reached the empty bed and dropped his duffel onto it. Forty pairs of eyes were riveted to him. He met their stares, and as he gazed up the row. Rourke, the bully, materialized out of nowhere beside Sunday.

"I don't hear anyone welcoming Boatswain's Mate Brashear," the chief remarked.

Rourke spat tobacco juice on the floor. "Fuck Truman. I don't care what he did. I don't bunk with no niggers, sir." Stooping, he grasped his sea chest in a brawny hand, heaved it onto his right shoulder, and brazenly strolled out.

When the other recruits saw that Sunday didn't reprimand him, they took that as their cue to do the same. One by one they hoisted their sea chests and filed out. The whole while, Sunday silently stared at Carl. Soon only Snowhill remained, nervously shifting his weight from foot to foot.

"Well, well. Your first day here and look at how much trouble you've caused," the chief said. "Have you anything to say for yourself?"

Through a window Carl observed the recruits filing

into an apparently empty barracks next door. "I'm surprised you didn't stop them, sir."

"Me?" Sunday said in exaggerated bewilderment. "You must have me confused with a baby-sitter. They're grown men. They can do as they damn well please."

"I just meant—"

"I know *exactly* what you meant," Chief Sunday snapped. "But this is the real world, not the utopia an idiot recruiter painted for you. If you were expecting a warm welcome, you deluded yourself."

"All I want is to be treated fairly, sir," Carl said.

"Who doesn't?" Sunday responded angrily, and they both knew he was referring to the hearing board. "But life isn't fair, is it? So it's hardly fair of us to expect the Navy to be any better." He cocked his head. "I just don't get it, Brashear."

"Get what, sir?"

"Whether you're a babe in the woods or as dumb as a brick." Sunday moved toward the doorway. "Some hatreds run deep, too deep to be pacified by presidential edicts. If I'd made those men stay, your life wouldn't be any less miserable than it's going to be. They have it out for you, and they're not the only ones."

"Does that include you, sir?" Carl asked, but the chief had turned and left. Now it was just Snowhill and him. "Are you going, too?"

"N-no," Snowhill said, and gazed around the near-deserted room in clear distress. "W-why'd they do that?"

"If you don't know, I'm not going to tell you." Carl squatted and lifted the lid to the sea chest at the foot of his bed.

"I'm f-from W-Wisconsin," Snowhill mentioned.

"Never been there," Carl said. Opening his duffel, he removed his father's radio, which he kept wrapped in layers of clothing to keep it from being busted.

Snowhill sat down. "W-we have a lot of c-cows, ch-cheese, and"—he grinned shyly—"g-girls."

Carl looked over. "Which do you like most?" he asked with a straight face, and for several seconds Snowhill appeared confused. "That was a joke," Carl clarified.

"Oh." Snowhill's forehead lined with furrows, then he laughed. "Oh! N-now I get it! Th-that was f-f-funny."

Placing the radio on the windowsill, Carl turned it on and adjusted the dial until an announcer came on, a sportscaster reporting a baseball game.

"... *Robinson strikes out again in this, his first season with the Brooklyn Dodgers. So far he has failed to live up to expectations, but it could just be first-time jitters ...*"

Stretching out on the bed, Carl laced his fingers behind his head. It was comforting to be reminded he wasn't the only black man bucking the system. He knew exactly what Robinson was up against, and he was rooting for the man all the way. One day he would like to go to a Dodgers game to see Robinson play in person.

"Say, Carl?" Snowhill said. "What's th-that?" He pointed above the bunk.

Twisting, Carl looked up. A note had been taped to the wall. Prying it off, he read the crudely scrawled message, his ears burning with resentment. *We're going to drown you, nigger.* Short and to the point.

"Wh-what's it say?" Snowhill inquired.

"Nothing," Carl said, tearing it into bits. "Nothing at all."

Ice-cold water swamped Carl, flooding his mouth, gushing into his nose. Befuddled by sleep, he sat bolt upright, gasping and sputtering and trying to remember where he was.

Chief Billy Sunday knifed out of the darkness. "Rise and shine, Cookie. Time for some training!"

Soaked, wearing only his underwear, Carl stumbled out of bed. By the clock on Snowhill's sea chest it was a few minutes past three. The middle of the night. Snowhill was sawing petrified logs, oblivious to what was transpiring.

Shaking his head to clear it, Carl shambled out into the brisk night and involuntarily shivered, his skin breaking out in goose bumps. The chief had stopped a dozen feet away and was facing him. "Sir?"

"Are you familiar with the principle of Boyle's law, Boatswain's Mate Brashear?"

"The wha—" Carl began, and was knocked kicking into the dirt by a tremendous spray of water. Sputtering anew, he thrust out a hand as he was pummeled mercilessly.

Sunday held a fire hose, securely cradled at his hip. "I didn't quite catch your answer, Cookie!"

"No, sir, I'm not!" Carl yelled to be heard over the torrent. He could scarcely breathe, but he dared not protest or try to run.

Sunday switched off the hose, threw it down, and stormed over. Seizing Carl by the shoulders, he hauled him to a fifty-gallon water drum. "Then it's time you learned." He plunged Carl's head into the drum and held him under.

Carl was stunned. He had anticipated this kind of thing from Rourke and some of the others, but not from the master chief. He couldn't understand why Sunday was so mad at him, or what he had done to deserve being hazed.

Sunday yanked Carl's head up. "Boyle's law states that at a constant temperature the volume of a confined ideal gas varies inversely with its pressure. Why is this law so important to divers?"

Wheezing like a bellows, Carl answered, "I don't know, sir." It was the wrong thing to say. He was shoved under again, and though he struggled, he was powerless in Sunday's firm grasp.

Sunday bent over Carl's ear to feverishly whisper, "You don't know and you're not ever going to know because you're just some dumb dirt nigger from Podunk. I know you, Brashear. Your scent hung in every shack I ever lived in as a kid. Your nigger face stared at me every time they made us leave because your daddy could farm cheaper than mine." Sunday shook Carl like a cat shaking a mouse. "Man drank himself into a seven-dollar casket, but that ain't going to happen to me! I don't drive mules. I am a Navy diver. Maybe next time you'll think of that when you imply we've got anything in common. You read me loud and clear, Cookie?"

Carl's lungs were about to explode. He nodded, and his head was jerked up as he was shoved backward.

"What did your record say?" Sunday said. "Seventh-grade education from Pickaninny U? I can't wait until they get a load of you in class. Hell, the math's damn near impossible and it's a cinch compared to the physics."

Carl thought that would be the end of it, but he was mistaken.

"You need an education, Cookie," Sunday said, re-claiming the hose. He aimed squarely at Carl's chest and bowled him over. "Come on, smartass. Quit now while you still can. Mamma's waiting!"

The stream battered Carl's head, his shoulders, his chest. Anger balled his gut into a knot, fury at Sunday for treating him no better than Rourke, and ire at himself for misjudging the man, for thinking Sunday was different from Rourke's kind. He had believed the chief was better than they were.

But most of all, Carl was angry at the suggestion he should quit. He would *never* quit. He would never let anyone keep him from doing what he had every right to do. Let them try their worst. He was going to be a Navy diver, and nothing they did could stop him.

Tucking his head to his chest, Carl contrived to keep most of the water out of his nose and mouth. He could endure the battering. He could take whatever Sunday or anyone else dished out. Screw them! he thought. Screw them all! And he laughed at the realization that he just might beat them at their own game.

Suddenly the torrent stopped. Sunday had turned off the hose and was regarding him as if he were an alien life-form. "You find this humorous?"

"Sure do, Chief," Carl said, recalling when Captain Pullman had essentially asked him the same thing. "You wasting all this water to get me to do something I'll never do. What would you call it?"

Sunday said nothing.

"So you're saying I'm somehow to blame for all the times your daddy was turned out of a farm because some black folks could do the work cheaper? If you need to blame someone, blame the damn landowners. They're the ones who treat sharecroppers like dirt. They're the ones always out to turn another buck, and they don't care who they hurt to do it."

The chief lowered the hose.

Carl wasn't finished. "We're a lot more alike than you're willing to admit. We know the dank smell of freshly plowed earth. We know the cutting feel of reins in our hands. We know what it's like to plod behind a mule hour after hour under a hot sun. We know things none of these crackers will ever know." Carl paused. "And we both know we were meant to be Navy divers."

Sunday slowly turned and headed off, but he stopped after walking a few yards to look over a shoulder. "Do you have a death wish, Cookie? Is that it?"

"Hell, no, sir. Why would you even ask?"

"Because what I just did to you is nothing compared to what some of the others will do. With them it's not personal. With them it's blind hatred. You're a marked man, Brashear. You're walking around with an X marked on your chest, and you're too dumb to realize it."

"Oh, I realize it, all right, sir," Carl said, rising stiffly. Mud plastered his back and his legs, and he could feel it sliding down his skin. "Let them try their worst. I'm ready for anything they can dish out."

"You only think you are," Sunday said. "This is diving school, not ballet class. There are a hundred and one ways they can do you in and make it seem like an accident. Do you want your mamma to shed tears over your grave?"

"She'd shed just as many if I were to give up," Carl said.

Sunday sighed. "You're a puzzlement, Cookie. A real puzzlement." He blended into the night, leaving Carl alone with the mud and the water and the stars.

The Hudson River was as cloudy as the sky overhead. Navy deep-sea divers were preparing to submerge, and the trainees were observing every precise, technically choreographed movement from an adjacent pier. They stood at attention, in a long silent row, Carl's black face standing out like the proverbial sore thumb.

"The men you are watching are Navy divers," Chief Sunday said. Scraping a match against a piling, he lit his cob pipe. "You bottom suckers, on the other hand, aren't fit to scrape their shoes. Avert your eyes."

The plebes heeled and did an about-face. Puffing smoke, Sunday moved down the row. "For those of you too dim to remember, my name is Chief Billy Sunday. There was a preacher by the same name who cleaned up

Chicago. Ran out all the whoring spics, drunken wops, and"—Sunday came to Carl—"motherfucking niggers who were making the place unfit for decent white folks to live. The only difference between that old preacher and me is that he worked for God and I *am* God." Removing the stem from his mouth, he growled, "Now why don't the first fifteen of you girl scouts step forward."

Some of the trainees swapped anxious glances as they haltingly obeyed.

"Good," Sunday said. "Back row, why don't you drop your cocks and pack your socks. You're shipping out."

No one moved. The trainees sensed it had not been a direct order. Befuddled as hell, they waited.

"I'm making a point, you jackasses," Sunday said. "Three-quarters of you standing here today will fail to become Navy divers." He fingered his pipe. "Any three of you who think you've got what it takes to make the grade, step forward."

A long beat of stillness ended when Carl impulsively took a step. Snowhill followed his example a fraction ahead of Rourke.

"Pay attention, ladies," Sunday taunted. "Of the unfortunates who do pass this school, only three of you will live to reach retirement. Think about that. Diving is the most dangerous job in the Navy." He swept the line with a raking scrutiny. "So who wants to live? Who wants to bail out now and save me the sweat of training your sorry ass?"

None of the trainees so much as twitched a muscle.

"Come on. Don't be afraid," Sunday urged. "I won't hold it against you. Better you should tuck your miserable tails between your legs and leave now. Get yourself a wife. Raise some kids. Have a nice, peaceful life and live to a ripe old age. End your days in a rocking chair, looking back on all the nice, peaceful things you did."

Still no one moved.

Sunday shoved the pipe back into his mouth. "Okay. I can see we'll have to do this the hard way. Which suits me just fine." He scanned the line and focused on Snowhill.

Out of the corner of his eye, Carl saw his friend squirm nervously.

The chief stepped up to the boy from Wisconsin. "I want you to look me in the face, son, and tell me that you believe beyond a shadow of a doubt you have what it takes to pass."

Snowhill couldn't do it.

"Let me guess. You were captain of the swim team, huh? You and your girlfriend used to practice the breaststroke?"

Flushing scarlet, Snowhill blurted, "M-m-my-"

Sunday leaned forward so they were nose to nose. "Your what? Say it like you've got a pair, girl scout!"

"My w-wife, Chief!" Snowhill managed.

"Oh, that's right. It's in your record. You knocked her up in your sophomore year, didn't you? You must have been practicing more than the breaststroke. Tell you what. Maybe you can bring the little woman by some night and we can all practice the breaststroke with her." Sunday's voice softened. "You were a hell of a swimmer, weren't you, son? State champ, your record says."

The chief grinned, and Snowhill must have thought the worst was over because he grinned, too.

"Y-yes, sir. I w-was."

Turning to the pile of gear they had brought, Sunday picked up a fifty-pound iron weight belt. He hefted it a moment, then suddenly threw it hard at Snowhill's midsection. "Here. Hold this."

The belt caught Snowhill in the solar plexus. Clutching it, he doubled over, gurgling and sucking air.

"What's the matter? Got the wind knocked out of you?" Sunday said. "Poor baby." He jabbed a finger in Snowhill's face. "If you let go before I say you can, you fail my course right now. Got it, swim champ?"

Snowhill started to acknowledge the question. But with a swift twist, Sunday grabbed him by the shoulders and propelled him over the edge of the pier. Holding on to the weight belt, Snowhill slammed into the muddy Hudson and vanished.

Sunday calmly clasped his hands behind his back. "Swimming does not have jack shit to do with deep-sea diving. If Johnny fucking Weismuller were in the soup wearing a two-hundred-pound Mark Five diving rig, he couldn't swim to fuck Esther Williams if she was buck naked three feet in front of him." Rotating, he stared directly at Carl. "The only way for any of you lame lunkheads to survive is to trust each other. Underwater all you've got is the man next to you, and that's why the only ones who make it through my class are the very best the Navy has to offer."

Carl and the rest of the trainees were staring at the undisturbed surface of the Hudson.

"Get out of my sight, all of you," Sunday said. "I'm sick of looking at you. There isn't one of you I'd call worthy."

The men began to break up and move off toward the barracks. But not Carl. Remaining at attention, he said, "Permission to relieve the man below, sir."

"What are you, Cookie? Some kind of goddamn hero? I've got no room in my class for heroes. Or stuttering swim champs with a wife and kids to worry about."

"If you want to flunk me, then do it, sir," Carl said. "Don't punish him just because he was decent to me."

Sunday snorted. "You think awful highly of yourself, don't you, sharecropper? The sun doesn't rise or set without your permission, is that it?" He nodded toward the water. "Well, I've got news for you. I did this for him. What if one day he's down at the bottom and in trouble? How the hell is he going to let topside know when it takes him half an hour to complete a damn sentence?"

Carl hadn't thought of that.

"As for you, I don't have to flunk your know-it-all butt. You're going to do that all on your own. Swim champ just didn't have any chance at all."

"Permission to relieve him anyway, sir," Carl persisted.

"So soon?" Sunday smiled. "It claims on his application he can hold his breath for over four minutes. It hasn't even been two yet. He shouldn't be in any trouble at all."

At that juncture Snowhill surged up out of the river and frantically gulped breaths.

"Well, well," Sunday said. "I believe Gunner's Mate Snowhill is a liar. Now, we're men of honor, aren't we, Cookie? We don't abide liars." Stepping to the edge, he bawled down, "You're out of my program, Snowhill! Pack your duffel and catch the next bus home." Turning, he brushed past Carl, saying as he did, "You have the whole barracks to yourself now, Boatswain's Mate Brashear. I'll be inspecting it at eighteen-hundred hours, and I expect the floor to shine."

Carl hurried to the ladder and reached down to assist Snowhill, who was quietly weeping. And still holding the weight belt. Carl took it and set it with the gear.

"C-couldn't get a b-breath b-before I went under," Snowhill mewed between sobs. "W-what he did w-w-wasn't f-fair."

There was that word again. Carl helped his friend to stand and they trudged along the pier. "I'll help you pack," he offered.

More tears gushed. "W-what w-w-will my w-w-wife th-think?" Snowhill said, stuttering worse than ever.

"She'll understand," Carl said. But no one could, not really, not unless they had been there. He gazed at the retreating figure of the chief. What Sunday had done was undeniably cruel, yet there was also no denying Sunday had a point. In an emergency, Snowhill's stuttering could cost lives.

"I t-tried. I really t-tried."

"I know you did," Carl said, and it struck him that sometimes trying one's best just wasn't enough. Sometimes the cards were simply stacked against a man. In which case, what real chance did he have of making it through diving school?

# CHAPTER FOUR

Three days later the trainees were lined up on the pier once again. Only this time they weren't there to watch experienced divers. This time they each stood in front of a pile of diving gear that they had signed for, gear exclusively their own for the remainder of their training.

"Go ahead, girls," Chief Sunday said. "Take a look. See if you can figure out what is what."

Carl bent and lifted a dented brass helmet. Under it was a tattered canvas suit, frayed lines, a scuffed mask, hoses that looked to be older than he was, half-rusted foot weights, and other equipment barely fit for use.

"Since there isn't one of you crybabies who knows his hind end from a hole in the ground, I'll have to go through the inventory one piece at a time. Check to ensure you have everything you need. A diver's life often depends on his gear."

Carl glanced at some of the other piles. Was it his imagination, or was his equipment just a bit older and more decrepit than everyone else's?

"Mister Pappy himself had a hand in choosing who got what," Sunday commented. "He's been watching each of you, marking your progress, taking note of how well you do."

Many of the trainees turned toward the tower. Carl

was one of them. Sure enough, the officer was up there with his binoculars trained on them.

"By the time your training is over, you'll be able to assemble your suits in less time than it takes to fart," Sunday said. "You'll be able to do it in the dark, do it blindfolded, do it underwater. Your suit will become your best friend. Treat it well. Take care of every article. Treat them as if they were your own."

Rourke held up a mask. "If this were my own, sir, I'd burn it and buy new stuff."

Chief Sunday smiled. "It's training gear for dumb-fuck trainees, not for real divers who engage in real diving operations. Hundreds of lunkheads just like you have used it and gotten by. You can do the same."

A lean, dark-haired man spoke up. "What if something gives out on us while we're underwater?"

"Then I hope you can hold your breath longer than Snowhill did, Isert," Sunday responded. "And I hope you have a better sense of direction than Crabtree."

They looked at one another. No one in their class went by that name.

"Two years ago, it was," Chief Sunday said, and idly waved a hand at the Hudson. "He was at the bottom practicing a routine drill when his air hose sprang a leak. Instead of signaling for help, the fool panicked. He thrashed around like a headless chicken, then swam toward what he thought was the surface. But in all that thrashing he got turned around, and instead of heading up, he went straight down."

Someone chortled.

The chief spun, his features flinty. "Laugh all you want now. But you won't be laughing when it's your turn down there. That river isn't no fish tank. It's so dark and foul, you can't see two feet in front of your face. And the bottom is nothing but muck and mud. One wrong move and you're stuck fast. Just like Crabtree."

"Did he die, sir?" Isert asked.

"Almost. I had to dive in and bail his sorry butt out. They took him to the hospital and pumped his lungs out, and he recovered. But he quit diving school. He couldn't handle it after that." Sunday paused. "That's the thing, you see. That's why I didn't save myself a lot of grief and boot most of you out the first day."

"Sir?" Rourke asked, confused.

"Until Crabtree panicked, I thought he had what it took. Every class is the same. There are those I think will make it, and those I think won't. But it doesn't always work out that way. Now and then a baby-faced mamma's boy will surprise the hell out of me and turn out to be a great diver."

Isert grinned. "So you're saying all of us really do have a chance?"

"Hell, no. I'm saying one of you, just one of you, deserves to graduate. The rest of you pissants are just going through the motions."

Day in and day out the routine was the same. Up at the crack of drawn, a quick breakfast, and then on to classes. Sunday hadn't exaggerated the difficulty. Carl slogged through the math with extreme effort, staying up long after lights out each night to go over the material again and again. He found that the longer he plugged away, the more of it he grasped, even problems involving multiplication and division, problems he would never have thought he was capable of comprehending. Little by little his confidence grew to equal his determination.

Along about the second week they were lined up on the pier in full diving gear, except for their helmets.

"Pass these down the line," Chief Sunday said, handing strips of cloth to the first man. "These, children, are blindfolds. I want each of you to put one on when I say so, and not before." He extended a pipe-fitting assembly known as a flange. "After you do, I'll say go, and you're to assemble the flange I'll give you as quickly as you can. Questions?"

No one had any. No one wanted to appear stupid.

Carl received his blindfold and passed the rest on.

Sunday was placing a disassembled flange at the feet of each man. As he straightened in front of Carl, he said, "Do your best, mule-skinner. And don't worry. You won't get any scars."

The order to put on the blindfolds was given, and Carl complied. Seconds later they were told to start, and he squatted, groping at the pieces, trying to make sense of what was what. From the tool belt at his waist he slid a wrench and set to work. He could hear Sunday pacing in front of them.

"Look at the lot of you! All thumbs! Fumbling like the bumpkins you are!" Sunday uttered a grunt of disapproval. "Isert, concentrate! Wilson, not so fast or you won't get the pieces to fit! Thomas, you go any slower and you'll be here until Christmas."

Carl felt the contours of each piece and tried to remember how the completed assembly had looked. He fit a rim onto a pipe and found a bolt to secure them.

"You're hopeless! You're all hopeless!" Sunday was bellowing. "There isn't one of you who has a clue what being a Navy diver is all about. So I'll enlighten you with my creed, as it were."

Sliding the wrench onto the end of the bolt, Carl carefully turned it.

"The Navy diver isn't a fighting man. He's a salvage expert. If it's lost underwater, he finds it. If it's sunk, he brings it up. If it's in the way, he moves it. If he's lucky, he dies young two hundred feet beneath the waves. Because that is the closest he will ever become to being a hero. Hell, I don't know why anybody in their right mind would want to be one."

Carl made rapid progress.

"When all is said and done, you'll take one thing away from this course, and one thing alone: respect. Not the respect of others, because that's so much hot air. No, I'm talking about *self*-respect, the highest kind there is. Make it through diving school and you'll never be ashamed to look anyone in the eyes ever again."

His fingers flying, Carl finished, set the flange down, and proudly rose, smiling at his accomplishment. He figured the chief would compliment him, but praise was not forthcoming. The scrape of shoes on the pier drew closer.

"Almost there, Machinist Mate Rourke. Another two bolts and you'll have it. Too bad the rest of you can't do as well."

Carl heard Sunday stop right in front of him. Surely now the chief would say something, but all Sunday did was make a *tsk-tsk* sort of sound and go on his way.

"Come on! Let's go! Isn't there one man among you who has what it takes?"

Later that afternoon the trainees paired off for signal training. Since no one wanted to work with Carl, Sunday ordered Isert to. They faced one another and took turns practicing. Carl had the signals memorized but Isert kept making mistakes. Now he tugged the line protruding from the helmet they were holding and gazed hopefully at Carl.

"No. That means 'take up my slack.' "

Isert closed his eyes, face screwed up. "Give me a minute. It will come to me."

Carl grabbed the other man's hand, wrapped it around

the air hose, and gave the hose a single, firm jerk. "This means 'I'm okay.'"

"I would have gotten it," Insert said, pulling his hand away. He glanced off at where Sunday was chastising a trainee, then whispered, "I'll be straight-up with you. I don't like you much. Because of you, Snowhill got kicked out."

"Don't blame me for what the chief did."

"I don't get you, Brashear. What makes you think Sunday and old Pappy will let you pass this course?"

"Because no matter what they say, they're not God. Just flesh and blood. They put their pants on one leg at a time, the same as you and me. So long as I don't mess up, I can outlast them."

Isert nodded. "Maybe so. Just the same, from now on I'm never going to partner with you if I can help it."

Stung by the rebuke, Carl let go of the helmet. He knew he shouldn't let these barbs get to him, but they did. He was flesh and blood, too, and his feelings could be hurt as easily as anyone else's. Steeling himself, he was about to say Isert could do any damn thing he pleased when he became aware that people were running wildly about, shouting to one another. Simultaneously, a siren wailed.

"What the hell?" Isert said. "Are we going to war?"

A sailor rushed excitedly by, slowing to exclaim, "Mister Pappy's dog got lost! Whoever finds it gets the first weekend liberty pass!"

The camp was in turmoil, more alive than Carl had ever seen it. The promise of liberty had brought everyone on the run and they were scampering about like deranged chipmunks in search of the bulldog.

Carl pivoted and joined in the madness. All the other trainees had joined in as well. To his surprise, Isert tagged along. They crisscrossed the area, past men who peered under vehicles and were poking into every nook and cranny. It seemed unlikely the dog could elude discovery for long.

Then Carl noticed that no one was anywhere near an equipment shack set off by itself not far from the tower. On a hunch he jogged toward it.

"What do you think you're doing?" Isert asked. "We're not supposed to go anywhere near that place. It's for real Navy divers, not trainees."

"We *are* divers," Carl said. And it was the one place no one else had thought to search. The door hung open, and he gingerly edged it the rest of the way with his toe. New brass diving helmets were aligned on a shelf on his right. Vulcanized canvas dry suits that put his own raggedy rig to shame hung from large hooks. One-hundred-foot coils of new air hose lay in neat coils at the rear.

"It's good for us the divers aren't here," Isert said. "They'd hang us by our ankles from the end of the pier and make us breathe water."

Carl glanced down. Muddy paw prints confirmed his guess. The tracks led to the left, to a row of storage lockers. From behind the lockers came snuffing and snorting and high-pitched whines.

Bending toward the wall, Carl saw a ten-inch gap. He reached around, snagged a handful of hair, and yanked. Out came a struggling dog—a beautiful female miniature collie, panting heavily.

"What on earth?" Isert declared.

Out strutted the bulldog, its chest puffed up, panting as noisily as the little collie.

"Why, you old dog, you!" Carl said, laughing. "It looks as if the only guy getting any in this camp is Mister Pappy's mutt." He gave the collie to Isert and hooked an arm under the four-legged stud.

"I'll be damned," Isert said, giving the collie the once-over. "Beats me what he sees in her, but to each their own," he joked.

Carl exited the shack, raised the bulldog over his head, and ambled toward the tower. Isert followed, holding the bulldog's sweetheart.

"Hey! Look at that!" someone yelled, and the refrain was taken up by scores of personnel as the news spread rapidly.

Carl turned from side to side, displaying his prize. Everyone smiled and clapped. For the moment, the color of his skin was of no consequence.

"Way to go, Brashear!" someone hollered.

"Ladies and germs, we have a winner!" another man cried, mimicking a sideshow barker.

Officers and sailors gathered around as Carl halted at the base of the tower. Up on top, partially shrouded by shadow, hovered their commanding officer.

Isert set down the miniature collie. "It looks like the only guy getting any around here is Mister Pappy's dog!" he said, swiping Carl's joke, and sparking raucous mirth.

All the personnel were at ease, truly enjoying themselves for the first time. A festive air reigned, but not for long. A booming command from on high brought their soaring spirits crashing back to earth.

"Put my dog down!"

The spectators fell deathly silent. Carl did as he had been instructed, his good mood evaporating like morning dew under a torrid sun. The bulldog dumbly sat there in a patch of shade, its tongue lolling.

Isert put down the frightened collie, too, and she scampered off. He started to back away but Mister Pappy thrust a finger at him.

"You!"

"Me, sir?"

"Fetch the red bucket."

"The what?" Isert said.

Carl had already seen it. Over the past several days a paint crew had been touching the old tower up. Piled next to a support were cans of paint, half a dozen brushes, a folded tarp, turpentine, and, at the forefront, a bright red bucket with a skull and crossbones painted on it, along with the word "lye." A brush handle stuck out the top.

"This one?" Isert said, grasping the handle and holding it so Mister Pappy could plainly see which he had grabbed.

Chief Billy Sunday arrived and stonily glanced from the red bucket to the man above.

"Wash the dog," Mister Pappy directed.

Isert gawked. "Sir, it's lye!" he called up. "It will burn his skin. Hurt like hell."

"Wash the damn dog! Now!"

"But, sir . . ." Isert said, moving woodenly toward the unsuspecting animal.

A lot of the others were just as confounded, but not Carl. He suspected why Mister Pappy was having it done—he didn't want his dog touched by a black man, and he was willing to torture the poor creature just to make a point. Revulsion seethed deep within Carl's breast. "Mister Pappy, sir!" Carl shouted. "I didn't mean no harm. He's just an old dog—"

"WASH HIM!"

Overcome by horror, Isert lifted the dripping brush and stood over the hapless canine. "I don't want to do this," he mewed. But he did. Suddenly leaning down, he ran the soaking wet brush over the bulldog's back, and at the contact the animal yelped and fell onto its side.

"AGAIN!"

Isert dipped the brush in the red bucket and stroked

it across the bulldog again. Yipping in anguish, the dog convulsed and shook.

Many of the onlookers couldn't bear the grisly sight and turned away. Carl started to, then changed his mind. He wanted to remember this day for as long as he lived, wanted to remember the depths to which those who hated him for an accident of birth would sink.

"AGAIN!" Mister Pappy thundered.

A week later Carl had another rude awakening. He was at his desk in the classroom. The instructor approached and slapped down a stack of textbooks, then moved to hand out identical stacks to each of the trainees.

"You think it's been hard so far? It hasn't. Everything to this point has been a primer to get you into the swing of things. Now we get to the meat of the course. To algebra and trigonometry and physics."

Carl opened the top book. A miasma of tables and figures confronted him, incomprehensible as a foreign language. He opened the next book, and the next. They were all just as confusing. For the first time since he arrived at Bayonne Diving School, the prospect of failing loomed large and real.

"I don't grade on curves," the instructor stated. He was an older, gray-haired man, only a couple of years shy of retirement. "You earn what you deserve. There are no teacher's pets in my class. I don't play favorites."

The last set of books was distributed and the instructor returned to his desk and leaned against it. "But I'm not entirely without heart. You're allowed to form study groups to help one another. Swap seats and sit where you see fit."

Rourke and several others began calling out the names of the trainees they wanted to join their individual cliques. Soon all the men had been selected, save Carl. Rourke sneered at him, then sat down amongst his own.

"Let's get started, shall we?" the instructor said, and moved toward the nearest group. He walked right by Carl, treating him as if he weren't there.

Carl took the hint. Gathering up his books, he left, trudging in abject defeat toward the barracks. He just didn't know if he could do it on his own. Diving practice was one thing; it was mainly manual labor, which came easily to him. But the intricacies of advanced mathematics had stumped men a lot smarter than he was.

Absorbed in thought, Carl almost walked right into a parked bus before he realized it was there. Two recruits who had washed out of the course were being seen off by the chief.

Sunday shook their hands and wished them well. The moment the door closed, he wheeled. "Well, look who it is. Albert Einstein." He reached for his pipe. "No. Wait. It's just Cookie pretending to be Albert Einstein."

One of the washed-out recruits had his pale face pressed to the window and was gazing forlornly out over the base.

"See him?" Sunday said. "You keep studying, because before too long it will be you in that bus." He walked off, whistling.

Carl moved on a few yards, but stopped at the sound of a screen door creaking. Carl looked up and saw Snowhill stepping from the mess hall wearing a stained apron. He was toting a full garbage can, which he carried to an open pit in which leftover and rotten food was dumped. The pit reeked, and no one ever went anywhere near it unless they absolutely had to. Scrunching up his face, Snowhill swatted at the swarm of flies that constantly covered the refuse. He upended the big can, dumping the contents onto the pile. Some stuck to the sides and had to be scraped out by hand.

Carl crossed over and stood waiting to be noticed.

"I h-hate this s-s-slop," Snowhill said to himself. Turning, he went as rigid as an ironing board.

"I'm sorry Sunday kicked you out," Carl said.

Snowhill set down the garbage can with a loud *bang*.

"Know why he did it?"

Sullen, Snowhill wouldn't answer.

"Oh, sure. He was pissed at you for being nice to me. But that's not why he washed you out."

Snowhill still wouldn't speak but he was listening.

"He washed you out because you stutter. Because if you were diving and were my buddy and you got in trouble, your stutter could get us killed."

"I w-w-wouldn't b-be—"

"Be my buddy?" Carl finished for him. "Hell, listen to you. You can't even insult me without sounding like a broken record."

"M-my fa-father used to say th-that."

"And folks laughed, right? They got to laughing and you couldn't stop stammering. What did your old man do next?"

Snowhill tried to say but his stutter was so atrocious, he spouted gibberish.

"Spit it out," Carl prompted. "You can do it. Take a deep breath and just say what pops into your head."

"He b-be-beat me."

Carl had figured as much, based on comments Snowhill dropped when they were bunking together. "That's a crying shame. You know why? As tall and strapping as you are, you couldn't put down an old bully like your daddy."

"He w-was my fa-father. I c-couldn't hit my fa-fa-father."

"Who said anything about hitting him? I meant to

stand up to him. But you didn't. And why? Because you're weak."

Snowhill struggled to respond but he couldn't form the words.

"Yep, weak as can be. Weak as mush inside. Oh, I know you're still here, and you've reapplied to the program. But you know what?" Carl hardened his tone. "You're not ever going to get back in because you think like a weak little man. So keep on doing as you're doing. Keep on slopping that pail, bu-bu-bu-buddy."

"Go to hell!" Snowhill snarled.

"What did you say to me, fool?"

"I said to go to hell!" Snowhill roared. "I thought you were my friend but you're not any different than all the rest!"

Carl took a step backward. "Listen to you! You got all that out without stuttering once! How'd you manage that?"

Snowhill blinked, in awe of his own achievement. "I was mad," he said, as plain as could be. "I was real mad."

"It shows you can do it when you have to," Carl said. "Maybe you can have the last laugh on Chief Billy Sunday after all."

"I can do it, can't I?" Snowhill raised his fingertips to his lips. "You did that on purpose. You were playing me. Why?"

Carl smiled warmly. "Because, you big lug, we're friends."

"Friends," Snowhill said, and whooped for joy loud enough to be heard in Massachusetts.

The gray-haired instructor moved down the aisle handing out graded papers. "Machinist Mate Rourke, ninety-one. Engineering Mate Yarmouth, eighty-seven. Engineman Crowfoot, sixty-nine." He reached Carl's desk and stopped. "Boatswain's Mate Brashear, thirty-seven."

The test plopped in front of Carl, the "thirty-seven" written in bold red letters. All the life drained out of him, and he sagged. He had tried. He had honest to God tried his best and he had failed spectacularly. It didn't help any that Rourke and the others were snickering at his expense.

The instructor hadn't moved on. "If you fail the next test, Boatswain's Mate Brashear, you will automatically be washed out of the course. It's the rules."

"Yes, sir," Carl said bleakly. It was no use kidding himself. He could study from then until doomsday and he wouldn't do any better. The next test would seal his fate. All those who wanted him to be booted out would get their wish.

Shuffling papers, the old instructor lingered. And then a miracle occurred. Barely moving his mouth, he said so softly only Carl heard, "There are seats of learning beyond the walls and control of this camp."

Carl was stupefied. The man had just offered him advice. Terrific advice, too, now that he thought about it. Carl turned to thank him but the instructor was already several feet away talking to another trainee.

"Ready to give up yet, black boy?" Rourke whispered maliciously.

"Not on your life," Carl replied good-naturedly, which incensed the bully and his cronies no end.

"You're just too dumb to know when to quit."

The barb rolled off Carl like water off a duck's back. *There are seats of learning beyond the walls and control of this camp.* Why hadn't he realized it sooner? Navy pay wouldn't make him wealthy, but he had enough socked away to afford a tutor, someone who could help him master the intricacies of the advanced lessons.

How to go about it was the pertinent question. Carl remembered his mother once took a course on quilt-making at the local library. It had been free of charge, and after it was over she had made each of her sons the nicest quilts they had ever seen.

Carl glanced at the clock, eager for class to end. He wanted to rush to the pay phone out near the gate and look through the Yellow Pages for the nearest library.

The instructor was coming back up the aisle. Carl looked up at him but the man avoided his gaze, and it dawned on Carl the instructor didn't want anyone else to know. It was to be their little secret. Odds were, if Mister Pappy found out, the instructor would be in a lot of trouble. Maybe even be discharged before his due date, adversely affecting his retirement.

The risk the man had taken touched Carl deeply. Just when he was beginning to think that everyone in camp was arrayed against him, Snowhill and the instructor reminded him that wasn't the case. Hope sprang anew.

Thanks to a man he hardly knew, Carl had a chance, a real chance, at achieving his dream.

Life was so strange at times.

So very, very strange.

It was late Friday afternoon, and the trainees and scores of other sailors stood in formation at attention, decked out in their best dress whites. To a man, they were grinning in keen anticipation of the privilege about to be bestowed on them. It was all they could do to contain themselves.

Chief Sunday, puffing languidly on his pipe, moving along the front rank, laying down the law. "Gentlemen, this is a weekend liberty. Not a week's liberty. Sure as hell not a month's liberty. One weekend is all you get. If your ass isn't back here by oh-eight-hundred Monday morning, you'll answer to me personally. Trust me—you don't want that."

Sunday saw Carl in the third row back, as spiffy as all the rest. "Remember, gentlemen, you're in the Navy. Your conduct reflects on your uniform. Do anything to besmirch that uniform, and again, you will answer to me."

The gates were closed but a pair of guards were ready to open them at the right moment. A local bus waited to take those who wanted into the city.

"One last thing and then I'll let you go," Sunday said. "One-night stands are over by morning but syphilis lasts a lifetime." He motioned. "Now get your raggedy asses out of my sight. Dismissed!"

As the horde of banshees screamed toward the entrance, the guards flung the gates wide and skipped aside before they were trampled.

"Lunatics unleashed on an unsuspecting world," Chief Sunday said, and smiled paternally, a father watching his sons leave the nest. Despite his speech, some of them were bound to get into hot water. A few would get into fights. Some would get so drunk they would pass out. Others would get laid. But most would simply wander the big city, taking in the sights.

Sunday watched Carl Brashear move out with the throng, and absently wondered what the sharecropper's son planned to do.

# CHAPTER FIVE

The sign on the lamppost read VILLAGE OF HARLEM, N.Y.

Carl Brashear smiled. He was in a thriving middle-class neighborhood bustling with well-dressed blacks. There wasn't a white person in sight. It had been so long since he was in a community of his own kind, so long since he could go out in public without being glared at, that he drank in the sights and sounds like a dry sponge drank in water. A matron with two adorable girls in tow went by. A man in a business suit gave Carl a friendly nod. Another man in overalls and a flannel shirt ambled past and smiled. Actually smiled.

Carl was in heaven. He pushed on, wrapping his left arm tighter around the books he had brought, rounding corner after corner, relying on his memory of the map he had studied to reach his destination.

At the next intersection a portly man was hawking flowers. "A bouquet for your beauty, son?" he said, displaying a marvelous bouquet of roses. "Every fella has a girl he needs to please."

Grinning, Carl shook his head and started by when it occurred to him a gift would be a nice gesture. "Why not?" Pulling some change from his pocket, Carl paid for some flowers and quickened his pace. He was running late. It had taken longer to reach the city than he counted on, and he might not get there in time.

Around the next corner reared an impressive stone building, the foundation composed of massive blocks. Wide steps led to double doors, and Carl scaled them three at a bound. Checking his reflection in the glass, he pulled his hat a little lower, smoothed his uniform, and went in. He had never been in a library before, never had any cause to, and the enormity of it stopped him in his tracks.

A whole new world unfolded before his wondering eyes. Towering bookshelves extended for as far as the eye could see, crammed with thousands upon thousands of books, more books than Carl ever conceived existed.

At a counter stood a nicely dressed woman of thirty-five or so. Carl walked over and held out the bouquet. He was going to introduce himself but she unexpectedly looked up and his tongue glued itself to the bottom of his mouth.

"Hello. I'm Mrs. Biddle. May I help you?"

Carl wriggled the bouquet.

"For me?" Mrs. Biddle eyed the roses as if they might bite her. "Have we met, young man?"

"No, ma'am," Carl forced his traitorous tongue to work. "We sure haven't." It sounded as if his mouth were full of sand.

Mrs. Biddle steepled her eyebrows. "What's the hitch? If there's one lesson I've learned in life, it's that men don't give flowers without a hitch. Usually it involves—" She caught herself. "Well, I can't say what it usually involves but it's how we get babies."

Carl deposited his diving books on the counter. "I'm not here to make babies with you, ma'am."

"Oh, really?" Mrs. Biddle said dryly. "I don't know whether I should be pleased or offended. There was a time when men couldn't keep their eyes off me, you know." She glanced at the stack. "Say, those aren't library books."

"No, ma'am."

"You're that young man who called, aren't you? Oh, dear. I told you. We're a public library, not a tutoring service." Mrs. Biddle looked longingly at the flowers. "Besides, I make it a point never to get involved with Navy men. They're all heartbreakers." Rousing herself, she tore her gaze from the bouquet and came around the end of the counter. "Now, if you don't mind, there's a Mr. Biddle at home and I'm sure he's aware it's Friday night. In fact, I bet he's brought flowers, too. Men are so predictable."

Carl didn't know what to say. When they'd talked on the phone she had led him to believe he would find what he needed at the library. He thought that meant someone to teach him.

Mrs. Biddle paused. "I'm not the only one who works here, though," she mentioned, her gaze drifting past him.

Carl had been vaguely aware of a muted squeaking. Swiveling in the direction Mrs. Biddle was looking, he saw a pretty young black woman coming toward them, pushing a book cart. Stopping at a shelf, the young woman slid a fat volume into its proper place. As she moved on, a book caught her interest and she pulled it out, flipped through it, and added it to a small pile on the bottom of the cart.

Carl was thunderstruck. She was the single most beautiful woman he had ever beheld. His mouth went dry and he mentally fumbled for the right thing to say.

Mrs. Biddle's face curled in a knowing smile. Raising her voice, she said, "I'm leaving now, Jo. Have a wonderful weekend. Don't forget to lock up."

Jo was lost in another book. "Ummm. Sure will. Have a nice one."

"And be sure to kick this handsome young sailor out," Mrs. Biddle said impishly. Winking at Carl, she clacked off in her high heels.

Jo had absently nodded. But now she glanced up sharply, realizing Carl was there. She had sharp, intelligent eyes, the brightest Carl had ever seen. "We're about to close," she said stiffly.

"Not for three minutes yet," Carl said, nodding at the wall clock. Placing the bouquet on the counter, he boldly took the book from her hand and turned it so he could read the title. It was a medical text. "Are you studying on nursing?"

Jo was miffed. "A person doesn't 'study on' anything, Boatswain's Mate."

Chuckling, Carl said, "Well, look out! The lady knows her rates and ranks. Get all that from one of these books, did you?" When she didn't answer, he opened the book to a complex diagram as complicated as those in his diving texts. "Understand any of this, Nurse . . . ?" he fished for her last name.

She didn't take the bait. Turning, she began to push the cart away.

In desperation, Carl stabbed for her arm and caught her wrist. He was afraid she might slap him but she only studied him aloofly, showing no fear whatsoever. "Look, I'm not here to flirt with you. I wish I was but I don't have the time. I'm in diving school across the river. It took me two years to get in and I'm not just good at it, I was born for it. But the thing is, I'm going to wash out if I don't pass my next exam. I need help. I need help bad." There. He had said what needed to be said. His future was in her hands.

"What's the last grade you completed in school?"

"Seventh," Carl admitted, wilting inside.

"No trigonometry? Physics?"

"No."

"Calculus? Basic geometry?"

Carl averted his eyes. He had never felt so inadequate, so uneducated, so plain outright stupid.

"Simple fractions?" Jo asked. Sliding her arm from his grasp, she moved off. "I'm sorry. I can't help you."

"Why not?"

Jo stopped. "Because it took me four years of working jobs like this to get through med school. And now I have six weeks to study for my finals. If I pass, I get to intern and maybe someday become a doctor. You're too far behind, Boatswain's Mate. I just don't have the time."

"Fine," Carl snipped. "Go back to walking around here reading to yourself and don't give me another thought. Go on."

"Don't you understand?" Jo said, not without sympathy. "You can't make up for five years of lost schooling in a few weeks. So whether I help you or not doesn't matter. You're going to fail anyway."

"I won't!" Carl declared passionately. "I can't!"

Jo's aloofness faded. "Why do you want this so badly?"

"Because they said I couldn't have it," Carl said. And no one, *no one,* was going to deprive him of his dream.

"I'm sorry," Jo said sincerely. "I wish . . ." She shook her head and pushed the cart on down the aisle. "We close in one minute."

Monumentally depressed, Carl watched her go into a back room. He couldn't blame her for refusing, not when her finals meant so much to her. By the same token, he couldn't just give up. He had to pass the next test no matter what. Scanning the bookshelves, he spied a sign. REFERENCE SECTION, it said, and underneath, in smaller print, Dictionaries, Encyclopedias. That was as good a place to start as any. Reclaiming his books, he headed toward it.

Jo slowly pulled on her sweater, guilt gnawing at her. The sailor had been so serious, so desperate, so much in need of help, but she'd had no choice but to turn him down. If she'd agreed, every minute she spent tutoring him was a minute less she had to study for her finals.

Walking from the room, Jo said, "I may know a professor at City College who can—" She got no further. The boatswain's mate was gone. Both relieved and somewhat disappointed, she turned off most of the lights and locked the door on her way out.

Her weekend passed uneventfully. On Saturday morning she did her laundry, Saturday afternoon she spent cleaning her apartment. Saturday night, when most women her age were out on dates, she buried her nose in books, studying until well past midnight.

Sunday was more of the same. Jo wanted to perform well on her tests. She was at the top of her class and she intended to stay there. If that meant endless hours cramming, so be it.

Monday morning arrived. Jo routinely put in a few hours at the library before attending classes. Usually, she showed up at 6:00 A.M., long before anyone else, and this morning was no exception. Her first order of business was to finish replacing the books returned the previous week. She retrieved the cart and had just started in on them when she was shocked to see a rose sticking from a book on a shelf ten feet away. Mystified, she pulled it out and sniffed it.

About twenty feet away was another.

Jo grinned, remembering the sailor's bouquet. A trail of roses led her deeper into the library, to a remote table in a far corner. Open books were strewn all over the place, and whole stacks teetered on the verge of collapse. Beside one of them, immersed in a volume, was the boatswain's mate. He looked tired and sported a two days' growth of beard. "You've been here all weekend?" she marveled.

"Yes, ma'am. I'm Carl, by the way. Carl Brashear," he introduced himself, and launched into, "Did you know Boyle's law describes the behavior of gases under varying amounts of atmospheric pressure? It says that if a diver takes a breath at a depth of one hundred feet and holds it while rising up to ten feet, the gases in his lungs will increase four times. Why is this important to diving? you ask. Because if a diver forgets to exhale on his way up, his lungs explode."

"My, my. Listen to you," Jo imitated him, more pleased than she had any right being. "But how did you get through all these books?" She gestured at the mess he had made. "The medical terms alone—"

"That's why dictionaries were invented," Carl interrupted. "I looked up the big words and turned them into little words. After a while it all started to make sense." Carl indicated a tin of fruitcake partially buried by more books. "Did you make this, by any chance? I found it in the back."

"Yes, as a matter of fact, I did," Jo said.

"It's possibly the worst fruitcake I've ever eaten in my life."

Jo's cheeks tingled. "I'm not much of a cook."

"Roger that, ma'am," Carl said, laughing. "But it kept me from starving, so it didn't go to waste."

He was so incredibly handsome that for a few moments Jo simply stared. Something deep inside of her stirred, something she had always suppressed, and before she knew it, she was saying, "I can work with you on Tuesdays and Thursdays from nine until midnight. But there are conditions. You're to ask me nothing about my personal life, and I want to know nothing of yours. This is strictly professional."

"I wouldn't have it any other way," Carl responded, his grin belying his statement.

"I mean it. And my time is precious. So the first night you go out drinking and fighting and leave me waiting here, our arrangement ends."

"Hmm. Tough choice. Spend hours each week with a beautiful woman who can help me make my fondest wish come true, or go off with the boys and get all rowdy." Carl scratched his chin. "What to do? What to do?"

Despite herself, Jo smiled, but she didn't let it linger.

"It's okay to smile, ma'am, even in a strictly professional relationship like ours."

This time Jo laughed outright. But she was deeply troubled. This sailor was doing things to her, kindling emotions she did not care to have ignited. Needing an excuse to tear herself away, she said, "I have to open the rest of the doors."

"I'll be here."

Jo reached into her pocket for the keys. As she drew them out, she inadvertently dropped them.

Carl was there in a flash, picking them up and gently placing them in her hand. "Here you go. Do you suppose you can tell me your name now or is it a secret?"

"Carlson. Jo Carlson."

"No fooling? My mama would say that was an omen."

"An omen?"

"You know. Carl. Carlson. She would say we were meant for each other." Suddenly Carl pressed a hand to his mouth. "Oh. Sorry. Strictly professional."

Jo couldn't believe how wonderfully giddy he made her feel. "You're going to be trouble, Mr. Brashear. Lots of trouble."

"Not me!" Carl exclaimed in mock innocence, and when she began to leave, he quickly said, "Jo. I like that name."

"Do you now? Thank my father. He'd always wanted a boy." Jo paused. "He was in the Navy, too."

"Yeah? Is he still alive?"

Jo's features clouded. "I wouldn't know. He ran out on my mother and I when I was nine years old." Shaking the keys, she pivoted. "I'll see you here promptly at nine on Tuesday night. Don't be late."

"Hey," Carl called out to her.

Wary of what he wanted, Jo turned, all her defenses up. She refused to let him get to her. "What, Boatswain's Mate?"

"Thanks."

"A bit premature, aren't you? You haven't passed your first test yet."

"With you helping me I have no doubt I will. You're an answer to my prayers. An angel."

"Oh, please. I shed my halo long ago."

"Then someone must have slipped it back on when you weren't looking. From where I stand, it's shining like the sun."

Jo bolted out of there as if he were an Amazon headhunter out for her head. Or her heart. She liked him, she liked him way too much, and the timing could not have been worse. As she went about opening doors to admit the public she couldn't shake the image of him in her mind's eye; his sparkling eyes, his rugged good looks, his smile, his laugh.

Under no circumstances would Jo let a romance flourish. She had meant what she said about being strictly professional. If he acted up, if he tried to get fresh or made lewd comments, she would gladly tell him to get lost.

The rest of the day slid by at a snail's pace. So did Tuesday. Jo was distressed to find she was looking forward to their appointment at nine. He was waiting for her, his diving books piled on his right, pencils and paper in front of him, raring to go.

"So you made it," Jo said a bit more harshly than she intended.

"Did you honestly think I wouldn't?" Carl replied. He made a show of squinting up at her. "Is it me, or is your halo on crooked tonight?"

"Let's get started," Jo said, taking a seat near him, but not *too* near.

For the next three hours Jo put him through his paces. She gauged the extent of his knowledge, where he was weakest, where he needed the most instruction, and zeroed in on shoring up his fundamentals so he would be prepared for the really hard stuff. His intensity was almost frightening. He tore into the instruction like a starved man into a chunk of meat, asking question after question, making sure he understood. And the whole time he was perfectly professional.

That night, tossing and turning in her bed, inexplicably unable to sleep, Jo admitted she was disappointed he hadn't made one solitary pass at her all evening. He had behaved like a perfect gentleman.

It was the same on Thursday. Jo sat a little closer and was a little more friendly but Carl never once brought up a subject even remotely personal. Toward the end of their time, she quizzed him on what she had imparted so far, and he rattled off the answers like a quiz show contestant, never missing an answer. He was exceptionally bright, yet another admirable trait.

The clack of high heels heralded the arrival of Mrs. Biddle, who was working late that night. She smiled and asked, "How are the two lovebirds doing?"

"Don't call us that," Jo said irritably. "We're friends, is all."

Carl's head snapped up. "We are? I thought we were tutor and student, nothing more, remember?"

"You know what I meant," Jo said, annoyed at the older woman for bringing it up. "Ruth just likes to tease people."

Mrs. Biddle tittered. "And goodness gracious, aren't you making a fuss over such a trifle? You'd think I had struck a nerve."

Jo was sure her face had burst into flame.

"Ah, to be as young as you two," Mrs. Biddle said wistfully. "To have your whole futures in front of you. So much opportunity. So much happiness." She turned to leave them in peace. "Don't squander a precious moment. We only get one lifetime, and if we let the things we care for slip through our fingers, we'll always regret it."

"Listen to her," Jo scoffed, but on her way home she kept thinking about the older woman's advice.

Over the next several days Jo spent every waking moment preparing for her finals. She tried to concentrate exclusively on her studies but couldn't. Time and again Carl's image floated before her, and she would daydream of them—together.

At their next study session Jo was more relaxed, and occasionally she let their talk stray into areas it was not supposed to. She learned about his family, about his sharecropper father, about the hardscrabble life they had lived. It increased her admiration for him. He was so dogged, so determined to succeed, to do what no other black man had ever done before. Become a Navy diver.

On Thursday Carl was not quite his chipper self. He yawned repeatedly and shook himself several times to keep awake.

"Am I boring you?" Jo asked.

"Not ever," Carl said. "It was a long day. We were up before first light drilling, and we spent most of the day at the river. The suits we wear aren't exactly light. After a couple of hours underwater I'm about ready to keel over."

A low rumble issued from under the table, and Carl looked down at himself in near-comical dismay.

"Did you have supper?"

"I haven't had a bite since breakfast," Carl said. "Toast and coffee."

"No wonder you're so hungry." Jo hopped out of her chair. "I'll call for takeout. What would you like?"

"You pick. I trust your judgment."

Jo's face caught flame again. "In that case, how about Chinese? I've been hooked ever since I was a little girl, and there's a place close by that can have the food here in fifteen minutes."

"Do I have to eat with chopsticks?"

"No, silly. They have forks and spoons. Or you can use your hands if you like."

"Darn. Usually I eat with my toes."

Jo made the call, and when the food arrived, Carl insisted on paying for it. She spread the boxes out on the table, then opened them. "Help yourself."

They ate in silence for all of one minute.

"I've told you about me," Carl mentioned, "but you've never shared anything about yourself other than your dad running out on you. What does your mom do?"

"She was a waitress for a while when I was young. Then she took up sewing and became a seamstress. She lives in San Francisco, in a small apartment with a cat and a cockatiel. I visit her at least twice a year or I never hear the end of it."

"So you live alone?"

"Very alone, thank you," Jo said, but it didn't quite come out the way she intended.

"Who would think anyone could be lonely in a city this size?" Carl said, and forked noodles into his mouth.

Jo was about to set him straight and explain the difference between being alone and being lonely when he unwrapped her favorite part of the meal.

"What are these?"

"My, you *are* a country boy. Those are fortune cookies." Jo leaned across the table and chose one. "We're supposed to break them open and read the fortune inside."

Carl picked up his. "It doesn't look like any cookie I've ever seen. Why is it so hard?"

"Chinese have sharp teeth," Jo joked, and broke hers open. Extracting the tiny slip of paper, she raised it to the light. In small bold letters was her fortune: *You will give your heart to another and much joy results.*

"What does it say?" Carl asked.

"I'll grow up to be witty and wise," Jo fibbed, quickly stuffing it into her pocket. "How about yours?"

Carl smashed the cookie onto a book, shattering it. He stared at the slip a few moments, then gave it to her without comment.

*"You face many obstacles,"* Jo read aloud, *"and must persevere or be lost."*

The gray-haired instructor rifled through the tests as he came around his desk. "The grades were not quite as high this time. Some of you slacked off. Machinist Mate Rourke, you weren't one of them. Another outstanding performance with a ninety-seven. Engineman Boots Crowfoot, seventy-nine. An improvement, Crowfoot, but you'll need to work a lot harder if you hope to get through the rest of the curriculum."

Carl tensed as the instructor halted next to his desk. Here it came. The rest of the trainees knew his career was on the line and were waiting for the ax to drop.

"Boatswain's Mate Brashear, you needed at least a seventy to keep from washing out." The instructor slowly lowered the test. "You managed a seventy-six, your best score to date. Congratulations."

"So he gets to stay, sir?" trainee Wilson asked.

"He gets to stay, yes."

Carl cradled the test as if it were a fragile egg. He would save it, have it framed, and hang it on his wall to remind him the impossible was possible if a person put their heart and soul into whatever they wanted to achieve. His father would be so proud when he broke the news. For the first time since he arrived at diving school, things were going his way. With a little luck, maybe he could make it through the rest of the course without too much difficulty.

And mules could fly, too.

# CHAPTER SIX

On Monday, a practical diving exercise had been scheduled. The twelve trainees who remained were taking turns diving and performing the required routine. As always, they dived in pairs. As always, Chief Sunday had to pick Carl's partner, and today it was Boots Crowfoot. They were suiting up to take their turn when the chief stepped to the end of the pier.

Air bubbles from the trainees currently below were breaking the surface. Sunday checked his watch and frowned. "Those boys stay down there much longer, they'll start getting mail."

Two junior instructors assisting the chief grinned. "Red Diver is done," one commented. "Green Diver is the one holding everything up."

"Again?" The chief made a beeline to the communications box and raised the microphone. "Green Diver, this is Chief Sunday. You have three minutes to get your patch hot and hung before I send the next team down. So let's hustle, Isert. Move your sorry Nebraska ass."

From the small speaker crackled Isert's tinny response. "This is Green Diver. I'm doing the best I can, sir. The patch just won't take."

"Do you have your cutting torch adjusted properly?" Sunday asked.

"I think so, sir."

"You *think* so?" Sunday rolled his eyes and his two helpers snickered. "Green Diver, I can't come down there and hold your hand. You should know the drill by now." He paused. "Red Diver, what's your assessment?"

Rourke's voice was as tinny as Isert's. "He keeps trying, sir, but the damn patch keeps sliding off. Mine went on without a hitch. Maybe the warm water has something to do with it."

The junior instructors were still snickering but Sunday silenced them with a slash of his hand. "What warm water, Red Diver?"

"The temperature has been rising steadily for the past ten or fifteen minutes. I figured it was from our torches."

Sunday lowered the mike and surveyed the Hudson. "Those things don't give off enough heat to warm an entire river."

Carl was as puzzled as the chief. The Hudson was always cold and murky, especially directly below the pier where a sunken ship lay, a mothballed freighter the Navy had scuttled years ago so trainees could work under simulated real-life conditions.

Chief Sunday clicked on the microphone again. "Green Diver, Red Diver, join us topside."

"This is Green Diver. Just give me another minute, sir. I can do it. I know I can."

Sunday hesitated, and suddenly the speaker squalled with a horrendous crash. Mixed with the earsplitting rend and creak of metal was a stifled scream. Everyone on the pier jumped up and stared at the surface. The water roiled and seethed like boiling stew.

"Red Diver! Red Diver! Do you copy? What is your situation?" Sunday anxiously inquired.

Static buzzed, and then Rourke came on, breathing unevenly, sounding shaky. "Topside, the whole ship just dropped out from under us. It fell about ten feet. We landed on something, Chief. And the water is hotter than ever. Hot as hell."

Sunday spun toward an upright plywood board to which charts and maps had been tacked. He ran a finger over the one that showed current flow and water temperature at various depths. Shifting, he nodded at a sprawling industrial complex across the river. "The hot water must be coming from that old factory. No one else is going down until we get on the horn and find out what the hell is going on." He returned to the communications box. "Red Diver, Green Diver, I want you both home. Now."

For a few tense seconds no one responded, then Rourke's voice blared urgently. "Negative on that come home order, sir. We've got a problem. Isert's air hose is tangled."

"Fouled, Red Diver. The proper term is fouled. Get it unfouled and get up here, now."

"I'm trying, Chief. But this wreck is lively. And the deck buckled under us when we hit. We're up to our armpits in twisted metal."

Sunday scowled and made as if to slam the mike against the box. "Why is it every accident has to turn into a full-scale disaster?" Pressing the button, he barked, "Status report, Red Diver."

"As near as I can tell, sir, Green Diver's line is caught in a mess of broken steam pipes. If I tug too hard it'll shred the hose."

"Keep trying," Sunday urged.

"Sir, I suggest we change out his line hose," Rourke proposed.

Carl and Crowfoot looked at one another. Changing out a line involved sending a diver down with a new air hose and lifeline. It would put the third diver at extreme risk.

Sunday had stiffened. "Change him out? You listen here, Rourke. He's your buddy. Take your time, follow his line back by feel if you have to, unfoul the damn thing, and get him the hell up here."

"I can't, Chief. There's no getting at it without fouling my own line and—"

From the speaker blasted another resounding crash, and this time both divers cried out, Isert shrilly, almost hysterically.

"Report! Report!" Sunday bawled.

More static sizzled like bacon in a frying pan for over five seconds, then another ten seconds. Finally Rourke came on again, shakier than before.

"Topside, this is Red Diver. She's dropped again, sir. Another ten to fifteen feet. Green Diver is more tan— fouled than ever. What do I do?"

"Stay put, Red Diver. Help is on the way." Sunday jammed the mike onto the jack and whirled.

Neither junior instructor appeared eager to do the honors. They had only graduated a few months ago and lacked experience.

"Hell!" Sunday said, and shucked his shirt. As he stripped off his shoes, he bobbed his chin at Carl. "Brashear, get over here and take off that gear."

Carl didn't budge. "You can't go down there."

"Who are you to tell me what I can and can't do?" Sunday snarled. "I warned you about that familiar tone of yours."

"Chief, that's two atmospheres of bottom pressure down there, minimum," Carl said, not intimidated in the least. "You can't dive that deep. It would kill you."

Sunday unfurled and started toward Carl with his fingers clawed, only to stop dead and swear a mean streak. "Damn your bones, you're right. All right." He surveyed the other trainees. "I need a volunteer."

"I'll go, sir," Carl said.

Refusing to acknowledge him, Sunday took a step toward the others. "Isn't there one of you with the guts to do the job? One lousy volunteer is all I'm asking?"

Carl moved toward the Hudson, donning his helmet. "We're wasting time, sir. Give me the extra line and hose."

Chief Sunday was practically beside himself. He brought them himself, and as he shoved them at Carl, he asked almost plaintively, "Why *you*? They hate your guts."

Smoothly securing his brass helmet, Carl slowed just long enough to say, "It's what a Navy diver does, sir."

Gloom mired the Hudson. If not for Carl's light he wouldn't be able to see his hand at arm's length. He moved as rapidly as the suit allowed, playing his beam over the freighter. The wreck had slid down a steep slope and come to rest on four huge factory discharge pipes, each large enough to drive a truck through. But they were never intended to support the weight of a submerged ship. Two of the pipes had already collapsed and fracture lines networked the other two. They could give way at any moment. When they did, the ship had another long sheer drop to the bottom of the river.

Carl angled toward the faint glow of Rourke's light. Rourke and Isert had been working in the engine compartment, and to get there, Carl had to navigate a maze of ruptured bulkheads and split decks. He descended with the utmost care, ducking, twisting, bending, working his way steadily nearer, conscious that Isert was doomed unless he got there in time. The freighter shivered and groaned around him. Popping sounds from the discharge pipes were added incentive—as if any were needed—to forge on without stopping, without slowing a heartbeat.

Passing through a wide gap in the bulkhead, Carl finally reached the compartment. Rourke cut him a spiteful look. Isert was on his back, his lines hopelessly fouled, just as Rourke had claimed.

"Topside, Blue Diver is here," Rourke reported. "He's got the fresh lines."

Sunday's response blared in Carl's helmet.

"Roger that. All right, Isert. You hold still now. Rourke's going to change you over and you'll be walking out of there."

Clearly frenzied, in a thin, boyish falsetto, Isert said, "I want to come up now! Can I please come up now?"

"In a couple of minutes," Sunday said. "Rourke, once you start, remember he's got five minutes of air in his suit. Don't screw the change, you read me?"

"I copy, sir," Rourke said, groping at his tool belt for the wrench he needed. "I won't let you down."

"You hear that, Isert?" Sunday said. "You're in good hands. Now stay still while he gets the job done. Don't panic. I won't be able to talk to you for a few minutes until he attaches the new line, so I want you to sing your favorite song while you're waiting."

Carl saw Isert's face twist back and forth. Isert was on the verge of losing it, and was breathing twice as fast as he should.

"I don't know any songs, sir."

"Then hum," Sunday said. "Listen to me, son. You've got to slow your respiration. Breathe nice and easy."

Isert began to hyperventilate. "Chief, I don't like it down here. I'm not made for this. I want to quit. Please. I just want to quit."

"Red Diver, change Green Diver out now!" Sunday commanded.

Rourke bent and wrenched Isert's air line off. It parted

with a shower of bubbles, and Rourke tugged on the new line to position it.

Isert's features contorted in raw animal panic. He was breathing in great hissing lungfuls, using up his air at an alarming rate.

Carl moved closer. "Stay calm, Isert," he said. "We'll have you out of there in no time. Just stay calm."

"I want to quit!" Isert sobbed.

Rourke worked swiftly, purposefully, as they had been taught. He started to turn the wrench, then lifted his helmet up. "What was that?"

Carl had heard it also. Loud, explosive pops from under the freighter. The last two factory discharge pipes had collapsed. He looked for something to hold on to as the ship sliced downward, gaining momentum quickly.

Isert screamed.

Rourke yelled in terror.

Clinging to what was left of a watertight door, Carl braced himself. The entire vessel trembled and quaked, threatening to rip apart at the seams. His headset flared, and Chief Sunday's voice nearly drowned out the din.

"What the hell is going on down there? Red Diver? Blue Diver? Report!"

Rourke had his arms wrapped around a hunk of rusted machinery. "Topside, the ship is dropping fast! She's tilting! I think she's about to capsize!"

"Not unless I say so!" Sunday blustered. "Stay with her, Red Diver! Change that boy! Get him up!"

Carl let go of the door and grabbed Isert's helmet, turning it so his light shone through Isert's faceplate. Isert's eyelids were fluttering and his pupils had rolled back in their sockets. "Topside, Green Diver is blacking out!"

"Shut up, Cookie! Dammit, Rourke, hook him up!"

Rourke tried. But no sooner did he affix the wrench

to the fitting on Isert's helmet than the old freighter started to roll.

It was every diver's worst nightmare, the one older divers dreaded most, the one they told younger divers to get clear of at all costs. The one scenario virtually guaranteed to kill a man every time.

Rourke had enough. "She's capsizing!" he wailed, and bolted from the compartment, powering his heavy suit up and out to safety.

Carl clung to Isert, doing what little he could to steady him. The ship crunched into the river bottom with bone-jarring force, spilling Carl onto his back. For hair-raising seconds the vessel teetered on the brink of going all the way over, but with a cataclysmic grinding and a dull boom, she settled on her side instead.

The ship's floor was almost vertical. In front of Carl's faceplate swirled bits of metal and debris. He was pinned under wreckage but he could still move his arms. Shoving heavy pieces off of his legs, he rose onto his knees and groped about until he found the new air line. He scrambled to Isert, who flailed helplessly, pinned Isert down with a knee to the chest, and applied a wrench.

Isert's eyes were blank, almost lifeless. He was slipping into unconsciousness. Another few moments and it would be over.

Carl turned the wrench once, twice, three times, to secure the fitting. The hiss of air rushing into Isert's helmet was one of the sweetest sounds he had ever heard. "Isert? Isert? Can you hear me?"

Coughing, Isert pressed both hands to his helmet. His eyes rolled down and narrowed as he focused. He smiled at Carl, then grabbed Carl's air hose and yanked firmly, once, the signal for "I'm okay." Carl grinned, and Isert laughed. The kid from Nebraska had just washed out and he couldn't be happier.

"Topside, the line has been changed out," Carl reported.

"We're coming home, Chief," Isert declared merrily.

A week later the trainees stood at attention on the parade ground, the morning sun bright on their strained faces. There were only eleven of them now, Rourke standing alone in front of the rest.

Carl watched Isert emerge from the barracks the white trainees shared, duffel in hand, and head toward the gate. Isert was shipping out. As Isert passed them, he deliberately looked at Carl, smiled, and nodded his thanks. All the trainees saw it.

Rourke, shamefaced, squared his shoulders at the approach of Chief Billy Sunday, who strode down the line with precise steps, stopped in front of Rourke, and pivoted to face him.

"Machinist Mate Warren Rourke, for valor above and beyond the call of duty, at the recommendation of your commanding officer you have been awarded the Navy and Marine Corps Lifesaving Medal." Sunday went to pin the medal to Rourke's uniform, then stopped.

Carl heard a loud creak. Although he was at attention, he glanced toward the old tower. Mister Pappy had partially emerged from shadow and was staring down at them.

Chief Sunday also looked up. Then, in disgust, he pinned the medal to Rourke and stepped back.

To Rourke's credit, he frowned, not pleased at all by the development.

"Dismissed!" Sunday said, and departed without congratulating Rourke or offering further comment.

The trainees sullenly dispersed, their heads bowed.

Carl did the unthinkable. He stared defiantly up at the squat figure in the tower, riveted by the realization his real enemy wasn't Billy Sunday or prejudiced trainees, but the commanding officer himself. Mister Pappy was a master manipulator, influencing men and events from behind the scenes to insure he never made it through diving school.

The medal wasn't all that important to Carl; the principle behind it was. He had earned the honor, not Rourke. By rights the medal should be his. Mister Pappy had nominated Rourke as a slap in the face, to put Carl in his place.

Boiling rage gripped Carl. He turned on his heel and got out of there before he said something that would get him in hot water. Which just might be what Mister Pappy was hoping he would do. Insubordination or disrespect shown a superior was more than adequate cause for dismissal.

Fortunately, it was time for Carl to head into the city for another lesson. Storming into the barracks, he gathered up his books and barreled out of camp, the world a red haze around him. He almost failed to hear his name being called. Halting, he saw Snowhill rush from the gate waving a sheet of paper.

"C-Carl! C-Carl!"

Carl wondered why his friend was stuttering again. He thought they had the problem licked. One look at Snowhill's face showed something was frightfully wrong. "Are you okay, buddy?"

"Th-this just c-came for you. T-t-telegram."

"Someone sent me a telegram?" Carl said, trying to think of who it might be. Belatedly, his rage dissipated and a terrible sinking sensation came over him. He gingerly accepted the telegram and tentatively unfolded it.

"I'm s-sorry, Carl," Snowhill said. "I h-hope it's not as serious as she makes it s-s-sound."

The words leaped up at Carl like hurled daggers, piercing his heart and sending a frigid chill down his spine. *Son,* it read, *please call home quick. Your father isn't well. He would like to hear from you. Love, Ella.*

Carl dropped the telegram, spun, and raced toward a phone booth down the road. He jerked open the door and leaned against the side, fumbling in his pocket for change, praying he had enough. He did, but only for a couple of minutes. His fingers felt like wooden dowels as he dialed and then fed the change into the slot. With rising dread he listened to the faint ring, once, twice, three times, before his mother finally answered.

"Hello?"

"Mama! Mama, it's me, Carl! I just got your telegram! How is Papa? What's wrong? How bad is it?"

"Carl," Ella said softly, so softly Carl barely heard her.

"Yes, Mama! What's going on? What happened?"

"It was his heart," Ella said. "He was out in the field, plowing. I was working on a quilt. It got close to supper so I went to the door to call him and saw him lying out there in the dirt."

"No!" Carl said. "What did the doctor say? How bad off is he?"

"Carl, your father is dead."

Racked by sorrow, Carl buckled as his knees gave way. The books fell from under his left arm and clattered all over the bottom of the booth. Limp, grief-stricken, Carl sagged, closed his eyes, and groaned. "It can't be," he sobbed. "It just can't be."

"The good Lord called him home, Carl. It was his time. He's in a better place now." His mother began crying.

"Why now?" Carl said, his senses reeling. "Why did he have to die on me now?"

"What do you mean?" Ella said.

"It's just—" Carl began, and bit his lower lip. He

didn't want to burden her with his troubles, not at a time like this. "I'm okay. Don't you cry, Mama. How are you doing? How is everyone else?"

"Your brothers are holding up as well as can be expected. As for me, I have bouts where I can't hardly stand for the tears." Ella paused. "Are you telling me the truth, son? Are you all right?"

Carl had never lied to his mother in his life, and he couldn't now. "No, Mama. I'm not okay. Not okay at all. I don't know if I can do this. I can't beat them."

"Don't talk like that. I have every confidence in you. So did your father."

"I wanted to show him what I could do before he died," Carl said, choking on the words. "I wanted Papa to be proud of me. Now it doesn't matter. Nothing matters."

"Don't talk like that. He was proud of you, Carl. Prouder than you can ever imagine. Almost his last words to me were to tell you—"

The line clicked dead. Their time was up.

"Mama?" Carl said in despair, and pumped the receiver's cradle. *"Mama!"* he cried. Then he slammed the phone down and staggered from the booth, stumbling over his books. Glancing down at them, he sneered, "Who needs you? Who needs any of this?"

The world blurred by tears, Carl shuffled down the road, moving mechanically, more out of instinct than design. He felt empty inside. He had loved his father dearly. The man had literally worked himself to death for them. Maybe his father had been a bit too stern on occasion, but he had always had their best interests at heart. Which was more than Carl could say about the Navy.

The glib recruiter had claimed the Navy was the one place in the world where men weren't discriminated against on the basis of their color. But it had been a bald-faced lie. The Navy was no different from the rest of the world. Blacks were treated shabbily, scorned as second-rate seamen who dared not step out of line or try to be more than the Navy said they should be. It was okay for blacks to die for their country, but they had to do it in the capacity the Navy dictated, not as they might want to.

What was he trying to prove? Carl asked himself. Why go on beating his head against the wall by fighting the status quo? Why endure endless abuse, when in the end the Navy would win? It always won.

Carl slowed, but his mind was racing. No, that wasn't quite right. The Navy wasn't to blame; it was the people *in* the Navy. Even then, it wasn't everyone. For every Rourke there was a Snowhill. For ever Mister Pappy there was someone like the old instructor who had suggested he seek help off base.

The majority were like Chief Sunday. Not truly bad or evil, they just did as they were told, or as pressure by their peers made them do. They always toed the yellow line in the middle of the road in order not to hinder their careers.

Carl's father had known men just like them. One lazy summer's day when Carl was ten or so, they had been off fishing and he had asked his father why it was that so many white people disliked coloreds.

"Remember that hill of red ants we found awhile back?" his father had asked. "How all the ants went about their work just as busy as could be without payin' much attention to the others? But when Red Tail brought a black ant over and dropped it among them, what did the red ants do?"

"They attacked it and tore it apart."

"Yet it was an ant, just like them. But they were red

and it was black, and that made it different." His father had gazed out over the pond. "Whether it's ants or people, the sad truth is they don't like things that are different. To many folks, being different somehow makes you bad. So a lot of whites treat blacks just like those red ants treated the black one."

"That's not right, Papa."

"No, it's not. But never forget there are whites who don't treat us like that. Whites who look at us and see a person, not the color of our skin."

"How will I know which they are?"

His father had smiled. "Trust me, son. They'll let you know. Just don't fall into the rut some blacks do of hatin' all whites because of it. In every basket of spoiled apples there are always a few that haven't gone rotten."

Carl had fished a bit, then asked, "What do we do, Papa, when whites treat us bad? Mama says we're supposed to be nice to everybody. But I don't want to be nice to people who are mean to me."

"Your mother is a fine woman. She was raised on the Good Book, and she believes in always turnin' the other cheek. She got me believin' it, too, when we were first married. But most of the time, you turn the other cheek, they slap that, too."

"So we treat them just like they treat us?"

"Do that and you'll end up behind bars. The prisons are full of black folks who couldn't take it anymore and snapped." His father began reeling in his line to cast again. "Don't ever stoop as low as those who hate you. Hold your head high. Go about your own life doing what you want and don't let anyone tell you different. Stand up for yourself, but do it smart."

*Stand up for yourself, but do it smart.* Carl stopped sniffling and wiped a sleeve across his wet face. How smart of him was it to give up? To turn his back on everything he had worked so hard to achieve? All because Mister Pappy had it in for him? If he quit now, it would be the same as slapping his father in the face, like saying that all his father ever did and said was so much bull. It would dishonor his father's memory. And if there was one thing Carl was *not* going to do, it was that.

Stopping, Carl looked up. He was startled at how far he had walked, and how much time had gone by. A car was coming up behind him. He looked back, and barely jumped out of the way in time as a swank maroon Mercury convertible roared past, missing him by inches. Thirty yards farther on it screeched to a halt, leaving broad skid marks on the road, and sat with the motor idling. A radio clicked on, and a song Carl recognized, Billie Holiday's "I'm a Fool For You," wafted on the breeze.

Warily, Carl approached. He thought it might be a redneck who had tried to run him down, but a mane of lustrous blond hair proved otherwise. A stunning woman was behind the wheel, adorned in a full-length fur coat. She was staring straight ahead, her expression as blank as a slate, a cigarette burning in her left hand.

"Are you okay, lady?"

The blonde kept staring. Not much over thirty, her beauty was marred by world-weary lines around her eyes and mouth.

Carl scanned the road. It was a desolate stretch, with only one building in sight. "Are you lost?" he guessed.

The woman smiled thinly and took a long drag. "Aren't we all?" she said. "I've been trying to get across that damn river to New York." Her other hand came out from under the fur coat. Tilting a near-empty bottle of gin to her red lips, she took a generous swallow. "Five years, and it's always the same. We were on our way to Roseland. But, as usual, we ended up having a fight."

A lovers' quarrel, Carl figured. She turned up the radio and an announcer came on.

*"You're listening to the sensational Billie Holiday live from Roseland. After a word from our sponsor we'll be right back . . ."*

"Bet they're having a grand old time tonight," the blonde said. "Everyone all dressed up. Dancing under those bright lights. We were going to be right there with them. People used to say he'd get all the plum assignments. Italy. Hawaii. New York. They never mentioned Bayonne."

Carl started to move on. Whatever was upsetting her, he couldn't help. But she pulled him back by asking a question.

"Want to hear the joke of it all, mister? When I came out back in the Garden District outside of New Orleans—"

Carl had no clue what she was talking about and it must have shown.

"Coming out. You know. The debutante ball. It's a dance." The blonde took another swallow of gin. "Well, they were holding it at this big hotel in the Quarter. And we just passed on the steps. I saw him first. Wearing that uniform." Her face glowed at the recollection. "Let me tell you, he was no boy. Not like the ones I was used to. He was a man. All man. And then he looked at me and it was pure electricity."

She had to be talking about an officer, Carl suspected.

"I went on into the dance. And do you know what he did? He sat out there in his car in front of the hotel the whole night. Waiting for me. Just waiting for me to come back out." Her world-weary lines deepened. "I could have had my pick of any boy at that party. The richest, most influential boys around. I could have lived like a movie star the rest of my days." She raised the bottle, but it was empty and she flung it from the convertible in disgust. "Do you think anyone ever gets what they hope for?"

"Sometimes. Maybe. I don't know."

Shifting, she looked at him for the first time. "You don't look like you're having such a great night, either."

Carl didn't say anything. The pain of his loss was too new, too overpowering.

"You're the one they talk about, aren't you? The Navy diver?"

"Trying to be. But it doesn't look good."

"Oh, hell. You're already there, you just don't know it yet." She smiled. "You good ones are all alike. Hell-raisers. Live for a challenge. Someone dares you, you can't stop yourself from taking them on. When life gets too peaceful, you make your own little wars. Crazy mothers, the whole lot of you."

Carl didn't know who she was talking about but it certainly wasn't him.

"Crazy," she said again. "Magnificently crazy."

"Well, if you're okay, I've got to go." Carl had forgotten about Jo and his lesson. And his books were back at the phone booth.

"Who said I was okay?" the blonde responded. "I just had a baby, but the baby wouldn't have me."

Perplexed, Carl studied her. Her body seemed too thin, too compact, for her to have just given birth. A tear streaked her cheek.

"Why can't I ever do anything right? Why is it that just when we think things are going great, life has to punch us in the gut?"

Carl had no answer for that one.

The growl of an engine preceded a speeding jeep crammed with rowdy sailors. Hooting and whistling, they shot past the convertible and on down the road.

"Maybe you should go home now, ma'am," Carl suggested.

"The name is Gwen. And God, no, that's the last thing I should do. I need life! I need a party! And someone to laugh with!" Gwen scrutinized him with renewed intensity. "Something tells me you could use that, too. A night on the town. Get away from it all. From all your cares and woes."

The idea had merit, Carl admitted. But he had responsibilities. "I appreciate the offer, Gwen. I just can't—"

"Don't you dare. A 'no' is unacceptable," Gwen interrupted, beckoning. "Know what I'm going to do for you, Mr. Navy Diver? I'm going to buy you a drink in a real Navy bar. One that caters only to sailors. How would you like to do that?"

Carl had never been in a Navy bar. They were whites-only. If he took her up on her offer, there was no telling what would happen.

"It's not that far," Gwen prompted, pointing.

Several hundred yards away was a run-down tavern. MOORE'S BAR, a peeling sign announced. From it blared faint music and the laughter of sailors having a good time.

"No one wants me in there," Carl said.

"Except maybe you. What do you say? Are you in the mood to live a little? Maybe show those boys that you're the kind of man who does as he damn well pleases?"

One drink couldn't hurt, Carl told himself. Besides, by walking in there he would be thumbing his nose at all those who wanted him to wash out. He would be saying to one and all that he was every bit as good as they were. When Mister Pappy heard the news, the commander was liable to burst a blood vessel. That alone made it worthwhile.

Carl opened the passenger door and slid in. "Let's go, lady."

# CHAPTER SEVEN

"That's the spirit!" Gwen said enthusiastically, and stomped on the gas pedal. The Mercury peeled out, burning rubber, fishtailing before Gwen straightened the wheel. "Drink! Laugh! Be merry!"

The convertible kept crossing the center line but thankfully no one was coming the other direction. Slewing into the parking lot, Gwen raised enough dust to cover half the state. She parked in front of the door, in a no-parking zone, then hopped out and crooked a painted finger. "Come on, Navy man. Don't chicken out on me now."

Carl regretted being so rash. Small signs by the door declared: NO LANDLUBBERS ALLOWED, and ARMY AND MARINE PERSONNEL ENTER AT YOUR OWN RISK. He opened the door for her, and she tittered.

"My, my, aren't you the gentleman. He used to be that way, too, until all the fighting began." Wrapping the fur coat right around her lush body, she sashayed into the bar as if she were the Queen of Siam.

The instant Carl crossed the threshold, the laughter and conversations ceased. The only sound was the blaring of Kitty Wells from the jukebox. Carl spotted Snowhill in a corner, showing a bar girl a photo from his wallet, probably the one of his wife he had shown Carl a hundred times. Other trainees were scattered about the room, among them Rourke and Mellegrano.

Gwen hopped onto a stool and patted one next to it. "This is for you, diver-man. Make yourself comfy." To the bartender, she said, "Donny, be a dear and bring us a couple of gins."

"We're out," Donny said. He was overweight and scruffy, with salt-and-pepper hair at the temples. A retired Navy hand, Carl guessed, who had opened up the bar to be near his own.

Gwen eyed the rows of liquor bottles behind the bar. "Make it scotch, then. Lucky for us you've got enough for the entire Second Fleet."

Reluctantly, the bartender set up the drinks, slopping some of Carl's on the counter. He was about to say something when he glanced past them, then sidled away as if they had the plague.

Carl swiveled his stool.

Rourke and Mellegrano flanked him, both glowering with their hands on their hips. "What the hell is this?" Rourke declared.

Gwen was a study in disdain. "Have a problem, do we, children?"

"You're not supposed to be in this joint, yourself," Rourke said. "So what do you think you're doing bringing *him* in here?"

"Having fun," Gwen said. "This establishment does cater to Navy men, doesn't it? And he *is* in the Navy."

Rourke balled his big fists. "Get out, Brashear," he snapped.

Carl came off the stool with his own fists bunched, ready to tear into the bully. He had taken all he was going to take from the other trainees. For his father's sake, and for his own, he wasn't going to let them tell him what to do. But just as the two of them raised their arms and were about to go at it, gruff laughter nipped their brawl in the bud.

"Well, I'll be damned! It's prom night here at the Moore Bar and someone forgot to let me know." Chief Billy Sunday materialized out of the crowd, holding an empty glass. He moved a trifle unsteadily and his cheeks were flushed. "Hell. I can't make up my mind who classes this joint up more, the fetching young woman in her expensive fur coat, or Cookie here." He looked at Rourke and Mellegrano. "Would you boys like a drink on me? Maybe you'd like to join us?"

Rourke and his buddy backed off, shaking their heads, wanting no part of bucking their superior officer.

Smirking at Carl and Gwen, Sunday leaned on the bar. "So, what did you two kids come here to do? Gwen, here, is big on dancing. Why don't you take a turn on the floor. It's a free country." Fire leaped from his eyes and his jovial mood disappeared. "You made a big mistake walking in here, Cookie."

"Don't blame him. This is my fault," Gwen apologized.

"It's always your fault!" Sunday growled, and pounded his fist on the counter with so much force, all the glasses on it shook. "Spoiled little rich girl gets her kicks dragging stray men to bars! Thinks we're just a bunch of sweaty rednecks she can shake up for the fun of it." Sunday nodded at Gwen, who gulped her drink in one swallow. "Look at her, Cookie, in that silly goddamn coat. Ask her and she'll tell you she's better than the rest of us. But give her two fingers of scotch, and woo-boy!"

By now Carl understood they knew one another. Extremely well.

Sunday winked at the nervous bartender. "Donny, be a dear lad and bring my wife a fresh soldier. You know she doesn't like to be empty."

Carl stared at Sunday in open contempt. He had taken about all he was going to take from him, too.

"What's the matter?" the chief said. "Think you deserve to be in here, don't you? Fraternizing among Navy men? Think you're as good as they are?" Sunday swept an arm at the stony patrons. "How about me, Cookie? Think you're better than me?"

It came out of Carl unbidden. "Damn right I do!"

Sunday turned to marble. Taking his pipe from his pocket, he smacked it down. "Noticed this, have you? General MacArthur himself smoked this pipe. I served with him at Leyte Gulf. Biggest damn naval battle in history. A kamikaze pilot ripped into the escort carrier I was on, the *St. Louis*, and she went down on a shallow reef. Me and six other boys were trapped in the fire room. There was only one way out."

"Flood the compartment and swim up," Carl said. The manual was clear on emergency procedures.

"Five decks, Cookie. Locked bulkheads. Dead bodies everywhere. You've got to have your balls screwed on tight for a swim like that." Sunday moistened his throat with scotch. "Anyway, the intercom was still working, and old MacArthur himself came over the squawk box. Any idea what he said?"

"No," Carl admitted.

"He said, 'Sunday, you cocky son of a bitch. I bet you can't hold your breath for the four minutes it will take to swim up out of there.'" Sunday chuckled. "Know what I said back? 'No, Mac, I can't. But I'll bet you that cob pipe of yours I can hold it for *five* minutes, because that's what it will take.'" Sunday clenched the pipe with mad glee. "So up we went, always pushing bodies out of the way, dead men staring at us like a legion of zombies. No air pockets. Nothing to save our asses if we ran into trouble."

Snowhill stepped up beside Carl and tugged at his arm. "C-come on, buddy. Th-this isn't worth it."

Carl wasn't moving. If Sunday was pushing for a showdown, that was fine by him.

"There are six men still breathing today because I led them out of that fire room," the chief declared. "And now, just because you pulled little Isert's white ass out of some rowboat sunk in a mud puddle, you think you're better than me? Some nerve." Turning, Sunday walked to a crude contraption on a wheeled cart: two brass diving helmets had been welded to a steel frame. "Let's just see, shall we? These collars are rigged so the helmets can be made airtight."

Carl had never seen a device like it. He started to walk over but Snowhill pushed against him.

"Let it go, man. Just let it g-go."

Chief Sunday stripped off his shirt and grinned. "Got any balls, Cookie? Or are you all bluff."

"You'll wish I was before I'm through!" Carl responded.

Now it was Gwen who tried to prevent him. "Please, no. Don't. This is all my fault. Let's leave, now. It will only get worse."

"I'm not leaving." Carl wasn't backing down to Sunday or any other man. Not tonight. Peeling off his shirt, he moved toward the cart.

"I told you," Gwen said after him, "hell-raisers, remember?" Shaking her head, she pulled the collar of her fur coat up around her ears and headed from the bar. "Fine. Be that way. It's your funeral, Navy Diver."

Carl grasped the helmet, then froze, astounded. Jo was there, over by the door! She seemed terribly hurt, her eyes pleading with him to stop. Others noticed, and whispers spread like wildfire. The bar became as still as a morgue. Gwen passed Jo on the way out and said something. Jo nodded, then fixed those immensely injured eyes of hers on Carl again.

"Well, Cookie? What's the holdup? You've got your very own cheering section now," Sunday taunted.

Carl dipped his head toward the helmet but stopped when Jo clasped her hands and silently mouthed, "Please!"

Everyone awaited his decision. Some had wads of bills out and were waiting for him to agree before placing a bet.

Sunday smacked his helmet. "Show your true colors, damn it! Or go back to following the hind end of a mule around all day."

Furious, Carl tore his gaze from Jo and nodded curtly. A vicious cheer resounded. Customers clapped and hollered and shoved money at one another in a wild orgy of frenzied gambling.

"What's the wager, Cookie?" Sunday asked. "How much are you willing to bet? I've got five hundred that says I'll skunk your sorry ass."

"No money," Carl said, struck by an inspiration. "If I win, you put Snowhill back in the diving program."

The chief was taken aback. "Snowhill? What in hell do you owe him that you'd go to this extreme?"

"I don't owe him. You owe him."

"Yeah?" Sunday laughed. "Fine. But if I win, then you have to hold up your end of the bargain."

"Which is?"

Chief Sunday seemed to grow several inches. "If I win, you ship out. You leave diving school. Tonight."

"No!" Snowhill shouted. "Don't do it, Carl! I'm not worth being kicked out! Forget about it!"

Carl grinned. "Did you just hear yourself? You didn't stutter once." Facing Sunday, he nodded. "Okay. You have a deal."

"And you just washed yourself out of the program. I've never lost, Cookie," Chief Sunday boasted. "Not once in over fifty matches." Snatching someone's scotch, he upended the bottle, chugging the amber liquor like it was water. Belching, he wiped the back of a hand across his mouth and wriggled up into his helmet.

Carl did likewise. Wasting no time, Mellegrano buckled him in while Rourke sealed in the chief. Rourke nodded at Donny, the bartender, who opened a spigot to which a pair of hoses had been attached.

"Get set!" Rourke cried.

A clammy sensation spread up Carl's neck as water bubbled up under his chin, rapidly climbing toward his nostrils. Through the faceplate he saw Sunday sneer. He filled his lungs a split second before the water covered his nose. It rose higher, blurring his vision, and through the helmet he heard a muffled outcry.

"Go!"

It had begun. Carl mentally willed himself to relax as he had been taught in diving school. As Sunday, no less, had taught them. He stared at the chief and only at the chief. Theirs was every bit as much a clash of willpower as it was lung power.

The room had grown quiet again except for a few last-moment bets being made.

From where Carl stood, he couldn't see the door, couldn't tell if Jo was still there. He was enormously flattered she had come all the way out to the base to find him, and wished he could have told her so.

"Thirty seconds!" Rourke bawled.

That was all? Carl was sure it had been a minute. He emptied his mind of distracting thoughts and filled it with reminisces of his father. Times they had gone fishing, played ball, indulged in checkers. This one was for Mac—and for himself. For all the times Sunday had mocked him. For the hosing. For the hazing. For Sunday always riding him. For the chief turning out to be Mister Pappy's real lapdog, not that unfortunate old bulldog. He was going to teach the chief a lesson, humiliate Sunday just as Sunday had routinely humiliated him. Once and for all he was going to prove the color of his skin didn't make him an automatic failure. Once and for all he was going to shut Chief Billy Sunday's obnoxious trash-talking mouth.

"One minute!"

Sunday had his brawny arms folded across his barrel chest. He was totally at ease, supremely confident. And why not? He'd boasted of never losing, and Carl believed him. Whatever else Billy Sunday might be, he wasn't a liar. Sunday has his own particular—some would say *peculiar*—brand of honor. A code old-time Navy men lived by. *Don't rock the boat. Always do as you're told. And don't take any lip off wet-nosed subordinates.*

Carl could never have made it in the old Navy. A life of galley duty wasn't for him. He wanted to carve out a career on his terms, not on anyone else's. If that involved stepping on a few toes, tough. He would do whatever it took to fulfill his dream. Including deflating Chief Billy Sunday's opinion of himself, and Mister Pappy's opinion of where black men belonged in the ranks.

"Two minutes."

Surprisingly calm, Carl matched Sunday's diamond glare. Two minutes were nothing and they both knew it. Any green kid brand-new to diving school could hold it that long, as Snowhill did that morning on the pier. When they reached the three-minute mark it would start to get rough. Four minutes would separate the braggarts from the men.

Carl thought of the pond, his hideaway when he was little. His haven. He had spent every spare hour he could there, swimming and cavorting. He'd chase the sunfish, or spook the big bass from its hiding place under a submerged tree, or play tag with the two wood turtles that called the pond their home by swimming after them and lightly tapping their shells.

Daily, Carl had dived to the bottom and stayed there as long as he could, always trying to remain longer than the time before, always striving to set a new personal record. Eventually he reached the point where he could stay under for minutes on end. Four, sometimes more.

Carl realized if it wasn't for the pond, he wouldn't be there at the bar, wouldn't be in the Navy, wouldn't be in the diving program. The pond was where he had honed the skills that enabled him to outrace the Navy search and rescue swimmer that day on the USS *Hoist*. The pond was why he had such a great love for the water.

"Three minutes!" Rourke shouted.

Chief Sunday's sneer widened, as if he expected Carl to give up soon.

To show he was in no distress whatsoever, Carl smiled. Sunday's sneer vanished, replaced by steely determination.

It was so unnecessary, Carl thought. Under different circumstances the two of them might have been the best of friends. They both loved the Navy, they both loved diving. But because Mister Pappy was using Sunday to make his life a living hell, they were at odds.

A dull pain in Carl's chest told him the four-minute mark was fast approaching. He always experienced a sharp pain about that time, but he could go longer by concentrating and not allowing the pain to dominate him. Staying calm was the key. Above all else, he must totally relax. If he tensed up for any reason it would reduce the amount of time he could keep holding his breath.

Chief Sunday squirmed and looked down at himself,

then glared. He was feeling the effect, too, but he wouldn't give up.

Sailors leaned toward them, anxious for the outcome, many clutching the money they had riding on the duel.

"Four minutes!"

The minute of truth, as the divers called it. The minute when most gave up. The minute that often meant the difference between life and death underwater. Few human beings could hold their breath that long.

The pain grew worse. Carl felt an urge to gasp for breath but resisted. Not yet, not yet. He had to make it to the five-minute mark. At least that long. If Sunday could do it, by God, so could he. He saw the chief seething at him. Shock gripped him as he saw something else; tendrils of blood were seeping from Sunday's nostrils.

The bounce dive, Carl thought. The dive that had scarred Sunday's lungs and brought about his transfer to diving school. The chief wasn't as young as he used to be, and wasn't quite as fit. All that smoking and drinking didn't help any, either. Maybe in his prime Sunday could hold his breath for five minutes, but certainly not now.

Rourke bent toward Sunday's faceplate. "Chief?" You're bleeding! It's over. The game's over." He reached for the handle that would break the seal on Sunday's helmet and let the water drain but Sunday grabbed Rourke's wrist, stopping him.

"But you're bleeding, sir!"

Sunday glared at Carl as if to say, "So what?" Seconds ticked by, weighted by anchors.

Carl's chest was aflame with torment, his lungs screaming for relief. He couldn't hold out much longer.

Suddenly Chief Sunday's eyes fluttered and he began to convulse. Another second and he passed out, slumping forward. Rourke instantly stabbed for the handle, venting the helmet.

Carl waited another couple of seconds, then vented his own. He shrugged clear and sucked in precious air as Rourke and others ministered to the chief.

Blood continued to dribble over Sunday's mouth and chin.

Rourke glanced up, spiteful as ever. "Satisfied?" he snapped. "Everybody knows how dangerous it is for him to do that. Pushing the chief to his limit could kill him."

"He challenged me," Carl reminded them.

"He's challenged all of us at one time or another," Wilson interjected. "But we had enough brains not to make him go that long."

Carl realized two things. The other trainees cared for Sunday, truly cared for him, just as all those sailors and officers on the *Hoist* had looked up to him. And second, he shouldn't take out his frustration and anger on Sunday for doing what Pappy ordered. Mister Pappy was his true enemy, not the chief.

Sunday was coming around. Raising his groggy head, he touched the blood on his mouth. "Damn! Whoever bet on Cookie came out the winner, huh?"

"Only one person was stupid enough to," Mellegrano said.

Most of the sailors stared at Snowhill, who was having money shoved at him from all sides. "Land sakes! L-look, C-Carl! I'm r-r-rich!"

Sunday slowly rose, supported by trainees. "You did it, Cookie. You honest to God beat me. Wait until word gets around. I'll be the laughingstock of the base."

Carl hadn't thought of that. But he refused to feel guilty. The chief had brought it on himself.

"Drinks all around, boys!" Sunday called out. "I want you to join me in a salute to Boatswain's Mate Brashear!"

No one moved. Judging by their expressions, they

would rather eat broken glass or walk through sheets of burning flame.

Outside, a car engine abruptly roared to life. Tires squealed, and someone yelled stridently, a warning, maybe. But it wasn't heeded. A tremendous, sickening crunch resounded.

For a heartbeat everyone in the bar was still, then they streamed toward the door, Carl among them. He burst out on the porch and saw Jo to one side, her collar pulled up against the chill.

"It was that blond lady," Jo said. "She got in her car and drove off like a crazy woman. Right for the river."

Had Gwen tried to commit suicide? Carl ran on. The Mercury convertible was a ruined, crumpled heap, steam rising from the shattered radiator. It had smashed head-on into a concrete mooring block Gwen hadn't noticed. If not for the block, the car would have plunged into the river and she would have drowned.

Sailors were already there, shoving bent metal aside and swiping at shards of glass with their bare fingers. Two men carefully pulled Gwen from the wreckage and carried her clear. In case the gas tank ignited, they didn't set her down until they were a safe distance from the car.

Carl shouldered through. Swaddled in her fur coat, limp and frail, Gwen slowly stirred and smiled dreamily up at him.

"Life strikes again, huh, diver-man?"

Someone bulled through the crowd, shoving sailors left and right. A hand gripped Carl and he was jerked back.

Chief Sunday reared over his wife, his shirt drenched, blood still caking his chin. "Gwen!" Kneeling, he tenderly clasped her hand.

"Hey, handsome," Gwen Sunday said. "We're going to have some explaining to do to the insurance guy, aren't we?"

"You ever try a stupid stunt like that again, I'll kill you," the chief said huskily.

Gwen laughed and pinched his cheek. "Why can't we be happy, Billy? Why can't we stop all the bickering and petty fights and be like normal couples?"

"Is there such a thing as normal?" Sunday said, quickly adding, "But we can if you want to. I'm willing to give it a shot."

"You've said that before."

"So have you."

Gwen sighed rather sadly. "I'm tired, husband of mine. So very tired."

"Come on, babe. Let's go home." Sunday slid his arms under her and gently lifted. Gwen's cheek fell against his broad chest as Sunday carried her through the hushed sailors toward the parking lot.

Carl watched them get into the chief's car. The love they shared was so strong, so obvious, he wondered why they were always at each other's throats. When one person loved another, they should be willing to give their all to the one they loved. He headed toward the bar to find Jo and glanced back one last time at the wreckage.

Beyond it a figure was walking hurriedly away along the edge of the road.

"Jo?" Carl bleated in surprise. "Jo! Wait!" But she did no such thing. Instead, she walked faster. He gave chase, overtaking her swiftly. "Jo? Where are you going?"

Jo had her arms wrapped tight across her bosom. She was shaken, drained. "I can't do this, Carl. I can't be part of this life again." She gazed at him in reproach. "I waited for you tonight. When you didn't show, I was worried sick you were hurt or dead. I flattered myself you wouldn't miss a lesson unless you were at death's door. You didn't even call!"

Stung, Carl asked, "How did you know where I was?"

"I knew. I pulled my father out of more Navy bars than I care to count. And this is the one nearest to the base."

"Jo, you don't understand what happened tonight—" Carl tried to explain.

"Oh, but I do." Jo reached into a pocket and waved a paper at him. "Look! I passed my finals. I couldn't wait to tell you but you weren't there."

"Oh." Carl had forgotten she was supposed to get the results that afternoon. "I'm so sorry, but it's not what you think."

"The point is, I'm starting an internship at Bellevue. Long hours are involved. I won't have time to see you anymore."

A pain far worse than the one Carl had felt while holding his breath spiked through his chest. "Jo, I made a mistake. It won't happen again."

"Yes, it will. You wanted to fight that man. I could see it on your face. You'd just been waiting for the right moment."

Carl couldn't deny it. But she didn't understand. He hadn't told her about Sunday, about the hazing and about his father.

Jo stopped and put her hand on his. "Don't you see? My mother went through this with my father, and it about destroyed her. I won't let the same thing happen to me."

"It wouldn't. I'm not like that."

"So you say." Jo's eyes were moist. "So they all say." She resumed walking. "The things I want out of life are smaller than the things you want. If I just work hard and keep my head down—"

"Your whole life will go by and you'll never really live," Carl finished for her.

Out of the darkness a cab appeared. Jo waved and it

braked across from them. "Carl, most of what's in those diving books you know better than I do. You don't need me anymore. You don't need anyone." Jo moved toward the taxi.

"I need you," Carl said, and when that didn't stop her, he blurted what they had both known since the moment they met. "I love you."

Jo stopped, swung around, and blinked. Tears poured, and she pressed a hand to her forehead. "Now he tells me."

Carl went to her, embraced her. Jo fought back the tears and pressed her lips against his, kissing him as he had never been kissed before, a kiss of passion, of yearning. It lingered on and on, until she finally pushed away from him.

"My mother is two thousand miles from here. I'm all alone. There's no one to stop me from falling hopelessly in love with you."

Carl smiled.

"Except me." Whirling, Jo yanked on the door handle and slid in. "Go!" she directed the cabbie. "Get me out of here!"

The taxi pulled out, and for several seconds Carl was rooted in disbelief. In one night he had lost his father and the woman he loved. An iron fist enveloped his heart and his legs grew weak. But only for several seconds. He refused to accept it was over. The fact she had come all the way out from the city to find him out of fear for his welfare was proof she cared for him just as much as he cared for her. Her kiss had confirmed it. If she let her go, if he let her slip through his fingers, he would never forgive himself.

Breaking into a run, Carl sprinted for all he was worth. The cab was gaining speed slowly, and he swiftly caught up. "Jo! Don't go! I love you! I mean it!"

Tinged by inexpressible sorrow, Jo's face appeared at the rear window. She was crying again, and her lips formed the word "What?"

The cab began to pull ahead. Carl couldn't sustain the pace much longer. In another dozen yards it would be out of earshot. Cupping his hands to his mouth, he bawled the one thing that would demonstrate his sincerity beyond a shadow of a doubt, "Will you marry me?"

The distance between them widened. Carl poured on a last burst of speed but the taxi's taillights were receding. "Please marry me!" he cried.

Out of nowhere a jeep bore down on him. Carl sprang to the right but would still have not made it if the driver hadn't spotted him and madly spun the wheel. Tires screeched, the horn blared, and the jeep swerved past, sailors leaning out to angrily shake their fists at him.

"Trying to get yourself killed, idiot!"

"Stay out of the middle of the road, moron!"

An incredible weight bent Carl's shoulders. His insides churned as he turned and trudged toward the base. *I've lost her.* He had lost Jo. The shock numbed him. He walked in a daze, hardly caring when he strayed out onto the road. If another vehicle ran him over, it would serve him right. "Jo. Oh, Jo," he said softly.

Carl had gone only a little way when a faint noise brought him up short. He looked back into the velvety darkness, sure he had heard a footstep, but no one appeared. Evidently he had been mistaken. He was about to go on when he heard another, and out of the night rushed Jo. Flinging her arms wide, she leaped into his and nuzzled her face against his neck.

Stunned, overjoyed, Carl held her tightly, savoring the feel of her body. Her scent, her perfume, were intoxicating. His head swimming, he never wanted to let her go.

"The driver said you were yelling something about marriage?"

Carl had to clear his throat to answer. "I asked you to marry me."

"While I was driving off in a taxi? Has anyone ever mentioned your timing leaves a lot to be desired."

"Will you, Jo?"

Jo tilted her face up. The tears were gone and she glowed with happiness. "On one condition."

"I work on my timing?"

"No more bars. Never again. I saw what it did to my mother and I refuse to put myself through that."

Carl tenderly stroked her chin. "I only went because I was upset over my father dying."

Jo gave a start. "Your father? Oh, Carl." Her arms constricted, hugging him close, nearly choking off his breath. "I'm sorry. Why didn't you say something?"

"Poor timing, as usual," Carl said, and they both laughed. Then her lips were against his again and the night blurred into insignificance.

# CHAPTER EIGHT

Chief Billy Sunday walked up to the door to Mister Pappy's quarters, raised his hand to knock, then hesitated. He had a hunch why his commanding officer had sent for him. Sunday didn't want to be there, but an order was an order. Rapping loudly, he waited until a sandpaper voice bid him enter.

As the door swung inward an acrid order hit Sunday like a stinging slap to the face. Breathing shallowly, he cautiously entered. All the lights were out. Except for pale beams of moonlight filtering through the window, Pappy's quarters were inky black. One of the moonbeams bathed a cramped kitchenette and a small table in the center. On the table were dozens of empty bottles of rubbing alcohol.

"Mister Pappy?" Sunday said.

In the darkness a shadow shifted, and the sound of running water filled the kitchenette. Pappy was at the sink, his back to Sunday, putting glass tumblers on a tray.

"Close the door, Chief. And try not to touch anything if you can help it."

"Yes, sir," Sunday said, wondering what in hell that was all about. He had never been invited to his commander's private quarters before, and he couldn't say as he ever wanted to visit them again.

The shadow lifted the tray and went into the next room. "Follow me."

A tiny fire crackled in a brick hearth. Otherwise, the living room was as dark as the rest of the place. In one corner an old windup Victrola played a scratchy Strauss waltz. Bed sheets covered most of the furniture. Sunday swept the room, trying to pinpoint his superior.

"Did you know ordinary house dust is composed primarily of human skin?" Mister Pappy asked. "Makes you think twice about who you invite into your home."

Sunday was drawn to a large winged-back chair near the fire. He couldn't quite see Pappy's face, mired as it was in shadow. "You sent for me, sir?"

Mister Pappy didn't reply. The tray he had brought in was now on a small oak table, and his pudgy hand lowered to the tumblers on it and arranged them in a neat line. "They're filled with rubbing alcohol."

"Sir?"

Mister Pappy produced several medals and dropped one into each of the glasses. "To clean these. To rid them of dust and contamination."

What could Sunday say? That it was the most ridiculous thing he had ever heard? "Yes, that should do it, sir," he conceded.

"Did you know, Chief, that two tablespoons of machine oil can contaminate a ship's entire fresh water supply?"

"I wasn't aware of that, no, sir."

"Some things just don't mix, do they, Chief?"

Sunday guessed where their talk was leading and became guarded.

"I've heard about the incident at the bar last night," Mister Pappy mentioned. "Not very bright of you, was it, to be shown up by Brashear? To be made to look the fool in front of everyone else? By one of their kind, no less."

"He beat me fair, sir."

"You were drunk. You have a bad lung. It was hardly fair." Mister Pappy paused. "You know why I've sent for you?"

"He's going to pass, sir."

"Is he?"

"He scored a ninety-four on his final. All he has to do is complete the exercise tomorrow and he's done it. One of the best in the class, in my estimation, sir."

Mister Pappy stared into the crackling flames. "Be that as it may, contamination is still contamination. His kind has already leeched into all aspects of civilian life. Doctors, lawyers, you name it."

"So what can one black Navy diver hurt, sir?" Sunday asked.

"Chief Sunday, there may come a time when a colored diver graduates from this school. But it won't be tomorrow. Not on my watch. Not as long as I have a say." Pappy's broad face swiveled like the head of a great oversized toad. "You agree with me of course, don't you, Chief?"

Carl hummed to himself as he stepped from the bus. Pelting rain failed to spoil his good mood as he strolled past the guards and on to his barracks. It was late and he needed to get some sleep before the big day tomorrow. Still humming, he opened the door and paused to shake some water off. Suddenly he stiffened. His radio played faintly at the back of the room, yet he was sure he had turned it off before he left. He moved down the aisle.

"Back kind of late tonight," Chief Billy Sunday commented. He was in a chair, leaning back, seated in the dark. The red glow of his pipe glared like a baleful scarlet eye. "And in a good mood too. Looking forward to passing tomorrow?"

"I just got married," Carl revealed.

The front legs of Sunday's chair thumped to the floor. "No fooling? The pretty girl who showed up at the bar the other night?"

"That's her," Carl said proudly.

"Well, well. Congratulations. I hope your marriage isn't as combative as mine." Grinning, Sunday took a slip of paper from his pocket and taped it to Carl's bed. "This one says, '*You'll never make it, nigger.*' I was supposed to leave it and go. But not this time."

"I always figured it was Rourke or one of the others," Carl said. "I never let myself think it could be you."

"Why not?"

"I saw your last dive, remember? But I guess I don't know you as well as I thought I did."

Sunday slowly rose to his full height. "Do you want to know who I am? I'm a sorry son of a bitch sent here to get it through that thick skull of yours that some things can't be changed."

"I deserve to pass."

"Since when does deserving mean anything? They're not going to have a colored diver. Because no matter what you do, how well you do your job, in their eyes you'll never be as good as they are. So, deserving or otherwise, you're going to fail." Sunday glanced at Carl's sea chest and picked up a framed photo of Carl's father. "This your old man? You look a lot like him."

"When you say 'they' you really mean Mister Pappy, don't you?" Carl asked. "The one who pulls your strings."

"Don't start. I'm being as polite about this as I can."

"Polite about ruining my life? Should I be grateful?"

"Just let it go."

"Never!" Carl practically roared. "I haven't come this far, haven't worked so hard, to quit the night before the last exercise. I'll be there, and I'll complete it, and he'll have no choice but to pass me."

Sunday shook his head. "God, you're stubborn. You just won't let yourself see the truth. It's over! Whether you show up or not, whether you complete the exercise or not, it won't matter. You're history."

"What about you, Chief? Where do you stand? Do you agree with him?"

"That's my business," Sunday said angrily. "What, you think I owe you this? I don't owe you or anyone else a goddamn thing! You've been fucked. It happens to the best of us and there's nothing we can do." In a fit of rage, Sunday savagely brought his hand crashing down onto the radio.

Without thinking, Carl lunged. But at the last instant he restrained himself; assaulting a superior would be grounds for a dishonorable discharge.

Sunday stared at the broken radio as if he couldn't believe what he had just done. He picked up a piece of the bottom, the piece with the letters A-S-N-F. "What did he ever say to you that makes you try so hard?"

"Be the best."

"Well, you are. But don't show up tomorrow. Mister Pappy will fail you no matter how good you do." Sunday walked off. At the door he stopped. "Know what the one drawback to Navy life is? Having to take orders from total assholes."

The door opened and closed, and Carl was alone.

Tendrils of mist shrouded the Hudson River, winding sinuously along the bank and blanketing the diving pier. To Chief Billy Sunday the brisk morning chill was a heady tonic. He breathed in deep as he moved toward five trainees in deep-sea diving suits perched on a long bench. Tenders were swarming over them, ensuring the suits were ready.

"This is your last challenge, gentlemen," Sunday greeted them. "The practical exam." He was both relieved and disappointed to see Carl Brashear was not among them. "You're the only ones left now, and today will decide which of you become full-fledged Navy divers."

Sunday moved to a nearby table where a pair of junior instructors had laid out a number of items. "We've been all through this but we'll go over it again. The object of today's test is to correctly assemble this underwater." He held up a complicated flange, the most complicated any of the trainees had seen to date. "We always save the best for last."

"Is there a time limit, sir?" Rourke inquired.

"No," Sunday said. "All you have to do is finish. Whether you take two hours or twenty doesn't matter." He grasped a small canvas bag and shook it so it tinkled. "The pieces you require are in bags like this one. Each of you will find a bag labeled with your name waiting for you at the bottom of the river. Once you've located it, return to your mark and call up for your tools. They will be lowered down and you can commence work."

"Piece of cake, sir," Mellegrano said.

"Be confident, not cocky," Sunday responded. "Take your time and get it right. That's what counts. We'll keep pumping air down to you for as long as you can stand the cold. If you don't complete the flange, you'll have wasted six whole months of your life."

"Sir!" one of the junior instructors interrupted, and pointed.

Carl had appeared out of the fog. Marching to the

bench, he sat down. The tenders looked at Sunday, and when Sunday nodded, they began to suit Carl up.

Twisting, Chief Sunday gazed at the tower. Mister Pappy was watching, as he always was, blanketed in shadow. Sunday swore he could hear the officer's teeth grind together from where he stood.

In due course Carl was ready and the tenders stepped back. The mist had begun to dissipate and pockets of sunlight dappled the pier.

Sunday faced the cream of his class. "Blessed are those who go down to the sea, for they shall know the wonders of the deep," he declared, a ritual he had performed on the last dive of every class. "Divers, approach the rail!"

The six men surged powerfully erect and clomped toward the river, their weighted diving boots hammering a staccato tempo. Oxygen compressors roared to life as the tenders fired them up. Six air hoses hissed and bulged as air gushed through them, and the tenders checked the hose connections, a final precaution.

"In you go!" Sunday directed, striding over to watch the divers descend the ladders. "Remember, once you've found your flange, call up for your tools."

In turn, the big brass helmets dipped into the Hudson and sank from sight. Sunday watched until Carl went under, then he moved to the communications box. It wouldn't take the men long to find their flanges. The bags had been scattered close to the pier to keep them from being carried away by the current.

The first voice to crackle over the box was Rourke's. "Topside, this is Red Diver. I've located my project bag and am on mark. Request tools."

At a nod from Sunday, a junior instructor attached a tool bag to a line and lowered it down.

Thirty seconds later another voice crackled. It was

Carl's. "Topside, this is Blue Diver. Request my tool bag."

The junior instructors looked at Sunday, who glanced up at the tower. Mister Pappy shook his head, and Sunday did likewise. In short order Yarmouth, Mellegrano, and the others called up for their bags, which were duly lowered.

"Topside, this is Blue Diver again. Where's that tool bag? I'm still waiting."

Sunday turned to the tower. Mister Pappy smiled grimly and nodded. Intense hatred coursed through Sunday but he did as he was ordered. It came with the territory, with being in the service. A good soldier always did as he was instructed. But he almost couldn't bring himself to nod at one of the junior instructors. Almost.

The man picked up Carl's tool bag. Sliding a knife from a pocket, he slit the mesh bag from end to end, then attached it to the line. "It's on its way, Blue Diver," the man said into his microphone. "Be looking for it."

Carl had been looking for it. For over five minutes. It had never taken so long, and he was beginning to suspect they weren't going to send it down but claim they had as a means of failing him. Up to his knees in the muck at the bottom of the Hudson, he craned his helmet back so he could see the surface. An object splashed down and sank toward him. The tool bag, he thought. Simultaneously, there were a dozen or so bright gleaming flashes of sunlight on metal. Not knowing what to make of them, he reached toward the tool bag, which descended with unusual slowness. When he gripped it he learned why. The bag was empty. He went to call up, to notify topside, then spied the slit in the mesh. Fingering it, the terrible truth dawned.

They had slit the bag and now his tools were scattered all over the place!

Carl wanted to scream with rage. He supposed he should be angry; he had been expecting them to try something. But now that they actually had, he was mad, damned mad, at how cleverly they had sabotaged him. He couldn't possibly assemble the flange now.

Or could he?

Carl surveyed the murky realm of the river. The tools were light and wouldn't sink very far. Those that had might leave telltale marks or holes. He should be able to find them and put the flange together. It would take time, lots of time, but there was no limit on how long it took to get the job done. He figured an hour to find the tools, maybe that long to assemble the flange, and it would be over.

Stepping away from his mark, Carl searched diligently. He was encouraged when half a minute later the dull glint of something at his feet turned out to be a wrench. One down, eleven to go. Holding the mesh bag so it wouldn't spill, he shoved the wrench into it and edged on. He moved with the utmost care in order not to disturb the muck any more than was absolutely necessary.

A little farther on, the handle of a screwdriver jutted from the ooze. Bending, Carl retrieved it, swirled it in the water to clean off the mud, and added it to his collection.

Carl settled into a pattern, roving in ever wider circles. He found a third tool. After that, nothing. He was sure they had to be within a dozen feet or so of the mark, but they might as well be on the moon, as thick as the muck was.

Twelve feet out from the mark, Carl stopped. He had been wrong. There were no holes, no marks to show where the tools had hit. The mud had swallowed them and re-formed. To find them, he must sift through the muck with his fingers. So much for locating them in one hour. More than that had already gone by. It would take forever. He risked succumbing to the water's chill long before he collected all twelve.

Tucking at the knees, Carl poked his fingers into the ooze and ran them back and forth, probing for contact with something solid. The tools had to be there somewhere.

They had to.

The moment the first tool bag sank into the river, Chief Billy Sunday had gestured to one of the junior instructors. "Start it!" he barked.

Hurrying to a large clock mounted to the dive shack, the young instructor flipped a lever to activate it. The minute hand moved, the sweep hand ticking off the seconds.

Sunday paced at the pier's edge, conscious of Mister Pappy's perpetual scrutiny. Conscious, too, that he loathed the man with every fiber of his being. It went against his grain to betray another sailor, yet that was exactly what Pappy demanded he do. So what if the sailor wasn't the same shade of skin? They wore the same uniform. That made them brothers in arms, and in Sunday's book that was all that counted.

Sunday glanced at the surface. Why the hell couldn't the kid have taken the hint and left? Why did Brashear have to be so damned stubborn, so damned determined, so damned noble?

None of the ready lines in the water m~~ved until eight forty-six. A dive tender reeled it up and attached to the end was a completed flange. The tender brought it to Sunday, who examined it and clinked the com link.

"Machinist Mate Rourke, one hour and thirty-seven minutes. Perfect assembly. You can come topside."

Next to tug his ready line and send up a finished flange was DuBoyce.

"Signalman DuBoyce, two hours and nineteen minutes. Perfect assembly. Get on up here."

Sunday moved to the end of the pier again. He couldn't understand why Carl was still down there. He assumed the young fool was hunting for the lost tools. A hopeless task, which even Brashear had to realize sooner or later.

Another diver succeeded and was winched up. Then a fourth. Eventually only Carl and Boots Crowfoot, always the slowest of the trainees, were left.

Clouds scuttled in from the west, gray clouds fat with the threat of rain. A drizzle began, pelting everyone with icy drops. Shortly thereafter a ready line jerked and up came another assembled flange.

"Engineer Boots Crowfoot, four hours and nine minutes," Sunday announced. "Better late than never, eh, Boots? Perfect assembly."

"I can come up?"

"With bells on," Sunday jested.

Crowfoot was hauled out. Tenders crowded around to strip off his dripping helmet and soaked suit.

"Finally!" Crowfoot said, his teeth chattering.

"How's the water down there?" Sunday asked.

"Remember that old saying about a well digger's ass, Chief? I was afraid I'd freeze to death before I got done." Crowfoot stared at the remaining air line. "Someone is still down there?"

"Boatswain's Mate Brashear."

"Hell, he won't be for long. He must be as cold as me." Holding his fingers to his mouth, Crowfoot warmed them with puffs of warm breath. "He'll signal to come up anytime now."

Sunday hoped so. God, how he hoped so. To all the

waiting trainees he said, "Take it inside. A hot meal and all the coffee you can drink will get your blood flowing."

"Shouldn't we wait for Brashear, Chief?" Crowfoot asked.

"He is one of us, sir," DuBoyce remarked.

*Would wonders never cease!* Sunday mused. Now the boys are Carl's best friends. "No, you go on to the mess hall. The tenders and I will stick around." Glumly, he focused on the air line as it moved a few feet. Still searching, Sunday guessed. Still trying to accomplish a miracle.

The phone in the dive shack jangled and a junior assistant rushed to answer it. "For you, Chief!"

Sunday didn't ask who it was. Entering, he shooed the junior instructor out and shut the door. "Chief Sunday."

"He hasn't come up yet?" Mister Pappy rasped.

"Not yet, sir, no."

"Good. Leave him. Take the tenders and go."

"I can't, sir."

Mister Pappy wheezed like someone having an asthma attack. "Are you refusing a direct order, Chief?"

"To commit murder? Yes, sir." There was a line Sunday wouldn't cross, and that was it. "If he dies, a review board will be convened. They'd take my stripes and toss me in the brig. I'm sorry. I've done everything you've asked, but that would be stepping too far out of bounds."

A long beat of silence ended with a curse. "Very well. I suppose you're right. A review board would be too messy, too public. Do you really think he'll stay down there as long as it takes?"

"Knowing him as I do, yes, sir."

Mister Pappy chuckled. "This could work to our benefit. He stays under too long, the cold will take care of him for us. We'll say he was too pigheaded for his own good, and it killed him."

"What if he manages to complete the flange, sir?"

"Need you even ask? He can't pass, you hear me? Do whatever it takes to ensure he doesn't. If he sends the flange up, have one of your subordinates drop it in the river before you can inspect it. Then haul the colored hardhead up and tell him that without verification, he fails the course."

"You never miss a trick, sir," Sunday said. He didn't intend it as a compliment but it was construed as one.

"I can't afford to. We're the last bastion against contamination, Chief. We're all that stands between upstarts like Brashear and the spread of their kind throughout the entire U.S. Navy. We must be vigilant. We must be strong. We must be clever."

The dial tone pealed in Sunday's ear. He slammed the phone down and stood for the longest while with his fists clenched, shaking with fury. Finally he composed himself, squared his shoulders, and marched outdoors.

It was almost noon. The lone air line moved a few inches. Brashear was still searching. The tenders and junior instructors had plunked down on the bench but Sunday walked to the end of the pier and stood with his arms folded.

*Damn you, Cookie!* Sunday thought. Thanks to the young upstart, he had been put in a no-win situation. Damned if he did and damned if he didn't. He didn't like being put on the spot, didn't like it one bit.

Sunday has always been a by-the-book kind of guy. He never wanted to make waves, never wanted to be put in a position where he had to even think about making waves. Making waves was bad for a man's career. It could have long-term, hugely unpleasant repercussions.

*Double damn you, Cookie!* Sunday reflected. And damn Mister Pappy for having it out for the scrappy boatswain's mate. As a result, here he was, caught in the middle in a deadly game of cat and mouse. A game that always ended poorly for the mouse.

Immersed in his musing, Sunday didn't realize how much time had gone by until one of the junior instructors hollered his name. He turned. It was past one now. But that wasn't why the instructor had yelled. A knot of seven or eight sailors were at the landward end of the pier, watching.

Sunday smiled and strolled over. "What are you fellows up to?"

"We heard about him at the mess hall, Chief," a kid not much over twenty said, and nodded at the Hudson.

"Him?" Sunday said, hoping it didn't mean what he suspected it meant.

"The guy still down there. Brashear. It's all they were talking about," the kid said.

"Who was?"

"Everybody, sir."

An older sailor piped in with, "A bunch of your boys were in there telling everyone about it. How the guy who is down there might freeze to death before he gets done. And all to pass the diving course, huh, sir?"

If Rourke and the others had been close by, Sunday would have strangled them with his bare hands. "Yeah, that's right. But it's not worth bothering yourselves over. Go on about your business."

"Oh, we're off duty, sir," another sailor said. "We'd like to stay and watch, if you don't mind."

Sunday minded, all right. He minded more than he could admit. But shooing them away would cause a lot of talk, maybe draw even more attention. He glanced toward the mess hall and saw other sailors approaching. Shrugging, he said, "Stick around if you want. Just don't get in our way, boys."

Word of mouth worked swiftly. Over the next hour

the crowd grew. Not just sailors, but clerical personnel and civilians who worked on the base. Thirty people, Sunday estimated, and still more came from all different directions.

At the forefront were Crowfoot, Rourke, DuBoyce, and the others. Sunday almost stalked over to give them a tongue-lashing, but refrained. What in hell were they thinking, he wondered, to blab as they had? Could it be that at long last, on almost the last damn day of the whole damn course, they had accepted Brashear as one of their own? It was preposterous, yet apparently the case.

The air line moved, but feebly. Sunday knew Carl had to be half-frozen. "Give it up, Cookie," he said softly. "If you go into shock down there, you may not wake up. Come on. This isn't worth dying over."

Another hour elapsed and the crowd doubled in size. Some had brought blankets to sit on.

The phone rang, and Sunday went to answer it himself.

"What the hell is going on down there?" Mister Pappy fumed. "Why are all those people hanging around?"

"They've heard about him."

"I gathered that!" Pappy screeched. "Order them to get lost. Tell them they have better things to do!"

"I can't do that, sir. They're on their own time. Some got permission from their superiors to come down. Everyone wants to be in on the finish."

"The finish?" Mister Pappy growled. "I'll tell you how the finish is going to be. You're not to bring him up until he stops moving. You hear me? Keep him down there until the cold finishes him off. Otherwise, every cook and shine boy in this camp is going to think they can pull a stunt like his."

"He's near dead now, sir," Sunday said.

"Not until he stops moving!" Mister Pappy stressed, and hung up.

Sunday went back out to the communications box, and clicked onto Brashear's line. What he heard was like a punch to the gut or a kick in the groin. Gasping, he leaned on the box and closed his eyes.

Over the line came Carl's voice, quaking but distinct. He was repeating the same thing over and over again: "My name is Boatswain's Mate Second Class Carl Brashear. I am a Navy diver."

# CHAPTER NINE

"My name is Boatswain's Mate Second Class Carl Brashear. I am a Navy diver." Carl's teeth were chattering nonstop and he could barely get the words out but he had to keep trying. It helped him focus. It helped him stay alive.

Carl was cold, so utterly, totally, miserably cold, colder than he had ever been, as cold as if he'd stood naked in a meat market freezer for the past six hours. He couldn't feel his toes and his lower legs were almost numb. Mechanically, he plunged his fingers into the muck for the thousandth time.

"My name is Boatswain's Mate Second Class Carl Brashear. I am a Navy diver."

*Two tools,* Carl told himself. Two tools were all he needed. The mesh bag contained the rest. But he couldn't complete the flange without the entire set. That was how the test was designed. Two more wrenches and he could assemble the flange.

Carl was south of his mark, closer to the pier than ever before. Bending back, he saw the pale surface. Saw, too, the blurred reflection of Chief Billy Sunday peering down into the depths. *Waiting for me to fail, aren't you, Chief?* Carl thought. To give up and signal to be winched out of the river. But that would never happen. Not so long as breath remained in Carl's body. Not so long as he could move his fingers, his hands.

The mud parted. A hint of metal drew Carl to the second-to-last wrench. Elated, he pulled it out, and there, right next to it, was the last wrench, the final tool. He put them in the bag and slowly turned. Willing his deadened legs to move, he returned to the mark, to the project bag, and opened it.

A terrible thought seared him. *What if they had tampered with the project bag, too? What if the parts weren't the ones he needed? Or it was the wrong flange?*

Carl gingerly removed a few pieces and was relieved to find they were the right pieces. He slid a wrench from the mesh bag and began to work on the fittings.

"My name is Boatswain's Mate Second Class Carl Brashear. I am a Navy diver."

His fingers weren't responding as they should. The cold limited his dexterity. He had to try twice to apply the wrench.

"My name is Boatswain's Mate Second Class Carl Brashear. I am a Navy diver."

Methodically, painstakingly, Carl attached the first couple of pieces. He thought of Jo, at her apartment awaiting word of how he had fared. Correction. *Their* apartment. He had promised to call her by lunchtime. He never imagined it would take any longer than that. How wrong he had been.

Tearing his mind from his new bride, Carl concentrated on the flange, and only the flange. He couldn't let his thoughts wander.

"My name is Boatswain's Mate Second Class Carl Brashear. I am a Navy diver."

Now that he wasn't moving about as much, the cold was more apparent than ever. It seeped into his muscles, his lungs, his bloodstream. He was exhausted and so god-awful sluggish. A snail could work faster. But he plugged away, forcing his leaden fingers to cooperate.

At the rate he was going, Carl estimated it would take him hours to finish. Hours more in that frightfully frigid water. Hours more of the cold spreading through his system.

"My name is Boatswain's Mate Second Class Carl Brashear. I am a Navy diver."

At sunset the tenders set up powerful spotlights and trained them on the Hudson and on the line that merely twitched now and then.

Well over a hundred spectators had gathered. Enlisted men, officers, civilians, nearly everyone on the base and some from outside.

Darkness claimed the river and its environs. Chief Billy Sunday lit his pipe and scanned the crowd. Jo had arrived a while ago and was gazing fearfully at the spot where her beloved worked underwater.

Unable to bear the sight, Sunday faced around. The air line twitched again. "Bring him up," Sunday commanded.

Almost immediately the phone in the dive shack jangled and one of the junior instructors moved to answer it.

"Let it ring!" Sunday said. "I told you to bring him up and that's exactly what you're going to do."

A tender headed for the winch.

The next second the public address system sizzled to life and out of the speakers thundered Mister Pappy's clarion command. "Sailor, you will disregard that order!"

Stopping halfway, the confused tender looked from the chief to the tall tower and back again.

"The trainee has not signaled to come up yet," Mister Pappy's voice reverberated eerily. "No one is to winch him up until he does."

The moment of truth had arrived. Sunday turned toward the winch but someone else was already hurrying toward it. The last person Sunday would ever have expected. The last person, no doubt, Brashear would have expected.

"I've got him, Chief," Machinist Mate Rourke said. "Say the word and I'll start reeling him in."

The speakers blasted shrilly. "Rourke? Rourke! What in the hell do you think you're doing? You are to stand down. You hear me?"

Rourke didn't stop.

Mister Pappy was beside himself. The speakers fairly vibrated as he shouted, "Chief Sunday, effective immediately I am relieving you of your command! Do you hear me? Chief Sunday?"

"I hear you, you miserable son of a bitch," Sunday muttered, striding to the edge of the pier. "Ready, Rourke?"

"Ready, sir."


Carl was frozen solid, a block of ice animated by a spark of life. He couldn't feel his body; couldn't feel his legs, his chest, his arms, his fingers, anything. It was as if the conscious part of him had become detached from the rest.

Yet his fingers were still moving. Carl had the last wrench flush against the last fitting and was turning it a fraction at a time. It was the best he could do. His grip on the wrench was weak, so weak that a freak gust of current nearly ripped it from his grasp.

His mouth no longer worked. His lips, his very vocal chords, were too cold to function. As he had been doing for what seemed like ages, he mentally recited the sum total of who he was, what he was: *My name is Boat-*

*swain's Mate Second Class Carl Brashear. I am a Navy
diver.*

Even the thought came slowly. Carl was slipping into
a frosty, empty haze. He had passed the limit of his en-
durance long ago. Now only raw will sustained him, and
that was fading fast.

Another tweak did it. The fitting was secure. Now all
Carl had to do was tug the ready line three times and
he was done. But when he went to reach for it his arm
wouldn't rise. He tried the other one with the same result. They were chilled to the marrow.

*MY NAME IS BOATSWAIN'S MATE SECOND
CLASS CARL BRASHEAR. I AM A NAVY DIVER.*

Carl threw all he had, every iota of strength and energy left, into grabbing the ready line.

"Reel him in!" Chief Billy Sunday bawled, and
Rourke began to turn the winch. Sunday stared at the
air hose, which had stopped moving, and was so intent
on it that he nearly missed the spasmodic jerk of the
ready line.

"Belay that!" Sunday yelled. "Not yet!"

Rourke stopped. "Sir?"

No more orders blared from the P.A. system. Mister
Pappy had realized the futility of intervening. The onlookers had pressed onto the pier and were thronged
around the diving shack and bench, Jo well in front of
everyone else.

Sunday leaned down over the pier. The ready line
jerked faintly a second time. Then a third. "Bring up the
ready line!"

Rourke nodded and cranked furiously, and within moments the flange burst from the Hudson River, completely assembled.

A cheer went up, a spontaneous roar that shook the

surrounding structures. People—many of them black—clapped in applause and men pounded one another on the back as if they were the ones who had completed the flange.

Sunday clicked on the communications line. "Blue Diver? Blue Diver, do you read me?" When no response was forthcoming, he cried, "Reel him up! On the double!"

The winch churned. The spectators pushed nearer still. A collective whoop went up when a brass helmet split the surface, changing to a gasp of dismay when the limp body under it was hauled into view. Tenders rushed to pull Carl onto the pier and laid him on his back, but it was Rourke and the other trainees who shouldered them aside and removed his helmet.

In the sudden silence, Jo knelt beside him. His eyes were closed, and he was a sickly shade. She touched his cheek, horrified at how cold it was. Like touching an ice cube. "Carl?" she said tenderly. Carl started to rise, and for a moment Jo thought he was standing on his own, but Chief Sunday had slipped an arm under him and pulled him upright.

Sunday stared at Carl a few seconds, then turned to the onlookers. "I want all of you to hear this. All of you are witnesses." He paused. "Boatswain's Mate Second Class Carl Brashear has passed the Navy diving course. As of this moment, he is a fully accredited Navy diver."

The cheer that rose to the heavens eclipsed the first.

Sunday glanced up at the tower but Mister Pappy was nowhere to be found. "Rourke! Boots! Get this man to his quarters."

The pair slid their shoulders under Carl's and hastened toward the barracks, the crowd parting so they could pass. Most of the spectators trailed along to see it through to the end.

Presently only Sunday and Jo were left. "Thank you," she said.

"For what? Shooting myself in the foot?"

"Carl has told me about you. He said you're basically a good man. What you did was right."

"What I did was stupid. I just sank my career." Sunday began to walk by her but stopped and put a hand on her arm. "Be sure he understands it was never personal. And tell him something for me."

Jo waited

"All those years he was plowing fields, I have to wonder whether the mule was in front of the plow or behind it."

Smiling wanly, Chief Billy Sunday vanished into the veil of darkness.

A week later Carl stood on the porch in front of his barracks, leaning on the rail. In the yard the rest of the trainees were gathered. Rourke, Mellegrano, Boots, and the rest were wearing pressed uniforms, their duffels packed. Their families and loved ones had arrived to pick them up, and a lot of hugging and kissing was going on. It was their last hour at the base. They were going into the world as Navy divers.

The one man Carl hoped to see wasn't there. Jo had told him what Sunday said. And the other trainees had related the events of that terrible day at the Hudson. He wanted to thank the chief but there had been no sign of Sunday since that evening.

Sighing, Carl stepped to the door.

"Carl! W-wait up!"

Snowhill rushed across the yard. Half out of breath, he sagged against the wall and stuttered, "H-hear wh-what happened? I j-just g-got word!"

"Slow it down, buddy," Carl said. "Take your time."

Flashing a self-conscious grin, Snowhill declared. "They've put me back in the diving program! I start training next week."

"Good for you." Carl needed to go in and lie down. He was still not fully recovered and tended to tire easily. "I'll talk to you later."

"That's not all!" Snowhill said. "Have you heard what happened to Chief Sunday?"

"No."

"Mister Pappy blew a g-gasket when Sunday passed you. Pappy busted him down a stripe and confined him to quarters. Sunday was sh-shipped out about an hour ago. So I guess he got his in the end, huh?" Snowhill checked his watch. "C-can't stay. On duty at the m-mess hall in four minutes. Be seeing you."

"Take it easy." Carl entered, frowning. Sunday hadn't deserved to lose a stripe. If anyone should be punished, it was Mister Pappy. But that was in a perfect world, not the real world. He would have liked to say good-bye, though. He owed Sunday that much.

Almost at his sea chest, Carl drew up in amazement. Resting on top of it was the old radio that had belonged to his father, the radio Sunday had smashed. It had been carefully restored. Leaning down, he switched it on, and the room filled with country music. The dial was set to the same station playing on Sunday's car radio that first morning out at the front gate.

Stupefied, Carl saw something had been added. Below the crudely carved letters A-S-N-F a small brass plaque had been attached, engraved with "A Son Never Forgets." "So that's what the letters stand for," he said, and laughed. Lying down, he twirled the dial to his favorite jazz station, set it on the window, and laid back to enjoy the music.

For the first time in a long time, life was sweet.

*     *     *

The club was called Harlem Nights, one of the most popular in Harlem. Not a white face in the house as the band leader announced the next number and the band swung into the rhythm with a vengeance; hot, brassy jazz, just the kind Carl loved. Which was why Jo had asked him to make reservations for New Year's Eve. But now, seated alone at a table, she checked her watch and wondered where in the world he could be.

The dance floor was jumping. Couples were strutting their moves in a frenzy of sensual abandon. A woman in a tight red dress sailed across the hip of a dapper young man, performing an acrobatic flip. Another woman was jiggling parts of her body Jo never realized could jiggle.

Jo wore her best dress and had done her hair just right. She had agreed to meet Carl there by eleven but it was pushing midnight and he still had not shown up. Remembering the bar incident, she began to worry she had made the same mistake her mother had.

"Pardon me?"

Jo glanced up. A smiling waiter held a magnum of champagne. "For me?" she asked.

"From the gentleman."

Only then did Jo spot Carl, framed in the entrance, grinning like a kid who had just been given his heart's desire for his birthday. She threaded through the crowd to meet him and they came together on the dance floor. Laughing, he swept her into his strong arms and spun, pressing her close. "Glad you could make it," she remarked.

"I told you I had to work late."

There had to be more to it than that, Jo mused. "You hate champagne," she said, thinking that somehow he had learned the secret she intended to break to him that night. When he grinned broadly, another idea occurred to her. "You received a diving assignment?"

"Brooklyn Navy Yard, standby diver," Carl disclosed.

"Oh, darling!" Jo stopped dancing and threw her arms around him. "Brooklyn? What more can we ask? We'll have our nights together, and on your days off we can go about the city doing what all married couples do. It's almost too good to be true."

"Baby, I didn't take the job."

"You what? A slot like that doesn't come along every day. We've been waiting, what, three years? How could you pass it up?"

Carl draped his arm over her shoulders. "Listen to me. The only reason I've been here this long is because Mister Pappy kept me on to spite me. He couldn't stop me from becoming a diver so he got back at me the best he could, by keeping me under his thumb and preventing me from rising in rank as fast as I should. If I went to Brooklyn it wouldn't be much different. I don't move up unless I dive. I'll never make master working as a standby. So I called on a friend and snuck a request for reassignment past Mister Pappy. And it came through."

Jo was almost afraid to ask. They had discussed this before and they always ended up arguing. "Where?"

"It'll sound a lot worse than it is."

"Where?" Jo demanded.

Carl grinned. "Guam."

A lightning bolt sheared Jo and she honestly thought she might pass out. Resisting the dizziness, she uttered, "It's half a world away."

"It doesn't matter as long as we're together. That's what we've always said, right?"

Jo looked at him. Sometimes he could be so mature, so considerate, and at others he was a ten-year-old boy with no concept of the consequences of his actions.

"Things are different. I have a practice now. I have patients who depend on me. If I leave now, everything I've worked so hard to build up will be lost. I'll have to start again from scratch."

"Honey, I need you. I've checked into it. The entire Pacific Fleet ships out of Guam. They have more dives and sick people than they know what to do with. You can start a new practice in no time." Carl rubbed her cheek. "What do you say?"

Jo bowed her head. Once again his timing could not possibly have been any worse. Lord, he had a knack.

"Baby, I can't be in two places at once. Understand? You need to come to grips with this. I ship out in a week. You can follow in a couple of months. Okay?"

Carl pulled Jo to him and they resumed dancing to a slow song but Jo's heart wasn't in it. She stared blankly at the ceiling, fighting back tears.

"Talk to me, will you?"

Jo had wanted the night to be extra-special, one they would remember for the rest of their lives, a reaffirmation of their commitment to one another. Now it was spoiled, and nothing she could do would salvage it.

"Look, it's not as if it's the end of the world," Carl said, trying to get her to meet his gaze. "We'll only be over there a couple of years, then I'll be reassigned somewhere nice. Europe, maybe. Or here on the East Coast. Just for you."

"It's not that so much . . ." Jo said.

"Then what?"

"Carl, I'm three months late. I had a test done and it came back positive. Do you know what that means?"

"We're going to have a baby?" Carl said in rapturous awe. And just like that, he was gone, darting off through the dancers.

Dumbfounded, Jo gaped after him, not knowing what

to make of it. She took a few halting steps and was
accidentally jostled. When she regained her balance, Carl
was back, holding her chair in one hand and her coat in
the other. "What are you up to?"

"Pregnant ladies shouldn't be on their feet. I learned
that much from my mama." Carl planted the chair in the
middle of the floor and guided her into it, then tenderly
draped the coat over her shoulders. "To keep you and
the baby warm."

Jo didn't have the heart to tell him she wasn't cold,
or that the baby was nowhere near developed enough
for her to need to stay off her feet. He was so sincere,
so concerned, reminding her of why she adored him so
much.

Nearby dancers had slowed to quizzically regard their
antics. Showing more teeth than a car salesman, Carl
shouted, "We're going to have a baby! A real baby! A
little one! And in honor of the occasion, we'll name him
after all of you! It'll be the only baby in the world with
twenty-nine names!"

Some of the dancers laughed, and Jo did, too. She
laughed harder when he knelt and peppered her hands
with kisses, then affectionately bent and kissed her
tummy.

"You hear me in there? I'm going to be the best damn
papa I can possibly be!"

Jo took his head in her hands and tilted it up. "Have
I mentioned lately how much I love you?"

The music stopped, and the dashing band leader
grasped the microphone to declare, "Ladies and gentlemen, and the rest of you low-down cats, it's time to ring
in the New Year! Are you ready?" A few of the revelers
answered that they were, and the band leader put a hand
to his ear. "I can't hear you so I'll try again. *Are you
ready?*"

This time the clamor nearly lifted the rafters.

The band leader began the countdown and every last person joined in, Carl and Jo counting aloud with the rest.

"Ten . . . nine . . . eight . . ."

Carl rested his forehead on Jo's. "This is the happiest moment of my life. One I'll never forget."

". . . six . . . five . . . four . . ."

"You do realize our baby will be born in Guam?" Jo asked.

". . . three . . . two . . . one . . ." Hundreds of balloons were unleashed from above and rained down in a cascade of bright colors. Couples hugged and kissed as the band broke into a jazzed-up rendition of "Auld Lang Syne."

"Happy New Year, baby," Carl said.

"Happy New Year," Jo responded. Balloons drifted down, covering them as his mouth covered hers.

Hundreds of miles to the south, in a ritzy club at the Pensacola Naval Air Station in Florida, a room packed with white officers and senior noncoms was a bedlam of blaring horns, yelling party-goers, and jovial cheer.

Senior Chief Billy Sunday and his wife, Gwen, were at a corner table with two other chiefs and their wives. Gwen melted into Sunday's arms and they locked lips with an intensity that brought playful wolf whistles from their companions.

"Happy New Year, beautiful," Sunday said when they broke for breath. She truly was gorgeous, one of the best-looking women in the club, and even after all the years, he counted himself fortunate to have earned her love.

"You, too, you big lug," Gwen said, pinching his cheek. She surveyed the scores of officers in their gleaming formal whites and the wives in their expensive, fashionable gowns. "I think we finally broke the jinx. I like it here. I really do."

"Just so you're happy," Sunday said as they sat back down.

"See? You were so mad at Pappy, but his pettiness backfired, didn't it? Why did he send you here, anyway? Why not some podunk base off in the middle of nowhere?"

Sunday indulged in some scotch before replying. "He was going to. He ranted and railed and said I was going to a place that would make Siberia seem like paradise. But I happened to mention that if word of what he had done ever leaked out, he would be up to his armpits in doo-doo. Some of the top brass don't take kindly to having their sailor boys hazed, even black sailor boys."

Gwen kissed him. "You did good. I was so proud of you."

"Losing my stripe doesn't bother you? The loss in pay?" Sunday drained his glass and motioned to a waiter for a refill.

"Since when have we ever relied on your paycheck?" Gwen said. "Hand to mouth is how it's always been. How it will probably always be." She shrugged. "I'm used to it by now."

Chief Pettigrew winked at Sunday. "That's some woman you've got there, you know that?"

"I surely do," Sunday agreed.

The din had faded and conversations were returning to normal. As the waiter brought more scotch, Sunday's ears registered a familiar voice, one he hadn't heard in years but one he would never forget. Like sonar homing in on an enemy sub, he raked the room and centered on a long table rimmed by officers. One was holding court with the saucy air of a medieval king.

"Bill?" Gwen said. "What is it?"

Sunday gulped half the glass and told himself to let sleeping dogs lie. "Just someone I know, hon."

"Who?"

"A grade-A asshole," Sunday said.

Gwen gnawed her lip and nervously glanced toward the long table with its shiny white tablecloth. "You're not going to start anything, are you?"

"Who, me?"

"Don't play innocent with me, mister. I've seen that look before. And it always spells trouble. Always."

Sunday laughed her worries off and stood. "I told you I've turned over a new leaf, and I have. To prove it, I'll walk over and introduce myself and come back to you without lifting a finger. You'll owe me an apology."

"Better yet"—Gwen pushed to her feet—"I'll go along with you to make sure you don't do something stupid." She hooked her elbow in his. "Please, Billy. You promised."

"I've kept my word, haven't I?" Sunday said as he guided her through the throng. "I've been a good little boy."

"See that you stay one. I'm warning you, lover. I wasn't kidding when I said I won't take any more brawling. I'll leave you. Sure as hell I will."

"Gwen, I always try my best for you. I let you talk me into going to a lousy therapist, didn't I?" Which, in Sunday's estimation, was a monumental waste of time. Psychiatrists were like fortune-tellers; they made it all up as they went along. The bozo Gwen had sent him to insisted that if he sorted through his psyche and came to terms with his "inner anger," he would never be angry again. He'd spend the rest of his days as peaceful as Mary's little lamb. The quack claimed Sunday's anger stemmed from frustration with himself. But the exact opposite was the case. It stemmed from having to put up with jackasses like Mister Pappy and the arrogant pup who sat over at the long table.

"I'll leave you," Gwen repeated quietly.

Sunday had heard that before. Since they'd said their "I do's," she'd left him five or six times, and she always came back. She always would. They were meant for each other. "We can't help being what we are, babe. There's no breaking the mold."

"There is if you try," Gwen said. "Take me, for instance. I gave up the life I loved, everyone and everything I knew, to be at your side."

"Ain't love grand?" Sunday said lightheartedly, but she wasn't in the mood.

"Yes, it is, but there are limits to how far you can push it. Push too hard, too often and eventually love will break."

"You know, maybe you should go to school and become a therapist. You'd be a hell of a lot better at it than Dr. Simpleton."

"Oh, Billy."

"What did I say now?" Sunday asked, but she wouldn't say. Which was just as well. They were almost at the table.

The young officer was still holding court. "—after I got done with him, he threw a salute and beat feet so fast it looked like his ass was on fire. I tell you, you've got to keep on top of these ignorant clods every minute of the day. The average seaman doesn't have the brains God gave a codfish."

Sunday came up behind the man's chair and tapped him on the shoulder. "Excuse me?" he said politely. The officer turned. And, as Sunday had surmised, it was Lieutenant Hanks. A few years older, a few years heavier, but still as smug and superior as ever.

Hanks's eyebrows knit. "Yes? Do you want something?"

Sunday nudged Gwen. "What did I tell you, hon? He doesn't remember me." Bending, he said, "Senior Chief Sunday? USS *Hoist?* You ended my diving career, Lieutenant."

Hanks looked Sunday up and down with stark contempt. "It's Lieutenant *Commander* Hanks. Yes, I remember. It was a long time ago."

Sunday nodded and straightened. "Ancient history. You're right. We just wanted to stop by and say hello. Auld lang syne and all that. Well, have fun."

"You, too."

Sunday didn't walk off, though. An irresistible urge to pound Hanks's cocky face to a pulp held him there until Gwen yanked on his arm, dragging him away. They were almost out of earshot when he heard Hanks's next comment.

"There goes the biggest drunk in the U.S. Navy."

The officers and their wives cackled merrily.

Gwen angled toward the dance floor. "I don't like that gleam in your eyes. Dance with me, Billy, and control yourself."

Sunday looped an arm around her slender waist and launched into a slow dance. He was trying, honestly trying, but his blood was on fire.

"See how easy that was? I'm proud of you," Gwen stated. "Did you try what the therapist said?"

"He told me to picture myself doing the most fun thing I can think of," Sunday quoted.

"And what's that?"

Sunday stopped, pulled her to him, and kissed her long and deep. Then he stepped back and said sincerely, "I'm sorry, baby. I'm so sorry."

"Billy, don't!"

Wheeling, Sunday threaded back through the tables

and came up behind Lieutenant Commander Hanks. He tapped the strutting peacock on the same shoulder.

Shifting, Hanks looked up in annoyance. "You again? What the hell is it now?"

"Your just deserts," Sunday said, and punched Hanks in the mouth. The blow rocked Hanks backward, but he surged out of his chair into an uppercut that sent him crashing onto the table. Wives screamed as some of the officers rushed to help. Sunday shook them off like a bear shaking off mongrels. Seizing Hanks by the shirt, he belted him in the gut, then again in the ribs. The thrill was exquisite.

The officers rallied and piled on, pinning Sunday down by the sheer weight of their numbers. Someone was screaming for the shore patrol and general confusion ran rampant. Struggling against overwhelming odds, Sunday happened to glance toward the entrance and saw Gwen on her way out, her fur coat around her body, her features downcast.

"I'm so sorry," Sunday said.

The hearing board was different from the last, held in a dismal room with no windows, no portholes, only a single bulb to illuminate the chair in which Sunday sat and the table where the review officers were arrayed against him. Unlike Captain Pullman years ago, sympathy was absent. No spectators were on hand to root for him, either.

The hawk-faced presiding officer cut right to the chase. "Senior Chief Sunday, your conduct was totally unacceptable. New Year's Eve or no, under the influence of alcohol or not, what you did was reprehensible. Only your otherwise sterling career keeps us from having you thrown behind bars." He paused. "You will be fined one half month's pay for six months, restricted to the confines of the base for two months, and are hereby reduced to the rank of chief petty officer. Have you anything to say on your behalf that might persuade us to reduce your punishment?"

What could he say? Sunday mused. That it had been fun? That beating the crap out of Hanks had been worth it? They would only add to his punishment, not reduce it. And he had already been punished enough, not by them but by Gwen. She was gone again. Without her, he always felt so lost, so empty. "No, sir."

"You're dismissed, then."

Sunday rose, saluted, and left. He needed to get off base for a while for a few drinks and some fun with the boys. Restriction or no, that was exactly what he was going to do. If he hurried, he could make it out the gate before official word of the restriction was forwarded to the shore patrol.

Half an hour later Sunday was on his favorite stool at his favorite watering hole. It was early afternoon and the join was fairly deserted. Business wouldn't pick up until six or so. Sunday was on his best behavior, and had limited his intake to four drinks. Just one more, he promised himself, and he would return to base. "Barkeep, hit me again."

"Here you go, Chief," Fred said amiably.

Sunday raised the glass and looked into the mirror behind the bar just as the front door opened and in strolled three Marines.

# CHAPTER TEN

*The Mediterranean Sea, 1966.*

The television in the galley aboard the USS *Hoist* filled with the paternal image of Walter Cronkite recapping an emergency news bulletin. "—thirty-six hours ago an American B-52 bomber went down in the Mediterranean. The bomber's crew has been recovered. Now the hunt is on for the fifty-megaton nuclear warhead they jettisoned shortly before impact. The largest naval search ever launched is in full swing."

"Tell me about it," Carl Brashear said dryly, and spooned the last of his pudding into his mouth. Soon he would be down there helping in that search.

"We'll be on-site any minute," Snowhill said excitedly without a trace of a stutter. "Damn, this is great!"

Carl shook his head in amusement. "Hunting for a nuke is your idea of fun? Man, you should have stuck with mess hall duty. A loon like you has no business going deep."

Snowhill laughed. "No, no. I meant being reunited. They've flown in divers from all over creation to help out. Crowfoot is on one of the other vessels." He sobered. "I guess you heard about Mellegrano?"

"No, what?" Carl had not heard anything about the other trainees since he left diving school. Of all of them, only Snowhill had bothered to keep in touch with an occasional postcard and letter.

"He was working a salvage job in the Pacific. Got crushed to death when a bulkhead gave way."

Carl felt no remorse. He had never gotten along with Mellegrano, even at the very end when the trainees treated him decently. "Heard anything about Rourke?"

"The Navy's blue-eyed poster boy for Navy divers?" Snowhill said. "Funny thing. After school, he applied for the most dangerous assignments around. Almost as if he were trying to prove something to himself."

Carl remembered that day at school when Sunday pinned the unearned medal on Rourke's chest.

"He saved a lot of lives, made a rep for himself as big or bigger than Sunday's was in his day," Snowhill detailed. "Made master chief already, too, if you can believe it. Last poster I saw extolling the glorious adventures of being a diver had him on it."

"How's your wife doing? And—what was it—three kids?"

"Five at last count. That's what I get for being so studly and virile." Snowhill grinned. "They're all doing fine. How about Jo and your boy? What's his name again?"

"Jackie," Carl said proudly. They had named him after Jackie Robinson. "Ten years old, going on twenty. Thinks he knows everything. We're living in Virginia now. I'm stationed at the Norfolk Naval Base." Carl looked at the wall clock. "She has no idea I'm here. They whisked me away so damn quick, I couldn't even phone. Right about now she's expecting me for supper. I'll need to do a heap of explaining when I get home."

"Too bad this mission is so hush-hush or we could get word to her."

Carl jabbed a thumb at the TV. "Hush-hush my butt.

Everybody in the world knows about it by now but the Navy still treats it as if it's a top-secret exercise."

Into the galley rushed a seaman who scanned the tables briefly before making a beeline for theirs. "Chief Brashear? Captain Hartigan requests your immediate presence on deck. We've arrived on-site and diving operations are about to commence."

Picture a gorilla in an officer's uniform, Carl thought, and that was Captain Hartigan. Unlike Hanks and his breed, Hartigan didn't have a snooty bone in his body. He never walked around with his nose in the air, putting on airs. He was friendly, fair, and cared about those under him. An ideal officer.

They were standing near the diving platform, watching tenders scurry to ready Carl's diving suit.

"Here's the setup, Chief," Hartigan said in his grave manner. "As best as we're able to pinpoint the coordinates, we should be right over the damn bomb. Or close enough that it won't take forever to find. You're going in first. Snowhill will be on standby." The captain motioned at the dozens of ships that dotted the whitecapped sea. "Most of them are sending divers to the bottom, too. But we have the prime drop zone."

"I won't let you down, sir."

"You never have, son." Captain Hartigan pulled a cigar from his shirt pocket, unwrapped it, bit off the end, and stuck it in his mouth.

A young ensign, new to the *Hoist* and eager to impress, lit a match and held it out. "Allow me, sir."

"Initiative, Ensign Culver. I like that. But it's not for smoking. My wife merely allows me to taste them nowadays."

"Sorry, sir." Ensign Culver started to draw back.

"However, she's not here at the moment," Captain Hartigan said, and bent to light the cigar.

A tender snapped to attention in front of them. "Sir, the diving suit is ready for Chief Brashear!"

"Over you go, Chief. I'll be monitoring from the bridge."

As Carl walked by, Hartigan grasped his forearm.

"Be careful down there, you hear?"

"Always, sir."

The tenders outdid themselves in suiting Carl up. After his brass helmet was lowered and sealed, Carl strode onto the driving platform and signaled to the winch operator.

The platform eased toward the choppy waves below, and Carl braced for contact. The water was rough but only at the surface. Once he was under, deceptive tranquility immersed him, a sense of serenity like the peace he always enjoyed at the bottom of the pond when he was a boy. But he had to stay alert. Given his proximity to the Atlantic Ocean, crosscurrents posed a potential problem.

In a way, though, the government was lucky the pilot had jettisoned the bomb when he had, in a relatively shallow area. The Mediterranean varied greatly in depth. At its deepest, in the Ionian section near Italy, it fell to fifteen thousand feet. Had the bomb sank there, sending a diver down would be impossible.

As standard prep for every dive Carl had boned up on the Mediterranean Sea, learning all there was of importance to the retrieval. More than four hundred kinds of fish lived in it but none posed a threat. Volcanic vents, like those found in the Pacific ocean, were absent. Nor were there any bottomless trenches to be wary of.

The bottom loomed below. Carl shifted to alight in a

clear area, then tested the com link by announcing, "This is Blue Diver. I am commencing my search."

From the helmet speaker tinkled Hartigan's response. "Roger that, Blue Diver. I'd appreciate if you would find that lost nuke quick. I'd like to make admiral before the week is out."

Smiling, Carl said, "I'll do my best, Captain." He began a sweep pattern, a grid system designed to maximize the territory he covered in a minimum amount of time. It was slow going at that depth, the water pressure hindering his movements. Jackie had once asked him what it was like to walk underwater way down deep, and Carl had told him it was like pushing through a wall of Jell-O.

Fish constantly whisked by, big ones and little ones. Several bluefin tuna glided out of the murk and seemed to be curious about the two-legged invader in their midst. Plant life was sparse.

Carl had been at it for over an hour when his light played over an object that glinted metallically, lodged in the sea floor. He immediately informed those up above. "Topside, I have an unknown metal object protruding from the bottom."

"Proceed with extreme caution, Blue Diver," Captain Hartigan advised.

"Roger that, sir."

Taking a deep breath, Carl vented just enough air from his pressure suit to enable him to sink to his knees. From his mesh bag he took a small brush and carefully stroked the top layer of silt to expose more of the object. Round and silvery, it was far too small to be a fifty-megaton nuclear warhead. Squinting through his faceplate, Carl slowly extracted it from the seabed and chuckled

"Care to share with the rest of us, Chief?" Hartigan prompted.

"It's a Coke can, sir. Disarmed and deactivated."

Hartigan laughed, and in the background, others were laughing too. "A goddamn Coke can? Bring it up, Chief. It's probably worth five cents at the PX. Should help the Navy pay for the search."

Carl rose and moved on.

"Blue Diver, need I advise you of the duration of your dive? It's about time to bring it up and let another diver take over."

"Give me ten more minutes, Captain," Carl requested. "I'm not cold, and not all that tired. I'd like to keep looking."

"Permission to proceed but—"

In the background a new sound intruded, a sound Carl recognized as the loud ping of the ship's sonar unit.

Hartigan barked at the operator without closing their circuit. "Sonar, shut your equipment down! We have a diver in the water!"

The sonarman's response was thin but audible. "Sir, that's not our sonar."

That was when Carl felt a disturbance in the water around him. Fish fled in panic as a rising rumble shook the sea floor. He turned, not knowing what to expect but never imagining it could be what he saw: the massive hull of a gigantic Soviet submarine bore down on him out of the aquatic gloom.

"Damn!" Carl blurted, and shifted to scramble out of its way. But he was moving far too slow. The man-made juggernaut swept toward him like a living leviathan, and only one thing would save him. Venting his suit, Carl flattened.

In a heartbeat the sub was above him, so close Carl could reach up and touch it if he wanted, the rumble of its passage like the rumble of a seaquake. The thing was gigantic. Longer than several football fields.

The rumbling went on and on, silt gusting against Carl's faceplate. Without warning, there was violent tug on Carl's line and he was yanked off the bottom. Tumbling like a rag doll, he realized his line had snagged on the submarine's rear rudder. Carl threw himself to the right, seeking to slip free before the line ripped.

It didn't work.

Conscious that mere seconds remained before the line would be stretched to the breaking point, Carl hurled himself to the left. For a few seconds he had the sensation of cartwheeling in free fall, followed by the concussion of impact. A cloud of silt mushroomed above him, obscuring the sub and the sea. He braced for a telltale hiss of air or the gurgle of water in his suit, but neither occurred.

Sitting up, Carl took stock. He was alive and unhurt, his suit intact, his lines functioning as they should. Nearby, his hand light reflected countless tiny particles of silt. Reaching for his headset, he realized it was blaring.

"Blue Diver? Report in! Carl? Carl?" Captain Hartigan was having a stroke. "Ensign Culver, put the standby diver in, now!"

Carl slowly rose. "I'm here, Cap," he said breathlessly. "It's a Soviet sub. They must be looking for the bomb, too."

"Where is it now, Blue Diver? I'll get on the horn to the admiral and he can raise hell with those devious bastards."

Carl stepped from the silt cloud and peered into the gloom. "It's gone, sir. And I hope it doesn't come back." A silvery shape a few yards away caught his eye. Dumbstruck, he moved closer.

"Next time you decide to scare the hell out of me, Blue Diver," Captain Hartigan joked, "do me the courtesy of letting me know first."

"Sir?" Carl said in awe.

"Blue Diver?"

"It's here, sir."

"The sub is back?"

"No, sir. But it kicked up half the sea bottom and uncovered what we're after. They found it for us, sir."

Hartigan was so flustered by the near tragedy that he didn't catch on right away. "Found what, Blue Diver?"

"The nuclear bomb, sir." Carl stared, mesmerized. A chill that had nothing to do with the cold water brought goose bumps to his body. "It's right in front of me, Captain." Bigger than he had thought, and deadly enough to turn a major city into ashes. His heart skipped a beat even though he had been assured the bomb wouldn't go off.

"Congratulations, Carl," Captain Hartigan said. "I'm writing you up for a commendation. But your job is over. You've been down there much too long as it is. Get topside, and I'll have Snowhill and the others handle the actual rigging."

Carl slowly reached out and touched the most lethal device on the planet. Inadvertently, he flinched. Were it to detonate, he would be vaporized into atoms in the blink of an eye.

"Blue Diver, did you hear me? We'll mark the spot with a buoy and reel you in."

"Fine by me, Captain," Carl answered, backing away. The thing gave him the willies. For once in his diving career, he looked forward to going up.

By late afternoon the recovery team was ready. Snowhill and two other deep-sea divers had rigged the nuclear bomb so it could be winched onto the USS *Hoist*.

The wind had picked up and the sea was exceptionally rough but Captain Hartigan radiated confidence. "The admiral will be here in forty-five minutes to personally thank us and take charge of the operation. We'll be on all the newscasts. People the world over will hear about this."

Carl wondered whether Jo would catch sight of him on the evening news. He had shed his diving suit and was on hand to supervise the retrieval. Another ship, the USS *Victory,* was at anchor close to the *Hoist* to assist if need be, and a thick cable had been stretched between them.

The crane operator was waiting. Carl nodded, and the man fired up the winch. Deftly working a series of long levers, the operator began to raise the nuke.

Practically everyone on the *Hoist* had ventured topside to witness the historic occasion, and the rails were jammed with craning necks. A helicopter circled overhead. Higher up were several planes. A few small boats bobbed near the line that linked the crane to the bomb.

"All this hullabaloo," Captain Hartigan exclaimed. "Wouldn't you like to see the looks on their faces if we brought up the Coke can instead?"

Carl laughed. "We'd be keelhauled, sir. And flogged, to boot."

"Not in this day and age, son. Haven't you heard? We're a kinder, gentler Navy."

The winch was grinding under the strain, and the crane operator watched it closely. All other eyes were on the line into the briny brink.

It was the greatest day of Carl's career. The commendation virtually assured he would make master chief well ahead of the curb. Another year or two should do it. Jo would be delighted, because once his dream came true he had promised he would settle down in one spot and live the life of a typical family man. Maybe instruct trainees, as Sunday had done.

Carl heard a faint sound he couldn't account for, like the sound a beer can made when he crushed it in his hand, and he looked around. The cable between the two ships had gone piano-wire taut, and the thick steel rail it was wrapped around was bending like so much pliable licorice. No one else had heard above the roar of the crane. He pivoted toward Captain Hartigan to warn him.

In the next instant, the rail ripped free. The cable uncoiled like a bullwhip, slicing across the deck toward a pair of unsuspecting deckhands who had their backs to it.

"Look out!" Carl yelled, and exploded into a full run. He covered the deck in a flash and catapulted himself at the deckhands, bowling into them and shoving them out of the cable's path. Tucking into a roll, he thought he was in the clear, but something slammed into his left leg below the knee and he was dragged across the deck. Part of the rail, Carl thought as he thrust out both arms and seized a deck cleat to keep from being hauled over the side to his death. Whatever it was that had hooked onto his leg snapped loose.

People were shouting. Feet pounded the deck, rushing toward him.

Dazed, Carl rolled onto his back and looked down at himself, glad no one had been hurt. Then he saw a shoe lying next to his chest. It was his own shoe. And his left foot was still in it, his leg bent back at an impossible angle.

Carl's world dissolved into a slow-motion tapestry of sights and sounds. The sky and the ship spun, changing places, as strong hands gripped him. His own ragged breaths wheezed in his ears, nearly drowning out the wild hammering of his pounding heart.

Captain Hartigan appeared out of the haze, bellowing for the medic, and Carl reached up, his arm seeming to rise from the depths of a fathomless black hole. He felt

Hartigan's fingers wrap around his and heard Hartigan say something. The black hole swelled in size, obliterating everything and darkness claimed him.

Carl Brashear felt sick to his stomach. With a start, he realized he must be conscious. He tried to open his eyes but they were heavy from sedation and for a few moments he thought he would pass out again. Blinking, he discovered he was in a hospital bed. Sunlight streamed through a window on his right. On the other side of the bed was a chair, and in it, sound asleep, sat the loveliest woman alive. He stared, marveling that of all the men in the world, she had chosen him.

Presently Jo roused, sat up, and saw he was awake. "Carl!" she squealed, rising. "I was so scared!" She tenderly embraced him. "So very, very scared!"

Carl didn't want to ever let her go. When she finally drew back, he saw how haggard she was. He also saw his left leg, encased in a cast and supported by elaborate traction cables. Only his toes were visible. They were grotesquely swollen from severe infection and tinged a putrid shade of green. The black hole yawned to engulf him again but he vigorously shook his head, fighting to stay conscious. "Dear God."

"You leg was nearly severed, Carl," Jo said, sitting on the bed. "It's going to take time to heal. Lots and lots of time. Eventually, you'll be able to walk some with a cane."

"Can I dive?"

Jo's lips pinched together. "I'm so sorry. They did the best they could. They say you almost died from loss of blood."

"I can't dive?" Carl groaned. "How am I ever going to make master?"

"You're not," Jo said bluntly. "They're going to retire you. But you should see the medal they— "

Carl cut her off with a raised hand. The greatest day in his career had turned into the worst nightmare of his life. They could keep their medal, for all he cared. He looked sharply away, and saw that some of his personal effects had been brought from the ship and placed on a nightstand. Among them was his father's old radio.

Jo noticed and asked, "Want me to get it for you?"

"Get it out of here is more like it," Carl said bitterly.

"Don't talk like that. It means the world to you. Since I can remember, you've always had it at your side."

"And what good did it do me?" Carl knew he shouldn't take out his heartache on her, but he could hardly suppress his frustration. "Baby, if I'm not a master diver, I'm nothing."

Jo stroked his brow. "That's ridiculous."

"You don't understand. You've never understood." Carl was close to tears but he refused to cry. He damn well refused. "It's my way of paying my father back. Of showing how much I cared for him." He bobbed his head at the cast, at what was left of his leg. "How can I pay him back how?"

"I never got to meet him. I don't know what he was like," Jo responded. "But from what you've told me, I'd say to do what he did. Keep your family together. Raise your son like your father raised you." She cradled his cheek against her bosom. "It's time to come home, Carl."

An inner wall burst, and Carl wept uncontrollably. Convulsively. Clinging to her as if she were a lifeline, he said, "I've failed, Jo. I've failed."

"Don't you worry, baby," Jo said, kissing his head.

"We'll get through this together. You, Jackie, and me. Like we're supposed to. Like a family."

Carl's sobs filled the room.

Far away, in the detoxification ward at the naval hospital in Pensacola, Florida, Gwen Sunday pulled her fur coat tighter around her body, then lit a cigarette. The admission's clerk was scribbling on a form Gwen had just completed.

From down the hall drifted her husband's voice, droning on drunkenly. "A chief petty officer shall not drink. However, if he should drink, he shall not get drunk."

The clerk looked up. "We're a thirty-day program with an excellent success rate. However, Mrs. Sunday, as you know, the Navy only pays for a portion of the expenses so the rest will have to come out of your own pocket."

"We're broke," Gwen informed her.

The clerk scrunched up her face like she had just sucked a lemon. "I wish you'd told me sooner. We're not a charity." She tore the admission form from the clipboard and crumpled it.

From the hallway echoed Sunday's recital. "If he should become drunk, he shall not stagger."

Gwen listened, all the vitality drained from her. They had hit rock bottom. Billy's career was in the toilet. The only hope they had was to purge him of the booze and claw their way back to some semblance of normalcy. It was all on her shoulders, though. He would be of no help whatsoever.

When Gwen thought of all the sacrifices she had made for that man, she wanted to go out and get a bottle of scotch herself. But rather than get drunk, she added another sacrifice to the long list. "Do you like my coat?"

The clerk had the crumpled paper poised over the wastebasket. "What's that?"

"My coat," Gwen said, running her hand down it. "One hundred percent real fur. Worth more than you can make in this place in a year."

"That would be most irregular," the woman said, but the desire her face mirrored belied her statement.

"Sister, life is irregular. We just have to make the best of what it dishes out. And this is a once-in-a-lifetime opportunity you're passing up." Gwen stood and shrugged out of the coat. "Here. Try it on for size."

"Oh, I couldn't." But the clerk did, and once she was enveloped in its luxurious softness, she was lost. Quickly removing it, she hung it on a hook behind the door, then moved around the counter. "Now where were we?" She unfolded the form and smoothed it out. "Oh. Yes. You can visit your husband every morning between the hours of nine and eleven."

"I'd like to see him once before I leave," Gwen requested.

"No problem. Follow me."

Two orderlies were playing cards at a small table just past the reception area. They had placed her husband in the first isolation room on the right. Gwen stepped to the small porthole and peered in. Her husband was flat on his back, his clothes filthy, blubbery innanely away, a stupid smirk on his grizzled kisser.

"If he should fall," Billy recited, "he will fall in such a manner as to cover up his rate so that passersby will think he's an officer." He cackled to himself.

"A wild one, is he?" the clerk asked.

"You don't know the half of it," Gwen Sunday said sadly. As she turned to leave, he howled at the ceiling and summed up her feelings exactly.

"Ain't life a royal bitch!"

# CHAPTER ELEVEN

For most Navy men it would be the honor of a lifetime. For Carl Brashear it was just another bitter reminder his career was over.

As predicted, the recovery of the nuclear bomb made headlines worldwide. So did the mishap that befell the man who recovered the bomb. As a human-interest angle, reporters pounced on the story like starving dogs on a bone, and every day for over a week, Carl was on the front page of every major newspaper in the country.

But there was more to come.

That Navy brass decided to capitalize on the heroics of their Navy diver by inviting the press to a formal presentation at his bedside of the medal he had earned. A captain in public relations broke the news to Carl the night before, and as soon as the officer left, Carl balled his fists and smashed them against the bed.

Jo and Jackie were there, Jo in her chair, their son over by the window, and both jumped at Carl's rare display of raw savagery.

"What's wrong, Papa?" Jackie asked, coming over. "Are you hurting?"

"Yeah," Carl growled, although not in a way the boy thought. It wasn't his leg. It was the unbearable idea of never being able to dive again. Of never achieving the rank of master chief. Of never fulfilling his dream.

Jo fished in her purse for a couple of quarters and extended them toward their son. "How would you like a candy bar from that machine down the hall?"

"Would I!" Jackie said. Snatching the money, he bounced on out of there, a limitless bundle of energy like all boys his age.

Carl shifted toward the window to spare himself from the distress marking his wife's face. "I know what you're going to say. Don't bother."

"I think I'll say it anyway to refresh your memory. He looks up to you, Carl. He thinks you're the greatest. You need to set a better example."

She was right, Carl admitted, but he had to release his pent-up emotions somehow. As it was, he could hardly keep from ripping the pillow to shreds.

"You've got to quit torturing yourself," Jo said in her calmly aggravating manner. "You've got to come to terms with what happened and get on with your life."

"What life?" Carl snapped without meaning to. "As a cripple? Tottering around on a cane? Put out to pasture before my time?"

"There's more to your life than your career," Jo said softly. "You have us, remember?"

For one of the few times in the many years they had been together, Carl gave rein to simmering resentment. "Don't you dare! I've always played straight with you. You know how much I love the two of you. You also know how much my career means to me. Lying here like this, all helpless and useless, is like being slowly smothered to death. I want to scream! I want to pound things! Break things! I want to curse God for turning His back on me!"

"Don't talk like that. Accidents happen."

Carl saw that it was no use and turned away again. Her dress rustled, and the bed bent to her added weight as her warm hand enfolded his. "Did I tell you we got a letter from your friend Chief Snowhill? He wants us to go visit him when you're up and around. Says he'll make some of his kids sleep out in the doghouse to make room for us."

Despite himself, Carl grinned. What he wouldn't give to be able to talk to Snowhill in person, or to Sunday, or any of the other divers. They would know exactly what he was going through.

"We also got a card from a Master Chief Rourke," Jo mentioned. "All it said was, 'Hang in there.' Is that the same Rourke who gave you such a hard time at diving school?"

"People change," Carl said.

"And you can, too," Jo kissed his cheek. "You can learn to live again. You can find something new to occupy you, something that means as much as being a Navy diver. Jackie and I will be right there with you every step of the way."

The word "step" brought Carl's rising spirits crashing down to earth. Glancing at the cast, he said flatly, "I can't wait until tomorrow."

Jo misunderstood. "That's the way! Wait and see. A year from now you'll look back and view this as a turning point in your life, not a tragedy."

Carl loved her dearly, but there were times when they were poles apart, and this was one of them. Slumping onto his back, he closed his eyes and wished the ceiling would fall on him.

The next morning was no better.

Over two dozen reporters were admitted to the ward for the special occasion. Enough Navy bigwigs to man a battleship were on hand, foremost among them Rear Admiral Yon, a kindly senior officer who conducted the proceedings. Standing beside Carl's bed, medal in hand, Admiral Yon addressed those crammed into the room.

"I'm here today to present this medal to Chief Brashear for his extraordinary heroism. Not only did he have the distinction of recovering an invaluable piece of military ordnance, but on the very same day he courageously risked his life to save the lives of two sailors who would surely have perished had he not acted with speed and fortitude."

Camera bulbs flared like firecrackers.

"Smile, Chief!" a reporter said.

Carl didn't feel like smiling. He felt like chucking them all out the window.

"Have you anything to say?" another newsman asked, and they all leaned forward, pens and pencils at the ready, hungry for a newsworthy morsel.

Carl considered several possibilities, none of which were printable in family publications. When he caught Jo staring, he settled for saying, "I did what I had to."

It provoked another flurry of bursting bulbs.

Admiral Yon beckoned for Jo to join them, then leaned down and attached the medal to the dress shirt Carl wore. "We're all extremely proud of you, Chief Brashear. Mend swiftly so you can go home and enjoy your retirement."

*Retirement.* Carl wilted inside, and just then a reporter for a syndicated chain snapped one last shot.


Billy Sunday had been mistaken. He thought his last therapist had been about as worthless as teats on a boar, but the therapist at the detox ward was either an escaped lunatic or thought he was counseling kindergarten kids. The man had the alcoholics making collages, for God's sake, using Elmer's glue and dull children's scissors so they wouldn't accidentally cut themselves. There they were, fourteen grown men and women, snipping pretty pictures from magazines and earnestly pasting them on sheets of cardboard.

"Remember, Mr. Schneider," the therapist said to a guy who kept licking the tip of the glue bottle, "select pictures that have meaning to you, pictures that reflect on your own life. After we're all done, I'm going to sit down with each of you and analyze each one."

Sunday squinted up at the sun. Their little exercise in human stupidity was taking place outdoors, on picnic tables near the facility. A shadow fell over him, and he gave the therapist the patented look he gave all imbeciles.

"Won't you reconsider and join us, Chief Sunday?"

"Not unless some of those magazines are *Playboy*."

"You're being most uncooperative, you know. How do you expect to make any headway when you refuse my help? The collage might seem silly to you but it has a definite therapeutic purpose."

"Better tell that to the guy guzzling your glue."

The therapist turned. "Mr. Schneider! Cut that out! We've discussed your aberration before." He walked off.

Sunday grinned, but it died when he saw who was a few yards away, staring at him in profound disappointment. "I didn't see you come up, babe."

"No fooling." Gwen sat across from him, a folded newspaper under her arm. "I was hoping you'd have turned the corner by now. Why couldn't you cut pictures out of the magazines like everyone else?"

"Is that why you came? To rag on me?"

"No," Gwen opened her purse and withdrew her flask. Uncorking it, she offered it to him. "Here. Want a drink?"

Sunday didn't take the bait. When she got like this, it

was best he keep quiet or they'd have another bitter fight.

"So do I," Gwen said. Only instead of raising the flask to her lips, she upended it, pouring the scotch onto the concrete. When the flask was empty she set it between them. "The first present you ever gave me and you didn't even buy it. You won it at that little county fair over in Cohoma. Threw three bull's-eyes in a row. I tell you, Billy, I felt like a sailor's girl that night. We had us some times, didn't we?" She laughed fondly.

Sunday laughed, too, but it died as quickly as his grin.

"Billy, you're never going to dive again. Deal with it."

"That was uncalled for."

"No, it was long overdue." Gwen wrapped her hand around his. "What you've got to do here, I can't help you with. It's up to you and you alone. So I'm not going to visit anymore. Or call you on the phone and cry. But when you leave, I'll be waiting in the car out at the curb. If you can promise me then that you'll never take another drink as long as you live, I'll let you get in and drive. If you can't, then, baby, you just keep walking. I've reached the end of my rope. No more reprieves. Get me?"

Sunday sullenly looked away.

"This is it, Billy. Either we pull ourselves together, or you dig your own grave and jump in. The choice is yours." Gwen rose, then put the newspaper next to the flask. "I thought you might like to see this. It's about someone else whose life you've made miserable."

Sunday opened his mouth to ask her to stay awhile yet but she was already hurrying toward the street. Absently unfolding the paper, he was jolted to find a photo of Carl Brashear in a hospital bed, flanked by the missus and the admiral. He devoured the story, then angrily slapped the paper down. "Never dive again!"

"Is there a problem, Chief Sunday?" the therapist asked.

"If you only knew," Sunday said to himself. On the next table were stacks of magazines, many of which he had read to while away the time. Recalling a particular article, he rose and tore into them like a madman, tossing one after the other down on the ground. "Where is it?" he fumed. "The damn thing has to be here somewhere!"

Reaching the bottom, Sunday looked up. It had grown unaccountably quiet. The rest of the patients were gawking at him, and the therapist appeared on the verge of calling for restraints.

"Who has the one I need?" Sunday demanded, and stormed among them to check the magazines they were cutting. An older man had the one he wanted, a fairly recent issue of *Aviation Weekly*. Snatching it, Sunday thumbed to the middle and grinned. The article was still there.

Taking the man's scissors, Sunday quickly snipped the article out. When he was finished, he straightened and nearly bumped into the therapist.

"I knew you would get into the swing of things eventually," the counselor said, beaming for joy.

Carl didn't have much of an appetite anymore. The doctors urged him to eat to keep his strength up so that he would heal that much faster, but he was in no great rush to hobble off into his twilight years. He was moodily picking at his lunch when an orderly entered.

"Package for you, sir."

Carl accepted the manila envelope. There was no return address. The postal stamp indicated it had been mailed from Pensacola, Florida, and he tried to think of who he knew who lived there. When the answer came to him, he inserted a fingertip into one end and slashed the envelope open. He expected a letter or a sympathy card but out tumbled a magazine clipping. Mystified, he read it, and as he did, the magnitude of the gift he had been given dawned on him.

Entitled "Heroes of the Air," it was about the daring exploits of Air Force pilots who had been wounded in combat and made phenomenal comebacks. One pilot had his leg shot off. A photo showed him back in action, standing beside his P-51.

"I'll be damned," Carl said, and lunged for the phone.

The next day, at one o'clock, Carl saw his room fill up again with people. Jo was there, of course, at his side, and so were Admiral Yon and a couple of junior officers. Carl's surgeon, Dr. Cudahy, and several medical officers were at the foot of the bed.

"All right, Chief Brashear," Admiral Yon said. "We have all assembled as you've requested. It's time for you to unveil your big secret. What was so important that you begged me to be here? So important that the good doctor and the rest of these men had to interrupt their busy schedules on your account?"

Carl saw Jo glance apprehensively at him. He deliberately hadn't told her for fear of how she would react. Sitting up straighter, he cleared his throat and said, "I want to come back, sir."

Admiral Yon, Dr. Cudahy, and the medical officers waited for him to say more, and when he didn't, the admiral said, "Back where, Chief?"

"Back to active duty."

Jo's hand fell from Carl's shoulder and she backed against the wall. Carl avoided looking at her and declared, "I want to dive again."

Admiral Yon's gentle features softened. "Carl, I understand but—"

"But it's not possible," a new voice inserted itself, brash and clipped, as a latecomer arrived. "Sorry I'm late. The lunch-hour traffic was atrocious." He nodded at the medical men and smiled at the admiral.

"Carl," Admiral Yon began the introductions, "I'd like you to meet Captain—"

"Hanks," Carl said hollowly. "We're acquainted, sir. From when we served aboard the *Hoist*."

"We did?" Hanks said, plainly at a loss. "Ah, well. So many enlisted men. It's difficult to keep track of them all."

"Not if you try," Admiral Yon said. "They're the backbone of the service. They deserve as much as respect as you or I."

"Of course they do, sir," Hanks said, his oily, placating smile as obnoxious as ever.

Admiral Yon turned to Carl. "Captain Hanks has been assigned as senior officer of the Personnel Policy Control Board at the Pentagon. He'll be spending a few weeks with us, meeting some of the men from the front lines. Getting a feel for their concerns."

"As for your concerns, Chief," Hanks addressed Carl. "You want to work as a Navy diver? With only one good leg and the other—how do I put this?—impaired? Be serious. Better yet, be realistic. We both know it's not possible."

"It is if you cut it off," Carl said.

Everyone in the room froze. Dr. Cudahy broke the awkward silence by saying, "You want to have your left leg *amputated?*"

"How will that help restore you to active duty?" Admiral Yon inquired.

Carl slid the magazine article from under the bedsheet. "It says here that pilots hurt in combat and other accidents have requested amputation of injured limbs and had a prosthesis fitted so they could return to active duty."

Jo moved to the window and stared out.

"I want to do the same thing, sir," Carl said. "I'm asking to have my left leg cut off, and to have it fitted with a special prosthesis so I can do what those pilots have done."

"What you're requesting has never been tried before," Admiral Yon commented, and pivoted toward Dr. Cudahy. "In your estimation is it even feasible?"

"It's feasible," the surgeon answered. To Carl, he said, "But do you appreciate the enormity of what you're asking, Chief? Once that leg is gone, it's gone for good. Granted, it's not fully functional, but at least it's your real leg. Perhaps you should consult with others who wear a prosthesis to learn what it's like."

"I don't need to consult anyone," Carl said. "I want to dive again. I want to make master chief. This is the only way."

Captain Hanks wore his trademark smirk. "I admire your courage, Chief Brashear. Misplaced as it is."

Carl sensed he had to make one last push to sell them. "It's my leg, isn't it? To do with as I see fit? Cut it off, then assemble a full medical review board twelve weeks from today. That's how long the article said it took the pilot to return to combat. I'll prove to you at that time that I'm fit to return to full active duty. If I don't, well, I'm no worse off than I am now. All I'm asking is the chance to prove myself."

Hanks opened his mouth but Admiral Yon spoke first. "You shall have your chance, Carl. And may God be with you."

The officers and the medical men filed out, leaving Carl and Jo alone. He set the article on the nightstand and took a long sip of water, still avoiding her.

"So you didn't ask anyone about this beforehand? You're not even curious about the consequences?"

Carl swallowed more water.

"I'm a doctor, Carl. My opinion might mean something here. But I guess it's too much to think you would turn to me in your time of need. I guess it's too much to have you depend on me, for once."

"I depend on you all the time," Carl said. "All those weeks and months I'm away at sea, I depend on you to take care of Jackie and hold our marriage and our family together."

Jo sat down next to him. "How are you going to come back with just one leg?"

"It'll work. I could barely read once. I found a way."

Nodding, Jo said, "I could put up with the months at sea. I could handle the dangerous assignments. But this, this is something else, something different."

"What do you want?" Carl countered, in more anguish than she realized. "For me to come home and put up a wheelchair ramp so I can go in and out of the house? How can I look at my own son?"

"Leave him out of this," Jo said. "You're not staying in the Navy for Jackie. You're not even doing it for your father. This is about you. It's always been about you!" She was livid, angrier than Carl had ever seen her. "Just when I was looking forward to being together again, you go and pull a stunt like this! But what do you care, right? So long as you get your precious career back!"

All the years they had been married, Carl reflected, and she still didn't really know him, still didn't know what made him tick.

Jo placed her hands on his chest, her eyes pools of sorrow. "Why are you doing this to me? I had dreams, too, you know."

Carl couldn't think of anything he could say that would explain it to her satisfaction, so he said nothing.

Rising, Jo griped his shirt and shook him in an agony of despair. "Answer me, goddamnit! Or so help me, I'm walking out of here and never coming back!"

"Your choice, baby, not mine."

It was the wrong thing for Carl to say, and he knew it immediately after the words had left his mouth. Jo shot up from the bed, emotionally shell-shocked, with tears brimming her eyes. "If that's the way you want it." She bent over, kissed him on the forehead, and walked quietly out of his life.

Emptiness seized Carl and wouldn't let go, a great, gnawing hole in the center of his being. Misery was his constant companion. There had been low points in his life but nothing to rival the torment oppressing his soul.

Carl tried to phone Jo that night but there was no answer. He tried a dozen times the next day. At six o'clock, in desperation, he called a neighbor and asked if she would go across the street and check if Jo was home. The lady replied there was no need; she had seen Jo throw a couple of suitcases into the trunk of their car early that morning and take off, with Jackie in tow.

Shortly before noon the next day, Carl was gazing glumly out the window when Dr. Cudahy walked in and cheerily asked, "Are you ready for the operation?"

The truth was, Carl had been so preoccupied with his family, he hadn't given the amputation much thought. The surgeon looked at him expectantly, and he hesitated. Here was a chance to set everything right with Jo. He could tell Cudahy he had changed his mind. He could take his cane and hobble off into the sunset, and all would be well. Jo would forgive him. They'd go back to

being as they were, his dream of being a master chief
forever shattered.

His dream or his wife.

Which would it be?

"I'm ready, Doc," Carl said.

It took a lot of getting used to.

Lying in bed that night, Carl stared at the stump that
had once been his left leg and shivered as much in horror
as in pain. He had done it, actually done it. His leg was
gone, or most of it, the stump ending just below the
knee. If his plan didn't work, the loss would be in vain.

Shaking in misery, Carl groaned. Maybe Jo had been
right. Maybe he had lost all sense of proportion. He had
sacrificed his wife and his leg, and for what? To follow
a dream? How sensible was that?

Not many people would have done what he did. Most
were content to accept whatever life handed them, to
make the best of their circumstances instead of going out
and molding those circumstances to fit their life's goal.
And now that he thought about it, what was so wrong
with that? Was his dream, was *any* dream, really that
important?

*Yes!* Carl almost shouted. A person's dream was everything, the driving force behind his life, and if he gave it
up, he might as well give up life itself. He had made his
choice and he would live by it, and if that meant losing
Jo, then that was her decision, not his.

Reaching up to wipe sweat from his forehead, Carl
glimpsed his wedding band. Angry at her betrayal of his
trust, he slid it from his finger, removed his dog tags, and
slid the ring onto the chain with the pair of metal tags.

If that was how Jo wanted it, fine by him, Carl reflected stubbornly. She had walked out on him, not the
other way around. She must make the choice to walk

back into his life. He had to move on. He had to concentrate on the challenge ahead—on being able to pass the review board.

Several days later Dr. Cudahy and a specialist showed up shortly before lunch. The specialist was a mousy little man whose glasses magnified the size of his eyes. Pulling out a tape measure, the man meticulously examined Carl's stump.

"This is Dr. Ferris," Dr. Cudahy introduced him. "He'll be responsible for fitting you with the prosthesis."

"Glad to meet you," Carl said.

Dr. Ferris squeaked like a small child's toy, his nose glued to the tape measure.

Carl was eager to get started on his training. "How soon will it be?" he asked.

"A week, a week and a half," Dr. Ferris said absently while looping the tape around Carl's knee.

"That's too long, Doc," Carl said. "I need to start training as soon as possible." When Ferris squeaked again, Carl gripped his arm. "Please. It's important. I need it as soon as possible. I don't have much time to train as it is."

Ferris unwound and drummed his fingers on his pointed chin. "I suppose I could phone in the order instead of mailing it in, and insist on having them process it immediately. And I could have the prosthesis sent special delivery rather than parcel post. In which case we can have you fitted and ready to go in, say, four days."

Carl came near to hugging the man. "Four days it is!"

True to Dr. Ferris's word, he was back in the allotted time with a box under his arm. "Here it is. Your artificial leg."

Like Jackie opening a Christmas gift, Carl slowly lifted the leg and gazed in awe at the object that would become every bit a part of him as his real limbs for the rest of his life. He ran his hand over it, marveling at how smooth it was.

"They constructed it according to your specifications," Dr. Ferris said. "It's three times as strong as a normal prosthesis." He grinned good-naturedly. "You could hold an elephant on your shoulders with that thing on."

"I might need to," Carl said, thinking of how heavy deep-sea diving suits were.

"Once you've become adjusted to it, you'll be able to return to some semblance of normalcy," Dr. Ferris said. "Just remember, though, Chief Brashear. It's an artificial device, and it has limitations. So long as you don't exceed them, you'll do just fine."

The very next morning Carl began training. His first task was to learn to stand. The next was to take a step without falling on his face. It required considerable conscious effort on his part since his sinews were naturally accustomed to performing a certain way with two legs. But by the late afternoon he could walk a dozen feet without falling.

From then on, Carl pushed himself relentlessly. Every waking moment was spent in the psychical therapy room. He practiced walking until he could do it for an hour without stop. To build up his atrophied muscles, he performed push-ups and crunches, worked with weights, and used the parallel bars.

Dr. Ferris stopped by a few times to see how the prostheses was working out, and was immensely pleased. Dr. Cudahy came by twice to ensure his leg was holding up under the strain. But for the most part, Carl was under the supervision of somewhat bored candy stripers who learned early on to stay out of his way. He was like a grumpy grizzly anxious to get out and about again after a winter of forced hibernation.

Eight days after the fitting, Carl arrived at the therapy

room minutes after breakfast. He went through his usual regimen, only this time he did thirty more crunches than he had the day before. He walked a while, then noticed a jump rope someone had left draped over a stationary bicycle.

It was much too soon to try using one but Carl couldn't resist. He glanced at the candy striper, who had fished a romance novel from her uniform pocket and was avidly flipping pages. Taking a breath, he swung the rope and gave a little hop. His artificial leg cleared it easily.

Encouraged, Carl tried again, hopping a little higher. Skipping rope had always been one of his favorite exercise. He smiled, and swung the rope a bit faster. Too late, he realized he had misjudged. The rope caught on his prophesis and snapped it out from under him. He flung out his arms to cushion the fall but only partly succeeded. Crashing down onto his stump, he howled with agony. His whole body erupted in violent spasms, as if he were being electrocuted.

"Chief Brashear?" the candy striper cried, and rushed to help. "My God! Are you okay?"

"I'll do it myself!" Carl rasped, mad at himself, not at her. Pushing the shocked girl away he clenched his teeth and rolled over. His artificial leg jutted from the stump at an unnatural angle. To align it, he had to stand.

Carl clawed toward the parallel bars, gripped an upright, and tried to lever himself higher. Another spasm racked his body, and he couldn't grasp it hard enough. He heard the candy striper crying and felt sorry for his enraged outburst. She was only a kid. Glancing up, he saw her bolt from the room, past a shadowed figure who had witnessed the whole thing from the hallway.

In strolled Chief Billy Sunday, grinning from ear to ear. "Damn, Cookie! Looks like I missed one hell of a party!"

# CHAPTER TWELVE

Under a sea-blue sky decorated by stray cumulus clouds, Carl Brashear and Billy Sunday walked toward some vacant benches near the hospital. Bright flowers lined the sidewalk, and in the trees sparrows chirped gayly.

Carl moved slowly, his stump still sore, his gait uncertain. It was his first excursion outdoors since the mishap on the *Hoist*, and he relished breathing in the scented air. "I want to thank you for sending the clipping about the pilots. It saved my life," he said earnestly.

"I hoped it would help," Sunday replied.

"What have you been up to?"

"In trouble, mostly. But what else is new?" Sunday chuckled. "The Navy gave me a second-class diving school to run down in Little Creek. It doesn't amount to much, but at least they're leaving me alone."

"And you took time off to come all the way up here to see how I was doing?" Carl carefully sank onto a bench.

"There's a little more to it than that," Sunday said. "When I read that article in the newspaper, it mentioned Captain Hanks was involved. That got me suspicious."

"Of what?" Carl said. "The admiral gave the okay, and Hanks agreed. It's all set. I'll be ready for the review board. Wait and see."

Sunday placed a foot on the bench. "I made some phone calls, Carl. Come this Friday, Captain Hanks is convening a medical review board for the express purpose of retiring your ass."

Staggered by the treachery, Carl blurted, "But today is Monday! I can't get ready by then! He can't do this!"

"Hanks has oversight of your case. The bastard can do any damn thing he pleases."

"But he promised I'd have twelve whole weeks!" Carl boiled with indignation.

"He lied. Cookie, he doesn't give a shit how many one-legged push-ups you can do. He'd trade you and me and every other old sea dog in the Navy for one glass-eyed electronics technician. And don't forget the most important thing of all."

"What's that?"

"Hanks doesn't like you. Never has. You showed him up on the *Hoist* and he's never going to forget or forgive. This is his chance for payback. He's going to retire you, then go off and brag to all his buddies how he put the screws to you."

"But I've got my leg back," Carl said, smacking the prosthesis.

"What you've got, friend, is a wooden stick on a stump. Maybe if you had the time you could do it, but he's not going to give you the time. You have no chance in hell of beating him at his own game."

Carl's throat tightened and he forlornly bowed his head. "All I ever wanted was to make master diver."

"All I ever wanted was to stay one," Sunday said bitterly, and pulled out his pipe. "Listen, I'm in your camp this time around. I want you to beat that sorry son of a bitch. But to do it, you've got to fight dirty. You've got to go around him. Right to the top."

"To Washington, you mean? The Chief of Naval Personnel?"

"They don't like cocky pencil pushers like Hanks any

more than we do. I might be able to pull a few strings and buy you that extra time."

"You also might get into a lot of trouble."

"Hell, Cookie. I've been busted so many times, I'm getting used to it." Sunday lit his pipe and grinned. "What are they going to do? Make me a fifty-year-old steward's mate? I don't even know how to set a table."

Carl gazed into the other man's eyes. "Why are you doing this?"

Sunday took a long puff, then declared with devilish glee, "To piss people off. And to get some payback of my own. I owe Hanks. I want to see the look on his face when we kick his teeth down his throat." He paused, casting an almost impish grin at Carl. "Figuratively speaking, of course."

"Of course."

Billy Sunday stood outside the chamber in which the review board had formally been convened. The polished mahogany door was cracked open several inches, so that he could observe without being seen.

Captain Hanks presided, and he had just called on Dr. Cudahy to present Chief Brashear for examination.

"I can't find him, sir," Cudahy sheepishly replied.

"What do you mean, you can't find him? Chief Brashear is the only black diver in the entire United States Navy, and he only has one leg. How hard can he be to locate?"

Dr. Cudahy wriggled like a fish on a hook. "Well, sir, he wasn't in his room when I went to get him. It seems he has been transferred."

"To where?" Captain Hanks demanded. "On whose orders?"

That was Sunday's cue. Nonchalantly ambling into the room, he announced, "He signed his own orders."

Captain Hanks stiffened as the rest of the officers on the review board glanced at one another in confusion. "You!" Hanks bleated in mixed surprise and fear, and immediately buttonholed an aide behind him. "Call the shore patrol! I want them up here—"

"Relax, Cap," Sunday said, advancing to the table. "I just want to talk. I'm not here to beat you up again. Although the idea is tempting."

"Don't tell me you have something to do with all this?" Hanks was slow on the uptake but he wasn't stupid. "Then you must know where Chief Brashear is. All right, spill."

Sunday calmly puffed on his pipe.

"I see," Captain Hanks said testily. "You refuse to answer? Suit yourself. As of this moment, Chief Carl Brashear is officially considered AWOL. I'll order the shore patrol to track him down and arrest him."

"No, you won't," Sunday said.

Hanks started to surge out of his chair. "Sunday, you arrogant, insufferable son of a—" Catching himself, he calmly sank back down. "But what else should I expect from the likes of you?"

Sunday dismissed the insult with a grin. "They'd never find him, anyway. I only have your best interests at heart."

"Sure you do," Hanks said sarcastically, and made a tepee of his fingers. "I'm on to your little game. Very well. What do you want?"

"Four weeks to train him. Then a full readiness evaluation and reinstatement hearing with the Chief of Naval Personnel."

"The Chief of—?" Hanks laughed. "At the Navy Yard in Washington? Preposterous! You must be kidding."

"Have you ever known me to kid you, Captain?"

"Forget it!" Hanks said firmly. "It's never going to

happen, and there's nothing you can do to convince me to give in."

"Think so?" Sunday rotated and nodded at Gwen, who had quietly entered and taken her place by the door. She opened it all the way, revealing a large group of reporters waiting in the hall, reporters Sunday had brought along as insurance. They burst into the chamber like a pack of wild dogs closing in for the kill, snapping photos and slinging questions.

"What's this about Chief Brashear being drummed out of the Navy?"

"Why was this review called behind his back?"

"Is it true the Navy went back on its word to him?"

Captain Hanks was a human beet. He raised his hand for silence, and when the reporters stopped, he said quietly to Sunday, "You seem placed on this earth to torment me."

"Can I help it if losing his leg to recover that nuke made Chief Brashear a national hero?" Sunday replied nonchalantly.

Hanks deflated like a punctured balloon. "You've outmaneuvered me this time, but I promise you it won't happen again." He wagged a finger for Sunday to lean closer so no one else would hear. "I'll grant your request on one condition."

"Name it."

"If he fails, you retire."

Sunday never hesitated. "He won't fail."

Facing the reporters, Captain Hanks said glibly, "Ladies and gentlemen, you've been woefully misinformed. Chief Brashear was allotted four weeks, and that's how many he'll have. I will personally schedule the evaluation hearing with the Chief of Navy Personnel."

"Captain," Sunday said, wanting to twist in one last barb. "You've done your uniform proud today."

*     *     *

The next month was grueling. Carl was pushed to limits he had never been pushed to, his body driven to the point of collapse in pursuit of his personal quest. From dawn until dusk he exercised; he walked, he ran, he skipped rope, he worked out on the parallel bars. Daily he did a hundred and one little things he had always taken for granted but now had to be relearned from scratch.

Billy Sunday stopped in two or three times a week to see how he was doing. At one point, seated on a weight bench while Carl did crunches, Sunday remarked, "Just watching you makes my gut hurt."

Puffing from the exertion, Carl softly counted, ". . . seventy-seven, seventy-eight, seventy-nine . . ."

"Have you heard from Jo?"

His concentration broken, Carl paused, but only for a moment. "No. Not yet. She won't let me down, though. I know she loves me."

"Always a fount of optimism," Sunday said. "Maybe that's why I hang around you—so some of it will rub off."

Carl slowed, galled his friend had so little confidence that he could patch things up. "Jo will be there when I need her. Wait and see. Gwen came back to you, didn't she?"

"About a hundred times. They should give awards for valor in wedlock. She'd be up for the equivalent of a Purple Heart." Sunday pursed his lips. "To be honest, I don't know how she's put up with me as long as she has. Things are finally stable, and I only hope I get to bring a little happiness into her life for a change."

"We do the best we can. No one can ask for more."

"Listen to you. Turning philosophical in your old age." Sunday snickered. "Now quit slacking off and get back to work. Or maybe you figure I'll carry you around piggy-back the day of your big test?"

That day came before Carl knew it.

A phalanx of officers and medicos were on hand to witness the initial challenge; Carl had to run a mile in the standard allotted time. He had on a T-shirt and shorts, his prosthetic strikingly pale in comparison to his good leg. Crouching, he awaited the signal.

Chief Sunday sidled over to where Captain Hanks and several companions were clustered. "It's a glorious day for eating crow, isn't it?"

"You've got it backward, as usual," Hanks said. "Are you ready to sign the retirement forms?"

"Never put your mule behind the plow, Captain," Sunday said.

"What the hell does that have to do with anything?"

Stopwatches were raised. A starter gun was fired. Carl exploded into motion, running smoothly, fluidly.

"Your boy is looking good," Hanks admitted. "Not that it will do him any good in the long run. Pardon the pun."

The officer's smug attitude disturbed Sunday. Hanks gave the impression the outcome was a foregone conclusion. "What have you got up your sleeve?"

"I'll never tell."

Carl was rounding the track at a remarkable clip but he wasn't going flat-out, not yet, not if he was to complete the four required laps. Sunday crossed his fingers, aware one slip was all it would take to end both their careers.

"Are you planning to be at the review board?" Captain Hanks asked.

"No law that says I can't," Sunday responded. Out on the track, Carl was pacing himself, just as they had

planned. Sunday checked his own stopwatch and smiled.
He scanned those in attendance, hoping against hope to
spot a certain pretty face. But Jo wasn't there. He considered phoning her, or having Gwen do it, even though
Carl had made it clear, in no uncertain terms, that they
were to do no such thing.

No reporters were present, but only because Sunday
hadn't deemed it necessary. The mile run was a prelimi-
nary, the outcome strictly on his friend's shoulders. There
was no way Hanks could rig it, unlike the review board
later that morning. That was when Carl would be most
vulnerable.

Carl completed the first lap. He sprinted by, streaming
sweat, his eyes fixed on the track, his profile the picture
of pure determination.

"Tell me something, Captain," Sunday prodded. "Why
do you go out of your way to make the lives of others
a living hell?"

"I'd resent that if it were true," Hanks said without
looking at him. "But the fact is, only those who won't
toe the line get my dander up. People like Chief Brashear, and people like you. Men who flaunt tradition and
discipline. It's not personal. It's a matter of decorum."

Where had he heard that before? Sunday mused. "You
know, I used to say the same thing. But it's not true.
Everything in life is personal whether we're willing to
fess up to it or not."

Neither of them had another word to say until Carl
approached the end of the fourth lap. He had slowed to
half his former speed but he was running strong, still
looking good. As he jogged past, Sunday pressed the
button on his stopwatch and crowed, "Look at this! One
minute and five seconds faster than required! See you in
court, Captain."

Hanks smiled. "I wouldn't have it any other way."

\*    \*    \*

Two hours later Carl stood in his skivvies in front of the full-length mirror attached to the bathroom door and studied himself. His muscles were toned, with a healthy sheen to them. He was a model of physical fitness, except for the missing limb below his left knee. Swallowing hard, as nervous as if he were about to make a dangerous dive in rough seas, he nearly jumped when a young sailor rapped on the outer door.

"Senior Chief Brashear, Admiral Yon's office has confirmed. You will be meeting with the review board in about one hour, at eleven sharp."

"Roger that. I'll be ready."

But would he? Carl asked himself. Hopping to the door, he closed it, then hopped to the bed and sat down. He hefted the artificial leg, holding his future in his hands. A glance at the phone brought a frown. Still no word from the one he wanted to hear from the most.

Bending, Carl cinched the prosthesis into place. His newly pressed uniform hung in the closet. Retrieving it, he slipped into the shirt and was about to don his pants when laughter from outside drew him to the window. Below, a Navy officer on crutches was hugging a young boy about Jackie's age. The officer's wife came up and they kissed, and the whole family moved off, arm in arm.

Memories stirring within him, Carl went to his suitcase. From it he lifted his father's old radio. The engraving on the plaque stared up at him. "A son never forgets," Carl read aloud, and ran a finger over the crude letters his father had carved. "I never will, Papa," he said softly. "I never will."

Carl dressed swiftly. At ten-thirty another knock on the door brought him from the bathroom.

"Are we set to go?" Billy Sunday asked, his face wreathed in pipe smoke.

"We're set," Carl confirmed. "How do I look?"

"One hundred percent Navy," Sunday complimented him. "And one hundred percent scared to death."

"Is it that obvious?"

"Only when you breathe." Sunday stepped aside. "After you. I have a cab waiting out front. Gwen went on ahead and is supposed to call if she gets wind of anything fishy."

Carl tried to stay calm. He honestly tried. But by the time the taxi pulled up in front of the mammoth building in which the examination was to be held, a horde of butterflies were loose in his stomach and his palms were clammy. He climbed stiffly out and craned his neck to see the summit of the imposing edifice.

"Don't let it get to you, Cookie. Navy bigwigs love to put on a show. The bigger the building, the bigger the circus."

Sunday shoved a glass door open and Carl entered. His unease mounted. For over a hundred years, the fates of Navy men had been decided in the hallowed halls ahead. He paused to read the director but Sunday snagged his sleeve.

"This way, Cookie."

Portraits of Navy legends adorned the walls, heroes all, men of renown. Carl had the ridiculous impression they were staring accusingly at him, offended by his impudence. Here he was, preparing to buck the system, to take on the top Navy brass and persuade them to bend the rules to allow him to do something no one had ever done before.

"Here we are," Sunday said.

A pair of husky Marine guards flanked a pair of ornate doors. One of the Marines glanced at a slip of paper in his hand as they approached, then moved to bar their way. "I'm sorry, sir," he addressed Sunday, "but we're under specific orders not to admit you."

Carl looked at his friend worriedly.

"Hanks," Sunday deduced, and sighed. "The man should have his name listed in the dictionary as a synonym for 'asshole.'" He clapped Carl on the shoulder. "I guess you're on your own. Get in there and show them what a real Navy man is made of."

Squaring his shoulders, Carl walked into the chamber. The immensity of the room was unsettling. It was monumentally vast, more fitting for a cathedral than a military installation. High polished walls arced toward a vaulted ceiling, wreathed by tobacco smoke from the scores of spectators crammed into every available seat. Some were civilians. A section near the front was exclusively reserved for the press.

A hush fell as Carl advanced toward a lone chair set apart from all the others. Beyond it, arrayed in tiered semicircles, were long tables occupied by some of the highest-ranking officers in the U.S. Navy. Among them was the kindly face of Admiral Yon.

Slowing, Carl scanned the crowd, praying Jo was present, but the only one he recognized was Gwen, seated near the rail. She smiled encouragement.

"Senior Chief Brashear, you may approach the board," an officer called out.

Ramrod-straight, Carl strode to the chair. He had never felt so small, so insignificant.

Directly across from him sat Captain Hanks. Speaking into a microphone, Hanks said, "You may sit down, Senior Chief Brashear."

Carl remained standing and executed a sharp salute. The move was another one of Sunday's tactical brainstorms, designed to make a favorable impression on the old-guard Navy officers in attendance.

Hanks was perusing a file. When he glanced up, he smirked. "The Army salutes indoors, Senior Chief. Not the Navy. Sit down."

"Begging your pardon, sir, but in the Navy I grew up in and have striven to serve, it is customary for a senior chief of my experience to receive a salute on an occasion of such gravity," Carl responded.

"We're in a new Navy now, Senior Chief. *Sit.*"

Carl held the salute. He was taking an enormous gamble but it paid off, judging by the expressions of sympathy that rippled across the faces of the older officers. Hanks noticed, too, but before he could do anything, Admiral Yon returned Carl's salute and Carl roosted in the chair.

"You know why we are here," Captain Hanks began frostily. "So let's get right to it. Expert testimony will be admitted into the record, testimony pertaining to your fitness with regard to possible reinstatement. Let the record show that you have met the standard physical requirements in prior examinations—"

"Sir, I thought I exceeded them," Carl made bold to interrupt.

"Yes, Senior Chief Brashear," Hanks said. "There is no denying you are in excellent physical condition. However, in light of your impairment, the question we must answer is whether you are capable of performing the duties required of a Navy diver."

The first expert Hanks called, to Carl's surprise, was Dr. Cudahy. Hanks asked a number of routine questions pertaining to the amputation and Carl's recovery, then showed his true colors. "So what you're saying, Doctor, is that in your esteemed opinion, Senior Chief Brashear is back to normal?"

"He has regained full use of his limb, yes," Dr. Cudahy said.

"That's not what I asked," Hanks snipped. "I specifically want to know if Senior Chief Brashear is as normal as, say, you and I. Can he do all the things a person with two legs can do?"

"More or less, yes."

"Elaborate on the less," Hanks said.

Dr. Cudahy cast a look of regret at Carl. "Well, he doesn't quite have the same degree of mobility someone with two healthy legs has. His agility and flexibility are reduced, but only slightly."

" 'Only,' " Hanks repeated meaningfully. "That's all, Dr. Cudahy."

The next man called up was a medical officer Carl had never seen before. Under Hanks's questioning, he presented a tedious account of how human weight pertained to buoyancy in water, concluding with, "If the subject were to become unconscious or deceased, his buoyancy patterns would fail to conform to current regulations."

Captain Hanks grinned slyly. "To break down what you've told us, if Senior Chief Brashear were to drown, he wouldn't float, right?"

"Yes, sir," the officer said.

Carl could only take so much. "Sir, I promise that if I'm killed at sea, I'll make every effort to die like a Navy man."

Many of the officers roared with laughter.

Hanks was not nearly as amused. "Your resolve is herewith noted, Senior Chief Brashear. But be advised that resolve is not always enough. You don't seem to think your artificial limb will hinder your performance. I say it's time to put it to the test." Hanks nodded at an assistant, who scurried from the chamber.

Carl's mouth went dry. Sunday had warned him Hanks would try something, and here it came. Shifting, he sur-

veyed the spectators once more, and once more was
knifed by disappointment by the fact that his wife and
son were not here to share in the most important moment of his life.

The officers were waiting for Hanks to get on with the
review. Some sipped water, others chatted quietly. They
all stopped what they were doing and glanced toward
the corridor when loud squeaking sounds issued from it,
like the creak of rusty wheels under an enormous strain.

Captain Hanks listened a few moments and smiled.
"Senior Chief Brashear, for the record, do you honestly
feel a man almost forty years of age, with just one good
leg—can you really compete with divers half your age?

"The question is, sir," Carl answered, "can they keep
up with me?"

More laughter greeted his comment, but it was sub-
dued as all eyes focused on the double doors. The two
Marines had just opened them, and into the chamber
rattled a huge four-wheeled cart being pushed by several sailors.

Carl's breath caught in his throat. On the cart was the
Navy's newest and best diving suit, and the most massive
ever constructed. A helium suit, it was called, and from
what he had heard, it was heavier than a ton of bricks.

"Senior Chief Brashear," Hanks said, a sneer in full
bloom, "you are looking at the future of Navy deep-sea
diving. It's the latest $HeO_2$ mixed-gas diving suit. It
weighs two hundred and ninety pounds. The men who
will use it will be required to walk twelve steps unassisted
before they can qualify to dive in it. Could you do that,
Senior Chief Brashear?"

Carl was utterly at a loss. When he had both legs, yes,
definitely, but he had no way of knowing if the prosthesis
could support that much weight. He had come too far,

though, to give up. "Yes, sir, I could," he replied confidently.

"I see," Hanks said. "Well, as much as I hate to prolong this another day, I will, in the interest of thoroughness, make arrangements for you to demonstrate your contention."

Carl's future was slipping from his grasp. "With all due respect, sir, I'd like to demonstrate it right here and now."

"Senior Chief Brashear, this is hardly the appropriate venue—" Hanks began.

"I want them all to see, sir," Carl cut him off, and nodded at the assembled officers. "I want to prove it in front of everyone."

"What you want is irrelevant," Hanks said, then suddenly reacted as if someone had driven a spear through his heart.

Sunday materialized at Carl's elbow. "I snuck in when the Marines were busy holding the doors open," he whispered, and swung toward the long tables to address the tribunal. "Captain Hanks, sir, I completely concur with your assessment. These slippery floors alone prohibit such a demonstration."

Carl couldn't say who was more bewildered, Hanks or himself.

"Chief Sunday, I don't need your advice," Hanks said icily. "If I were you, I'd head right back out that door. You're in enough trouble as it is."

An old admiral at the end of the table, older even than Admiral Yon, leaned forward and asked, "Who is this man?"

"Chief Leslie W. Sunday, sir," Sunday said before Hanks could answer.

"Weren't you the one who swam out of the *St. Louis* at Leyte Gulf? Held your breath for four minutes?"

"Five, sir."

"Those were the days," the admiral said fondly, and bobbed his head at Hanks. "Chief Sunday can stay."

Hanks rolled his eyes in exasperation.

To hide a grin, Carl looked toward the seats and was electrified by the sight of a pair of faces that had not been there previously, faces that leaped out at him, that set his blood to racing through his veins. In his overwhelming excitement he nearly heaved up out of his chair and ran over to them, but common sense prevailed. "Jo," he breathed in love and gratitude. His wife and son had slipped in unnoticed and were right beside Gwen. Suddenly he realized someone had said his name, and he tore his gaze from his loved ones and swiveled toward the review board. "Sir?"

"Is there a problem, Chief Brashear?" Captain Hanks asked.

"No, sir."

"Then let's get back to the point of this discussion, shall we? Namely, this is hardly the time or place for you to attempt a demonstration."

The others officers were watching Carl, waiting for him to prove otherwise. "Captain, I've spent most of my life in the Navy, trying only to succeed. I have never asked for a favor. However, my quest has come at great personal cost to those who love me. They, too, have made sacrifices. They, too, have endured great pain to support me. If I stop now, their suffering, their sacrifices, will have been for nothing."

Carl looked at Jo and she gently nodded. She understood. She was with him, with whatever he decided to do. The chamber blurred and he lowered his chin to his chest as if in thought when in reality he was composing himself, afraid he would start weeping out of pure happiness in front of all the ranking officers. Coughing to clear his tight throat, he continued, "So I'm begging you, sir. If I walk these twelve steps today, reinstate me to active duty. Give my career back. End my suffering. End the suffering of those who care for me. Let us go home in peace."

Captain Hanks gestured impatiently. "Chief Brashear, the business of the modern Navy is—"

"Forgive me, sir," Carl butted in, "but to me, the Navy isn't a business. It's an organization of people who represent the finest aspects of our nation. We have many traditions. In my career, I have encountered most of them. Some are good, some not so good. I would, however, not be here today were it not for our greatest tradition of all."

"And what would that be, Chief Brashear?" Hanks walked into Carl's trap.

Carl looked at Sunday and they both knew he was referring to him. "Honor, sir."

A majority of the officers smiled and nodded. Hanks saw they had been favorably impressed, particularly the admirals, and he exhaled loudly and grumbled, "Very well, Senior Chief Brashear. Get on with the demonstration. But I remind you—should you fail, your reinstatement as a Navy diver will be denied."

# CHAPTER THIRTEEN

Tension crackled. Spectators whispered and pointed at the bulky helium suit, and the officers grew somber.

Captain Hanks became his smug self again, confident his ploy would achieve the result he desired.

The tenders helped Carl in the monstrous suit under the watchful eyes of Billy Sunday. Sunday double-checked everything: every snap, every buckle, every lace, every fitting. "It looks okay, but I've never used one of these babies before," he whispered.

Carl grinned. "Did I hear right? Your first name is Leslie?" he chided.

Sunday ignored him. "How much weight can that leg of yours take?"

"I don't know. I requested a reinforced prosthesis to handle the extra weight of a diving suit, but not a diving suit this big, *Leslie*."

Sunday's nostrils flared like those of a riled bull. "It was my dad's name. Do you have a problem with that?"

"Oh, no, Leslie. No problem at all."

"Call me that again and I'll pop you in the mouth."

"In front of all these bigwigs . . . Leslie?"

Squatting, Sunday examined the artificial limb. "Carl, get serious. This thing won't support that much weight for long. It'll snap like a matchstick."

"Not if I keep most of the weight on my good leg," Carl said.

"Two hundred and ninety extra pounds on one leg? You'll pass out by the eighth step."

"Don't you get tired of always looking at the sunny side of things?"

Sunday muttered something Carl didn't catch, and stepped back. "Hat that diver!" he commanded, and the tenders moved to comply. Lifting the heavy helmet, fighting under its weight, the tenders slowly brought it down and secured it over Carl's head. As they worked, Sunday paced off a dozen even paces, then pivoted with parade ground precision. "Are you ready, Senior Chief Brashear?"

"I'm ready," Carl said. He had never been more ready for anything.

"Navy Diver, stand up!" Sunday ordered.

The tenders jumped to assist Carl but were waved off by Captain Hanks. "Leave him. He has to do it by himself."

Sunday's temper surged. "Captain, if I recall the regulation manual correctly, the diver may be helped to his feet. That's a lot of brass to sling up from a seated position."

"It's spun copper, Chief. We haven't used brass in a decade. You would know that if you bothered to keep abreast of new developments." Hanks smiled at the two of them, a smile as wicked and ominous as a hurricane on a dark horizon. "Furthermore, the new manual states that the diver must rise unassisted."

"That's what it says in the new book?" Sunday said skeptically. "If I may ask, Captain, how would you know?"

Hanks had them right where he wanted them and

couldn't resist gloating. "Because, Chief," he conde-
scended to say, "I'm writing it."

Carl's heart dropped. So there it was. The test had
been rigged from the beginning, but Hanks had cleverly
waited until the last moment to play his trump card. Now
they had no choice except to play by his rules or bow out.

Sunday was struggling to control himself. "I see, sir.
Too bad no one let us know so we could properly prepare. But never let it be said a Navy man isn't
adaptable."

"Proceed with the demonstration," Captain Hanks instructed impatiently.

"Navy Diver, stand in!" Sunday boomed with an authority born of thirty years of experience.

Carl took a breath and pushed upward, but to his con-
sternation, nothing happened. The suit wouldn't budge.

"Diver, square that rig and approach the rail!" Sunday
rang out.

Again Carl tried, every muscle straining. The weight
was incredible, far more than an ordinary suit, far more
than he had anticipated. He thought he heard his bones
creak. He did hear the prosthesis groan as he slowly
unfolded, sweat breaking out all over. Finally struggling
to a fully erect position, he swayed slightly and quickly
transferred most of the weight to his right leg. His knee
wobbled, threatening to give way, but after a couple of
seconds it stopped.

"Start walking!" Sunday thundered, and began counting the steps aloud. "One!"

The artificial limb made a horrendous popping noise
as Carl brought it down, and once more he switched the
weight to his good leg. A single step, and already he felt
more tired than he had after jogging a mile. To advance,
he had to push off on his right foot, then jerk the pros-

thesis forward in short hops so as not to place too much pressure on it.

"Two!" Sunday cried.

Carl carefully pushed off, carefully lurched forward, and just as cautiously slid his artificial leg up beside his foot. As he applied his full weight the prosthesis crackled loud enough for everyone to hear.

"Three!"

Marshaling his strength, Carl repeated the maneuver. His entire body quaked under the tremendous load, and for a terrifying moment he teetered on the brink of collapse. But with steely determination, he completed the step.

Sunday's eyes bored into the faceplate, into Carl's eyes, compelling him to keep going, to keep moving, because if he stopped his career was over. "Four!"

Licking his dry lips, Carl lumbered on. He vaguely recalled hearing a myth once about a guy who supported the whole world on his shoulders. At that instant, he was that guy. He was supporting what seemed like the weight of the entire universe. The heavy suit relentlessly bore down, grinding at his body, at his bones and joints, so that he walked awkwardly, shambling like the Tin Man of Oz, always a heartbeat away from keeling over. He managed another stride, and another. On the seventh he made the mistake of bending forward a bit too much and almost pitched onto his face. Regaining his balance, he launched into the eighth step. A distinct, sickening *crack* came from low down, but it wasn't the artificial limb that had succumbed. He halted as a moist, sticky sensation spread down his right leg.

Captain Hanks partly rose and stared at Carl's feet. "Good God. His leg is broken. Please, let's end this." Hanks glanced at Admiral Yon, and Carl saw the admiral sadly nod his assent. "Senior Chief Brashear, you will stand down."

To the astonishment of all those present, Billy Sunday shouted, "Diver, you will disregard! This is my detail!" It wasn't Billy Sunday, washed-up alcoholic giving the order. It was Billy Sunday in his prime. Sunday the master diver, Sunday the senior instructor at the Bayonne Diving School, who commanded respect and obtained the very best out of the men in his command. "Damn it, Cookie! Move your ass! I want my twelve!"

Gritting his teeth, Carl propelled the massive suit onward. Agony speared up his leg but he blocked it from his mind. *I won't give up!*

"Nine!" Sunday bawled, and commenced reciting the creed he had drummed into every trainee. "The Navy diver isn't a fight man. He is a salvage expert. If it's lost underwater, he finds it. If it's sunk, he brings it up."

Through sheer force of will, Carl shambled another step.

"Ten! If it's in the way, he moves it. If he's lucky he will die young two hundred feet beneath the waves, for that is the closest he will ever come to being a hero."

Carl's right leg was soaked below the knee, his left thigh was a wellspring of torment. Jerking like a man on high stilts, he took another uneven pace.

"Eleven!" Sunday smiled fiercely. "Hell, I don't know why anyone would want to be a Navy diver. Now you report to this line, Cookie!" He pointed at the shiny tips of his shoes.

Darkness sucked at Carl's mind, seeking to plunge him into unconsciousness. Resisting, he thrust his broken leg forward and followed through with the prosthetic, taking the last step. The helium suit tilted, and for a few harrowing seconds he thought he would fall on top of Sunday. Every muscle screaming, he righted himself and stood grinning deliriously at his accomplishment.

"At ease," Sunday said proudly, and shoved a chair up.

Carl collapsed into it, his temples pounding so loudly he almost missed the official pronouncement.

"The United States Navy hereby reinstates Senior Chief Carl Brashear to active duty," Captain Hanks said bitterly, and slammed a gavel onto the table, ending the examination.

A thunderous roar rose to the vaulted ceiling as everyone shot to their feet and applauded.

For Carl, the next several minutes were a whirlwind. At Sunday's crisp command the tenders sprang to strip the helium suit off. The moment they were done, Dr. Cudahy knelt and examined his leg, saying, "Your leg is definitely fractured. I need an X ray to gauge the full extent. I'll go for a stretcher. You sit here and rest."

Carl was too exhausted to do anything else. Officers and onlookers filed past, congratulating him, shaking his hand, wishing him well. Reporters snapped photographs and one even gave him a business card so he could call at his convenience and give an in-depth interview.

Admiral Yon walked up. "Chief, you've made this old warrior feel young again. It's men like you who are the backbone of the Navy."

Then the two people Carl had been waiting for stepped out of the crowd. Despite Cudahy's instructions, Carl struggled to his feet. "Jo," he breathed.

"Carl." Her face was haggard, fraught with worry.

Jackie looked up expectantly and Carl lifted his son, heedless of the discomfort. "I'll quit. I don't need a stripe on my arm to tell me I made it."

An eternity winged by, and a smile finally bloomed on Jo's lovely face. "The man I married never once quit in his life. Besides, how could I sleep at night knowing I deprived the Navy of such a fine master chief?"

Carl set Jackie down and Jo filled his arms. Jo, with her sweet scent and the delicious taste of her mouth and tongue and the velvety warmth of her body against his, in a kiss of total bliss. When she placed her cheek on his shoulder, Carl tenderly pulled her close, relishing the moment. His gaze drifted over the crowd and alighted on a figure at the periphery. Carl grinned.

Billy Sunday did something Carl had never seen him do; he snapped to attention and performed a salute. As Sunday's arm lowered, Gwen melted into it, and the two of them stared, smiling brightly.

Carl wanted to call them over to thank them, but a knot of officers passed by, blocking his view, and when the officers moved on, Billy and Gwen Sunday were no longer there.

"Did I hear something about a stretcher?" Jo asked.

"The doctor is making a fuss over my leg," Carl said.

Jo kissed his neck. "I intend to make a fuss over you myself once I get you home. A fuss you'll never forget."

A grimy bus hissed to a stop at the entrance to the Bayonne Naval Base. A young black sailor stepped down, claimed his duffel, and showed his orders to the shore patrolman on duty. The patrolman waved him in without batting an eye, saying, "Barracks C. Four blocks down, on the right."

The young sailor entered the base, his bucket hat at a jaunty angle. The streets were paved, the buildings recently modernized. Bayonne had a nice, clean, thriving spirit the young sailor liked.

The building that would be his home for the next six months was right where the shore patrolman had said it would be. Fifteen other young sailors lounged in front of it. Three of them were black.

A gangly white seaman ambled over and offered his hand. "You're just in time. Any minute now the senior instructor is supposed to show up. A real hardass, they say."

"I hear he's the guy who found that nuke," the black sailor said. "You know, over in the Mediterranean that time. I read about it when I was a kid."

"Me, too," the gangly seaman said. "Wow. He must be an antique."

A commotion ensued as the trainees scrambled to line up at attention. A solitary figure was striding toward them. His bearing, his appearance, his very uniform, radiated authority. He walked down the line, inspecting each of them. "So you think you want to be Navy divers?" he said, and gave them a look that implied they were out of their minds. "I'm Master Diver Carl Brashear, and I can tell you right now that only four or five of you will make it through this course. You think that you know what being a diver is all about, but you don't have a clue." Carl paused, then recited with passion, "The Navy diver isn't a fighting man. He is a salvage expert. If it's underwater, he finds it. If it's sunk, he brings it up . . ."

In 1968, Carl Brashear became the first amputee in U.S. Navy history to return to full active duty. Two years later he became the first African-American to become a master diver. He did not retire from the Navy for another nine years.

# A Note From the Editor

What follows has been excerpted from the transcripts of two interviews conducted by Paul Stillwell of Master Chief Carl Brashear at the U.S. Naval Station in Norfolk, Virginia. One interview took place on November 17, 1989, the other on March 2, 1990. As a non-continuous excerpt, every care has been taken to retain the integrity of the exact words spoken by both men. However, slight editing and transposition were necessary in some places to retain the flow of the narrative. Any unspoken additions, marked in brackets, are those of the editor. Furthermore, the reader will note that certain elements of the novelization are expanded or altered from the facts present in the interview, owing to dramatic license. This in no way, however, detracts from the true essence of Carl Brashear's heroic life story.

The full and unedited transcript of this oral history is available on demand, and can be purchased in its entirety from the U.S. Naval Institute Press. For more information, you may access the company's Web site at www.nip.org or call their customer service department at 410-224-3378 (local) or 1-800-233-8764 (toll-free). You may also contact them at the following address:.

Customer Service
USNI Operations Center
2062 Generals Highway
Annapolis, MD 21401–6780

# United States Naval Institute's Interview with Carl Brashear

To become the first black master diver in the Navy, Carl Brashear used a rare combination of grit, determination, and persistence, because the obstacles in his path were formidable. His race was a handicap, as were his origin on a sharecropper's farm in rural Kentucky and the modest amount of education he received there. But these were not his greatest challenges. He was held back by an even bigger factor: in 1966 his left leg was amputated just below the knee because he was badly injured on a salvage operation.

After the amputation, the Navy sought to retire Brashear from active duty, but he refused to submit to the decision. Instead, he secretly returned to diving and produced evidence that he could still excel, despite his injury. Then, in 1970, he qualified as a master diver, a difficult feat under any circumstances and something no black man had accomplished before. By the time of his retirement, he had achieved the highest possible rate for Navy enlisted personnel—master chief petty officer. In addition, he had become a celebrity through his response to manifold challenges and thereby had become a real inspiration to others.

Carl Brashear's composite portrait is of an individual motivated by a thirst for excitement and adventure. He found it in the Navy, and he found himself driven by a motivation to excel. He prided himself on looking sharp and doing his job well. His remedy for the obstacles he faced was hard work. His story is an example of what an individual can achieve when he is determined to meet his goals.

Paul Stillwell
Director, History Division
U.S. Naval Institute
February 1998

Paul Stillwell: Could you please tell me when and where you were born and what you remember of your early childhood?

Carl Brashear: I was born in Tonieville, Kentucky, in January 1931. That was in Larue County. When I was about six weeks old, we moved to a farm that was about three miles out of a little town called Sonora in Hardin County, Kentucky. My father was a sharecropper. I lived on the farm until age seventeen. During my early childhood, I attended school in a one-room schoolhouse.

PS: Segregated, I presume.

CB: Yes, a segregated schoolhouse with broken-out windows and hand-me-down books. I attended that school from the first to the seventh grade.

PS: I'm sure you learned a lot about hard work at that farm.

CB: Yes. We all had our chores to do. I'd get up before daylight in the morning. I milked three or four cows, chopped wood, and then I walked three miles to school. We went to school in the rain, snow, sleet, or what have you. Then, when we got to the schoolhouse, we had to build [a] fire in a potbellied stove. It would be around nine o'clock before the schoolhouse got warm enough for us to start our classes.

PS: What did you have in the way of brothers and sisters?

CB: Including my father and mother, there were nine of us in the family. I'm number six. We lost a sister when she was about six weeks old. The rest of my brothers and sisters are still living. My father passed away in 1974.

We lived on the farm. We thought that was a good way to live. We didn't have electricity, didn't have running water, but we were happy. We had a lot of love in our family, a lot of togetherness. The entertainment in the evening was my father telling jokes and playing with us.

PS: When did you first encounter prejudice?

CB: When I was about five or six years old. When we would be walking to school in the sleet and the mud and snow, the white kids would be riding the bus. That's when I realized what was going on. Of course, there were no movies in the little community that I lived in, but we would go to Elizabethtown, which is about eleven miles from where we lived, to see a movie or something like that. When we did, we'd have to go in the back of the bus. This was when I realized that there was prejudice.

PS: And apparently that segregation was a situation that was accepted by both sides?

CB: Oh, yes. It certainly was. We didn't know any different. We thought this was the way of life, and we just accepted it. Now, of course, in the little community that I lived in we didn't feel it as much as once we went to a larger city. Because in the little community we lived in, everybody knew each other.

PS: Did you have friends in the white community?

CB: Oh, yes. We had a lot of friends in the white community. They would come to our house and help sharecrop, and we'd all be around the same table. Or we'd go to their houses and sharecrop. They called it "swap working." We would all be in the same area—eating, laughing, and talking. If we had to stay at somebody's house, a lot of times they would sleep in the same bed. So we didn't feel the brunt of the prejudice in my community.

PS: Did you set goals for yourself in that period? What did you hope to be?

CB: I didn't set any goals for myself during that period. But looking back on my life now, I always was doing things that were exciting, daring things. I recall when I was thirteen years old, and this guy had a Harley-Davidson. He needed a part for a car, so I rode the motorcycle over to Elizabethtown to get it. Well, my mother found out about this. She ran down to the little station where you crank up one of those telephones to try to get the policemen to stop me on that motorcycle. But before she could get a telephone call through to the next town, I had been to the Western Auto, picked up the part, and [was] on the way back, riding a big Harley-Davidson.

PS: What other things did you do like that?

CB: Well, we had a creek called the Glendale Creek. I used to swim across that creek. I used to cut church on Sundays and swim certain distances. Gee, I was just a young kid when I went swimming in those lakes. That was a pretty daring thing to do. One time my father gave me a horse and a saddle, and I'd take him uptown, and he'd stand way up, you know. Then I had rope where I could rope a cow and things like that. I was always doing daring things.

PS: By the time you got to your late teens, did you have a better idea of what you wanted to do with your life?

CB: Yes. My brother-in-law was a soldier, and so at a very early age, I'd say around fourteen, I wanted to be a soldier or a military man. When I was seventeen, I went to enlist in the Army. The Army people were screaming and yelling at me. They had me so scared I didn't know what I was doing, and I failed the entrance exam. I was supposed to go back and take it in the next couple of days, but instead I joined the Navy.

PS: Why did you make that switch?

CB: Well, when I came back from Fort Knox, I stopped in Elizabethtown. I saw the Navy recruiting office and stopped in to talk to the recruiter. The chief treated me so nice, and I told him that I'd been to Fort Knox. He said, "Well, let me talk to you about the Navy."

PS: It's interesting that one person can make that much difference in your life.

CB: Yes. He didn't scream at me like the one at Fort Knox. Also, [the Army] had me in a very cold barracks where I was supposed to take an exam, set aside from other people, and I just failed the exam.

PS: What year was that?

CB: That was in 1948.

PS: That was the year that the services were officially integrated.[1]

CB: Yes, 1948. So I joined the Navy and never went back to enlist in the Army. Looking back now, I think I was better off, anyway, by coming into the Navy.

PS: Did you then go to boot camp?

CB: Yes, I went to boot camp in February of '48 in Great Lakes, Illinois. We were in an integrated company when I took my basic training there. From there I went to Key West, Florida.

PS: Great Lakes is a cold place to be in February.

CB: Very cold. Snow, sleeting, and raining I made it through boot camp okay.

PS: What do you remember about the training?

CB: Well, the training was very strict, and everything had to happen on time. They would do things to you to try to get

[1]On 26 July 1948, President Harry S. Truman issued Executive Order 9981, which said, "It is hereby declared that there shall be equality of treatment and opportunity for all persons in the armed services without regard to race, color, religion, or national origin."

you angry or see how much you could take, just a lot of harassment during the training. But the training was very effective. I didn't much like the food when I first went to boot camp. But about four or five weeks into the boot camp, I was eating everything I could find. I stole a pie one day.

The chief petty officer came and saw me and said, "Son, you stole a pie, didn't you?"

I said, "Yep."

He said, "Was it good?"

I said, "Yes, sir."

He said, "Did you enjoy it?"

I said, "Yes, sir."

He said, "Well, that's fine. We like to see people eat." He was talking to me just as nice as he could.

This was at noontime. And, man, I was telling all the kids I stole a pie and got away with it. At four o'clock, who'd I see standing in front of the barracks but the chief. He made me pull my watch cap down over my face, and then he had me walk in front of the Navy exchange, hitting on an empty pie pan with two spoons saying, "I stole a pie. I stole a pie." [Laughter] So I had to do that for two hours . . . I never stole another pie. As a matter of fact, I never stole anything else.

PS: Did you ever get any adverse treatment during your training because of being black?

CB: No, I did not, not in basic training. They treated us all equal and all the same, it seemed to me. There wasn't any favoritism or anything like that. If there was, I didn't notice it.

PS: How much choice were you given in what you could be right after you got out of boot camp? Did you have any other choices besides steward?

CB: Not immediately. I was assigned as a steward for squadron VX-1 at Key West, Florida. I didn't enjoy Key West too much. We were living on the seaplane base, and the only time that we could go swimming in the pool was on Saturday mornings. That was from nine o'clock until twelve, one day a week. We lived in, of course, the stewards' barracks, and Key West was segregated. We had one street we could go to for liberty.

But [it was] where I got out of the steward branch. I met Chief Boatswain's Mate Johnson, who used to work at Kinnock Ford here in Virginia Beach after he retired. I met Chief Johnson in sort of an unusual way. One day I went fishing over where the Navy crews were beaching the seaplanes, and I watched them. I met Chief Johnson there, and he arranged for me to get out of the steward branch and come over to work for him as a beachmaster. That's where I developed a love for the sea—from swimming out the side mounts to beach those seaplanes.

PS: Where does this myth come from that blacks can't swim?

CB: Well, I don't know where that came from. I recall we had a meeting in Washington, D.C., after I became a deep-sea diver—there was a lot of talk about why blacks couldn't swim. One guy said it was due to the bone structure. One guy said they had too much negative buoyancy. But my theory is that blacks just weren't exposed to that environment. They weren't exposed to swimming pools.

PS: So it's more a cultural thing, really.

CB: Yes.

PS: Were there any overt examples of discrimination and prejudice when you were out on liberty in Key West?

CB: Well, we couldn't go to the nightclubs that the rest of the people went to. I recall one night we wanted to go into the Club Tropics, and they threw us out. But as far as getting along, we never had any violence.

PS: How much chance did you have in that job to grow and learn and develop?

CB: Well, I learned how to get along with people, how to respect other people and do my job without somebody coming around watching me. I developed an attitude that "I'm as smart as you are, and all I have to know is what you want me to do, and just let me do it." I didn't develop an attitude that people were picking on me or people were putting me in a different assignment. I just grew up, and had a good attitude there. I didn't have that type of attitude in the steward branch [though], because I didn't think I should be shining shoes and waiting on officers and doing menial tasks. Even though I had a seventh-grade education, my GCT[2] was sixty.

PS: Sounds as if Chief Johnson was an effective "sea daddy" for you. What kinds of things did he teach you?

CB: He taught me basic seamanship up one side and down the other. He taught me how to be a good sailor, how to dress appropriately. He developed a liking for me, and he would take me out to his house sometimes and just sit down and talk to me. He told me how to do

[2]General Classification Test, an aptitude test administered to recruits.

things, how to adapt to various situations, and how to be a good sailor. That's the bottom line: to be a good man and a good sailor.

PS: There are a lot of things about shipboard seamanship that a boatswain's mate needs to know that you couldn't learn in the squadron. How did you pick up those things?

CB: Well, I had already advanced to third-class boatswain's mate there in Key West. When I went to my first ship, which was the USS *Palau*, I was a good wire splicer. You had to splice a lot of wire for the gear for those seaplanes, and we had to put in a lot of metallic sockets. The beach crew had a sewing machine in the beach house there, and I could sew well.

When I went to the *Palau* and reported in as a boatswain's mate, being the first time on a ship, well, he started me off in the sail locker—splicing wire, sewing, and what have you. I already knew how to use a boatswain's pipe, but I hadn't been on a ship to do it. I started off putting in extra hours, learning the fuel rigs and the anchoring and mooring methods.

PS: Did you enjoy shipboard life?

CB: I enjoyed shipboard life very much, but I didn't enjoy the USS *Palau*. I wanted to be a diver. Well, when I put in a request to be a diver, they disapproved it, and from there we just didn't get along well after that. The same thing happened aboard the USS *Tripoli*. I wanted to be a diver.

PS: What motivated you to want to be a diver?

CB: Well, what first motivated me to be a diver hap-

pened at Key West. We parted the lower block on a
buoy, and they brought out the YSD[3], a yard diving craft.
The guy put on a face mask and a shallow-water diving
rig and fixed our block. That was my first encounter with
seeing a guy dive.

Then when I requested it on the USS *Palau,* it was
disapproved, and they transferred me to the USS *Tripoli.*
We would ferry. We'd load up in New Jersey and go to
Bremerhaven, Germany, or Copenhagen, Denmark, or
somewhere in France and places like that. Then we de-
ployed to the West Coast, and were [also] just off the
coast of Korea. [Once] when the USS *Tripoli* was an-
chored off the coast of Corpus Christi, Texas, one of our
aircraft, an old TBM Avenger, rolled off of the jettison
ramp. This time they brought out a barge and made it
into a moor and dressed a guy up in a deep-sea diving
suit. I said, "Now, this is the best thing since sliced bread.
I've got to be a deep-sea diver." So I started requesting,
requesting, requesting to be a deep-sea diver. I finally
got into school in 1954.

PS: At what point did you feel that you needed more
education?

CB: Well, I realized I needed more education right after
I made third-class boatswain's mate. That's when I enrolled in the USAFI[4] correspondence courses.

PS: Were there any instructors on board, or did you have
to do it all yourself?

CB: All yourself. It wasn't like it is in today's Navy.

---

[3]A designation for a self-propelled seaplane wrecking derrick.
[4]United States Armed Forces Institute.

PS: That's a tough way to go to high school.

CB: Right. I took my GED[5] test and passed it in 1960. My first phase of diving school didn't require a high school diploma. But when I got into mixed-gas diving, they required [one].

PS: When did you make second class?

CB: I made second-class boatswain's mate in 1953. Right before I went to diving school.

PS: What do you recall about the diving school?

CB: The diving school was in Bayonne, New Jersey. That involved a lot of psychological stress, a lot of hard work. When I reported to the diving school, the training officer thought I was reporting there as a steward or a cook. When he found out that I was there to be a student, he called me in and said, "Well, I don't know how the rest of the students are going to accept you. As a matter of fact, I don't even think you will make it through. We haven't had a colored guy come through here before."

PS: That's a real welcome, isn't it?

CB: Yes. And he said, "But that's what you're here for." I said, "Certainly that's what I'm here for."
  I had about a week to hand around before the school started. One of the chief boatswain's mates needed some wire spliced. So I spliced a lot of wire and did a lot of work before the school started. When school started,

[5]General Educational Development test, equivalent to a high school diploma.

somebody in the school was trying to get to me. They would put notes on my bunk: "We're going to drown you today, nigger!" "We don't want any nigger divers."

So one day, I was going to quit, but I heard from a man named Rutherford; he was a first-class boatswain's mate from Arkansas. He was on the staff. He said, "Meet me at the dungaree bar this afternoon, Brashear." That's when you could go drink beer in dungarees. So I met him at the bar, and he said, "I heard you're going to quit."

I said, "Yeah, well, I'm not going to take this mess."

It made him mad, see. And he said, "You son of a bitch. I can't whip you, but I'll fight you every day if you quit." He said, "Those notes are not hurting you. No one is doing a thing to you. Show them you're a better man than they are."

And then we started drinking beer, see. And before you know it, man, I perked up. [Laugher] So I continued on in school. I graduated number sixteen out of a class of seventeen. I wasn't the anchor man. [Laughter] I was the first black man to graduate from that school.

PS: What do you remember about the actual training? What sorts of things did you study?

CB: Well, in diving school in those days, you started off with your regular PT[6] in the morning. Then the first week was orientation. The second week was physics. And then diving medicine and diving physics, of course. Then you had a period of nothing but just pure diving, where you do all your projects: your flanges, your underwater welding, cutting, hydraulics, and what have you. That was for

[6]Physical training.

four weeks. Then you had two weeks of demolition. We studied how to make boom-booms using primer cord [and] TNT. During those days it was composition C3, a plastic explosive.

Then the last few weeks we had salvage. That's when you learned all about beach gear: the mechanical purchases to pull stranded vessels off the beach; belly lift gear to lift heavy objects off of the bottom; and putting in metallic splices.

PS: Did your seventh-grade education handicap you during the classroom work?

CB: No, it did not. Believe it or not, I adapted. I picked up that training. I made good marks in the classroom. I'd write good papers. I never flunked an exam in salvage school. Not even physics. And you couldn't use a slipstick or a calculator either. [Laughter] I studied, because I knew they were looking at me. I couldn't fail, because I think if I had failed one exam, they would have put me out of school with the attitude there.

The diving school is geared to put a lot of stress on you. I know that, because I've been an instructor in diving school myself. It's geared to see how it can break you down, see how it can get you angry. One time I was putting a breastplate on one of the divers and dropped a wing nut. The chief saw it. So he made me walk around the parking lot with a deep-sea diving helmet on my head. [Laughter] Then I had to come back and do push-ups with that deep-sea diving helmet on me.

PS: I bet you were in good physical condition.

CB: Oh, yes. I was in fantastic condition. Even today, I'm in good shape. I go to the gym, work out, and fight a couple of rounds. I've always been a nut for physical fitness.

PS: Well, please describe that experience of going down in the heavy suit.

CB: Well, every dive is different, and when you get down there in the suit, you can't see. The lights would go out in Bayonne, New Jersey, after you put your head below the surface. It's a different world down there, and you know how the people are thinking about you up topside. You know they've got to pull you up. But you've got to have faith in those people up there. Even though they don't like you or they want to see you wash out, they're not going to do anything to you down there. So you've got to depend on those folks to bring you up. I always felt that they would be tending and taking care of me as a diver like they would somebody else.

PS: How far down did you go during that training course?

CB: The deepest place up there in Bayonne was 64–65 feet when we were making our dives. They would try to extend your bottom time so that you were required to make a couple of decompression stops. It was mostly ten-foot stops.

PS: This was to avoid the bends.

CB: Yes. Having the bends means nitrogen bubbles in the bloodstream or the tissues.

PS: So it's a matter of coming up gradually to avoid that.

CB: Yes. That's the purpose of the staged decompression.

PS: Are there any of the specific techniques that you remember from Bayonne about welding and demolition?

CB: Judging how to advance your rod—that makes a good weld—and how steady you are with your rod, because it's a self-consuming method. You have to touch the metal. People [who are] not hull technicians or ship-fitters make better marks in underwater welding than the hull technicians and the shipfitters. The shipfitters think, "Well, I'm a welder up here on the surface. I know what I'm doing." So they have a tendency not to be retrained. I didn't listen either when I was in a seamanship class in diving school. You're just overconfident. So I think that's what happens to the shipfitters. They don't listen, and they just don't want to be retaught how to weld.

PS: What do you have for a light source when you're working down below?

CB: In muddy black water, you don't have any light source. A light only works in clear water. You just feel. That's where good mechanical ability comes in, you see. You've got to be mechanically inclined. If you're not, you're not going to get your job done. That's very important in being a deep-sea diver.

PS: What do you remember about the explosives work?

CB: Well, we knocked some windows out of some people's houses in Swinburne Island. [Laughter]

The instructors would have us put two or three pounds of explosives together and go over and shoot it. Well, you know, we were good, so we put in a little more explosive. Well, this one particular day, the clouds were a little low. When you do a demolition job on a cloudy day you have to cut your explosives down if you've got a residential area or buildings somewhere, because it will only go up so far. [But] we mixed up some C3 and some dynamite and went over the hill and shot it. The sound wave went up and hit those clouds and blew against the hill and knocked out the people's windows, see. [Laughter] And the diving school got a telephone call.

PS: Was safety a big part of the curriculum?

CB: You know, they didn't stress safety like we do now. We weren't that safe. And, believe it or not, we didn't have that many accidents. A lot of times we didn't change the oil in our compressors or the filters or the loofah sponges like we were supposed to and get our air analyzed like we do today. We just didn't pay that much attention to it. We would breathe air off a compressor, and we'd come up and we'd feel oil on our lips.

PS: Was it straight air you were getting, or a higher proportion of oxygen?

CB: No, salvage school was just straight air.

PS: How long was the course?

CB: Sixteen weeks. I was accepted very well.

PS: I'm sure that was a great feeling of satisfaction for you.

CB: Well, when I graduated from that school, I could have stepped over the building. That was one good feeling when they called me up there and handed me that diploma. And it was sort of exciting, too, the way they did it. I graduated number sixteen out of a class of seventeen. And, of course, they gave the anchor man a spiel about the fact that he could have held the class back. Shoots was his name. Shoots and I were standing there looking at each other, didn't know which one was going to be the anchor man. [Laughter]

PS: They built a little suspense.

CB: Yes. So I was number sixteen out of a class of seventeen, but we had started with thirty-two people.

PS: So you were really sixteen out of thirty-two.

CB: Yes. We lost almost half of that class.

PS: What were the living conditions like when you were there?

CB: Terrible. Barracks with broken-out windows, and the windowpanes weren't making tack. One time it snowed, and we had to stuff blankets in the windows to keep the snow out. We lived in the old building right on the pier head where we dove. They said, "If you're going to be divers, you must be rugged."

PS: Did you have any choice in where you would go for your first duty assignment as a diver?

CB: No. I was only there TAD[7] from the *Tripoli*, so I returned to her.

[7]Temporary Additional Duty.

PS: Did you have a chance for New York liberty during that period?

CB: I lived with my first wife on 126th Street in New York.

PS: How had you met her?

CB: I met her back in Elizabethtown, Kentucky, when she was going to high school. All the family knew her; she used to hang around with my sisters when she was a little girl. We started dating and got married in '52. Then she finished beauty school and [became] a cosmetologist. We went to New York in 1953 and lived on 126th Street, because the USS *Tripoli* was homeported out of New York. When I got my orders to go to diving school, the ship was in Mobile, Alabama, and I came back over and started my diving school.

PS: What was your wife's name?

CB: Her name was Junetta, and we stayed married for quite some time.

PS: Did you have regrets about going back to the ship after this exciting work?

CB: Yes. I didn't want to go back to the USS *Tripoli,* because there were no divers aboard.

PS: What was the point of sending you back then?

CB: Because I was TAD. So I went back there in December of '54, and the exec, I guess, pulled some strings for me. I left in March of '55 to a diving ship, an ARS[8], the

[8]A designation for a salvage ship.

USS *Opportune*. She was homeported in San Juan, Puerto Rico. But she'd already got orders to change home ports to Norfolk, Virginia. I went aboard the USS *Opportune* and did a lot of diving jobs while I was aboard.

PS: Tell me some of the ones you remember.

CB: A gas barge sank in eighty-six feet of water off of Charleston, South Carolina, and we went down there to raise her. That was our first salvage job.

PS: How did you go about that?

CB: Well, we went about that by patching and blowing. We'd blow a hole in it for it to level out on the bottom. It was a YGON[9], and on the decks you had three hatches each side, port and starboard. So we patched it, and then we'd take off each one of those hatches and put a blow and a vent pipe on it. When we made her tight, then we pumped air into it using Leroy compressors.

But when you're blowing something like that, you've got to be very careful. The first time we raised it, we didn't watch our gauges and got too much pressure in it and ruptured her seams, and she went back down. What you're supposed to do when you start blowing is start cutting down on your air so you won't have too much air pressure inside [and] bring it up gradually. But we brought it up a little too fast, and she ruptured and went back down. Then we step-raised it and patched it and pumped it after that.

PS: How many men were involved in the job?

[9]A designation for a non-self-propelled gasoline oil barge.

CB: Well, an ARS has about eighteen divers aboard total, and the crew is about 100–105. That's a diver's paradise. I was a salvage diver, and of course, you had first-class divers and second-class divers. We didn't have a master in those days on board the *Opportune*. I think the Navy had only about six or seven masters during those days. So that was my first salvage job on board the *Opportune*. And there's quite a bit involved when you're salvaging something. Even salvaging a wreck, it's always miserable, it's always dangerous, and the weather seems like it's always bad. There's no pleasant salvage job.

Then we were on a training mission off the coast here out in the Virginia Capes laying beach gear. Remember an aircraft called the S-2[10]?

PS: Antisubmarine plane.

CB: Yes. We were in a two-point moor, getting ready to do some seamanship evolution, and we heard the plane sputter and mutter. Finally, she crashed. Well, we put ourselves in a dangerous situation. We took a work boat and put bottles of oxygen in it, because it was too shallow to get the ship in. We put a gauge on an oxygen bottle and dove and salvaged those people in that airplane on pure oxygen. And there was grease all over the water. Can you imagine diving?

PS: How deep was it?

CB: Fifteen, sixteen feet. You could see part of the plane sticking out. But we were diving on pure oxygen around all of that oil and grease.

[10]In 1962 the Grumman S2F Tracker was redesignated S-2.

PS: Why pure oxygen?

CB: We didn't want to put a big old compressor in our little work boat. We thought we were dong the right thing and dove on pure oxygen. You know, we could have blown up. We brought a YSD over there and picked that plane up, put it on the ship, and got the bodies out. We had to put wire straps onto different structures and pick up the plane piece by piece. When we would pick some of it up, well, it would break apart and go back down. Sometimes you'd have to go down and take a choker strap and put it around part of the plane. The safety officer on those jobs always wants the black box. Then you'd have to get out there in the mud and search for that black box.

PS: What other jobs do you recall?

CB: We had a job at Labrador, where we had cold, cold weather. We had to lay an underwater fuel line into the Air Force base there in Saglek Bay, Labrador. So we got the fuel line laid, no problem. Then the ship was coming up to make an anchor and tie up to the buoy. He was going to drop his anchor out here and then drift over to the buoy and then hook up his fuel line. But he lost his anchor, so we had to go find that anchor for that old merchant ship. The diver was a first-class petty officer name[d] Luzon, and we were exceeding the capabilities for a diver in the shallow-water suit. At that time, we weren't supposed to dive but sixty feet in a face mask. We were down about almost one hundred. Well, when you get down to that depth, you don't have the volume in the hose to get the air down to you. Do you know what I mean? So he dove at almost one hundred feet in that shallow-water gear, [with] that old "can-do" spirit.

And we gave Luzon a signal by tugging on the air hose and lifeline, and he answered. Then we gave Luzon a signal, and he didn't answer. We gave him another signal; he didn't answer. So we brought Luzon up; I was the tender. There he was—passed out, no mask on. He was starting to turn blue, so we gave him artificial respiration and brought him around.

PS: That makes your point, again, about the safety being sort of lax back then.

CB: Yes, it was.

PS: Please tell me more about the teamwork that's involved in a dive.

CB: Diving requires tremendous teamwork. You've got to know each other's capabilities. You've got to know a lot about your fellow man. Each diver requires two tenders. The minimum you can have for diving is four. You need the tenders, a timekeeper, and a supervisor. But in your deep-sea diving mode, you require more personnel. You have to have a compressor watch. You have to have two tenders. You've got to have a supervisor. Plus, your ship has got to be in a two-point moor. It requires quite a few people.

PS: How reliable was the equipment back then?

CB: The equipment was very reliable. As a matter of fact, in the 1970s I was the master diver at the Naval Safety Center for two years, and we researched records. We went back as far as we could go and found only two equipment failures that caused accidents. Most of it was personnel errors [such as] not following safety precautions. Most of the time they don't follow the decompression profile, or they'll dive a person that is tired, or they'll dive a man that is just not physically fit to be diving that one particular day, or weather conditions [are unsuitable].

PS: Sounds like that "can-do" spirit can get in the way of safety.

CB: That "can-do" spirit can do you in, and I'm a good example of that with my leg.

PS: Did you make first class on board that ship?

CB: Yes, I made first class on board in 1955 in Argentia, Newfoundland. My wife and I didn't have any kids in those days, and I didn't tell her I made first class. One day I came home in my uniform, and I had my new first-class crow[11] on while I was sitting around the house. So she was wondering when I was going to take my uniform off. [Laughter]

PS: You were wondering when she'd notice.

CB: Oh, yes, but she never did notice it until I finally told her, "I made first class." Boy, she was excited. Pay got up to $230.00 a month. We lived on 126th Street during those days, and my first son was born there on 126th Street. Then we moved to Long Island, and in 1956 I had my first tour of shore duty, in Rhode Island.

PS: Please tell me about that.

_____
[11]"Crow" is the nickname for the sewn eagle design that is part of a petty officer's rating badge.

CB: Well, I went to Quonset Point, Rhode Island, as a first-class boatswain's mate, and I was in charge. I was the leading petty officer at the boat house and, of course, for diving. That was a two-year shore duty. During those two years, I picked up a lot of dead people and a lot of airplanes, including one Blue Angel[12]. So the job up there consisted of picking up the airplanes that had crashed and running those boats. And during that tour of duty, I got a letter that I would be assigned with President Eisenhower for about 180 days.

PS: You weren't stationed at the White House, were you?

CB: No. When he would come to Rhode Island to play golf at Newport, I would take the 104-foot crash boat and meet the *Barbara Ann*[13] at Delaware and escort it to Rhode Island. I had thirteen people, two 20-millimeter guns on each wing of the bridge. I would carry Jim Hagerty and Secret Service people and what have you. One time Mamie rode with me when I escorted the *Barbara Ann*. I was very fortunate that I got picked for the job. One day I asked Jim Hagerty how he knew who I was when he came aboard my boat. He told me, "Son, we knew you long before we got there." [Laughter]

I really don't know how I was picked for it, because we had three first-class boatswain's mates there at the boat house and quite a few first-class boatswain's mates on the station. But when I was a second-class boatswain's mate and won "Sailor of the Year," they started calling me "Mr. Navy." I took a lot of pride in my uniforms, took a lot of pride in my appearance—peculiar some-

---

[12]The Navy's flight demonstration team.
[13]*Barbara Ann* was the presidential yacht.

times, I guess. I'd be on the ship and on some dirty job like the one I had this morning. Well, before I'd go back to work in the afternoon, I'd have on a clean set of dungarees. I was always sort of a nut for looking sharp. It could have been something down through the years that caught the eye of somebody. I really don't know.

PS: Did you get to meet the President?

CB: Yes, I met the President. He didn't talk to me as much as Mamie. Mamie talked to me about three or four times a week. But Ike didn't talk to me but about, maybe, once a week. But when I left, he gave me a little knife that said, "To Carl M. Brashear. From Dwight D. Eisenhower, 1957. Many, many thanks." And then I got an invitation to go to his funeral, too. The skipper of the *Barbara Ann* asked me to request to be assigned to their staff and they'd [put in a commission to] make me an ensign. But I had to turn that down, because my goal was to make chief and to become the first black master diver in the Navy.

PS: What else do you remember about the tour at Newport?

CB: Well, one of my sons was born up there. That's what I remember mostly. My number-two son was born in North Cranston in Rhode Island.

PS: Where did you go from Quonset?

CB: From Quonset Port, Rhode Island, I went to a ship repair facility in Guam. And there I stayed two years in a diving job with the exception of about seven months

of that TAD on an ATA[14] that belonged to the ship
repair facility. During this tour of duty, we did a lot of
underwater work on destroyers and a lot of demolition
work. We blasted out a channel while I was on board
going into a place called Merizo, which was a LORAN[15]
station during those days. We shot something like 60,000
pounds of explosives to deepen this channel three feet
to fifteen feet so they could get a fuel barge in. Sometimes we would shoot electric; sometimes we'd fire
non-electric.

On one particular day, we had a 500-pound bomb that
we had rolled under a coral head, and theoretically, if
you fire non-electric, it would have to go off—no other
way, it would have to explode. So we set our charge and
pulled the igniter. Then I held it to my ear, hearing it
burn. Then we'd go in to the beach and wait for it to
explode. It never went off. Now, this was supposed to have
been impossible. So now what were we going to do? We
gave it another thirty minutes, another thirty minutes,
another thirty minutes. We said, "Well, we've got to go
check it." Just as we were getting into the boat, that 500-
pound bomb went off. If it had been fifteen more minutes, we'd have been right on top of it. That was a close
call. Very close.

PS: Did you take up scuba diving yourself?

CB: Oh, yes, but I trained as a Navy scuba diver. We
phased in scuba in '56 and '57. I got about three weeks
of it while I was in Rhode Island, and we phased in with
the Scott hydropack.

---

[14]A designation for an auxiliary ocean tug.
[15]Long-Range Aid to Navigation.

PS: What are the advantages of that over the rig you'd been using?

CB: Mobility. Depth control. Freedom of movement. That's scuba over deep sea or the cumbersome diving suit. Quick jobs. During those days, you could dive to sixty feet in scuba; now you can dive to 130. And you don't need a tender if you dive with a buddy. You don't have to be tethered. If you dive in the buddy system, you would just keep contact with your buddy.

PS: What was Guam like as a place for your family?

CB: Very nice. A lot of recreation. It was just a very nice place to have a family. I liked it so I put in for a year's extension, and it was approved. So that would give me three years on Guam. I took the exam for chief and made it in about 1959. I put my new uniform on in '60, and they canceled my extension. So I said, "By God! You make chief, and it's a disadvantage." So then I had to buy all those winter clothes and come back to the States. But that's where I made chief.

PS: Where did you go from there?

CB: I left Guam and went aboard the USS *Nereus* in San Diego, California, and then on to first-class diver school in Washington, D.C., in 1960. The stay was short. I flunked out of first class. Blew it. Every diver that went to that school as a salvage diver and flunked out of first-class school left as a second-class diver. Many of them had flunked out. First-class school was a hard school, very hard.

Physics. Medicine. Decompression. Treatments. Ratio proportion, mixing gases to the proper ratio. I mean,

God, it was hard! Flunked it. They called me in and told me, "You're leaving as a non-diver." I could have gone through the floor. I'd been diving for seven years and left as a non-diver, went back aboard the *Nereus* and had to show up there as a non-diver, chief petty officer.

PS: That was probably the lowest point in your career.

CB: Man, I hit rock bottom. I said, "I've got to get off of this ship." So I got a set of orders to the fleet training center in Hawaii. I went there as the chief master-at-arms, non-diver, just regular chief boatswain's mate. A second-class diving school was in Hawaii, also. The man in charge of that school was Billie Delanoy. I knew Billie when he was much younger.

I called him, and I said, "Billie, I'm over here at the fleet training center."

He said, "What the fuck you doing at the fleet training center, Brash?"

I said, "I'm over here in the chief master-at-arms billet."

He said, "You always could lie good." But I convinced him I was over there [at] the fleet training center as chief master-at-arms. He said, "Come over here and see me." So I went to see him. And he said, "Well, shoot. You got to be on a diving billet."

I said, "Bill, I'm not a diver." Of course, we got into the details that I had gone to first-class school and flunked out and left as a non-diver. He hit the overhead.

So he saw my executive officer, and I went to second-class school from the fleet training center, graduated as a second-class diver, back from a salvage diver to a second-class diver to graduate.

PS: You mentioned to me that you had done some diving on the hull of the *Arizona*[16] when you were out in Hawaii.

CB: I recall diving on the *Arizona* the last of '61 and early '62 to determine how much of a list she had prior to putting a memorial on it. Of all the diving I did in my time, this gave me a different feeling. I got down and thought about those shipmates down there that didn't make it out. It seemed like it was a different atmosphere, a different experience. You get a different feeling diving on the *Arizona* than you did any other place.

PS: What was your next duty?

CB: While I was still at the fleet training center, I got TAD orders and went to Joint Task Force Eight as a diver for nuclear testing. I did my 180 days there at Joint Task Force Eight on Johnston Island and Christmas Island, testing those nuclear bombs. The Thor missiles. I ran YTB-262[17] while I was there. I was there as a tug skipper and as a diver. I was recommended for the Joint Service Medal and got it. So that was an exciting tour, watching them shoot the Thor missile [and the] high altitude bombs over there.

PS: Was there any concern about radiation during those tests?

CB: Yes. Film badges would read a little high, you know, and a couple of guys had to leave the island a couple of

---

[16]The battleship *Arizona* (BB-39) was hit by Japanese bombers while moored at Pearl Harbor on December 7, 1941. The ship burned for three days; of the 1,514 crew members 1,177 were killed. It became a permanent memorial in 1962.

[17]A designation for a self-propelled harbor tug.

times. When they shot the Thor missile at Christmas Island, my wife took pictures at Hawaii just like daylight. The high-altitude bombs on Christmas Island—oh, my God! That was a fireball up there! And the aftershock. You'd have to get in a kneeling position and be under this tent. You couldn't look at it. When they'd shoot one of those twenty-or thirty-megaton bombs, it would rock that island.

PS: What do you remember about your duty on board the USS *Coucal*?

CB: Lot of hard work with the four-point moors, training for rescuing personnel out of a submarine and just preparing myself for first-class school and going to sea a lot, making the WestPac[18] cruises. We went to Okinawa and the Philippines, Japan. Our skipper was George Stenke. He invented the Stenke hood [that] is used for making a buoyant ascent out of a submarine; you can breathe freely all the way to the surface. He was the daddy of the Stenke hood, and I helped him quite a bit on it and worked with him. I've trained with it quite a bit since then. It was a good tour of duty. I learned a lot on there. We had a master diver there named Flanagan, and he would help me prepare myself for first-class school.

I studied math from 1961 to 1963, day and night. Got a set of orders to go to the first-class diving school in Washington, D.C. Now, I'm reporting into the school with the attitude that, "Hey, I'm a salvage diver. I only have to go fourteen weeks like the rest of the salvage divers and just get the mixed gas, physics and medicine and split and mixing and analyzing."

[18]Western Pacific.

The training officer come and told me, "You know how long you're gong to be here?"

I said, "Yeah, fourteen, sixteen weeks. Whatever it takes for me to cross-train."

He said, "No, you're not." He said, "You're going to be here twenty-six." He made me go through the complete school just like I'd never been a salvage diver. I went through twenty-six weeks of school.

We had seventeen graduate out of that class.

PS: Why do you have mixed gases as opposed to straight air?

CB: Well, when you dive deeper than 300 feet, you have to have some kind of breathing medium to [help] keep the mental and physical controlling center form an artificial atmosphere, cut down on the nitrogen narcosis. They had done the research years and years ago and found that helium and oxygen mixed in the proper ratio was a good breathing medium for that purpose. Because, see, when you dive below 300 feet, you actually exceed the partial pressure of oxygen. So you would go into oxygen toxicity—oxygen poisoning. That's the reason you breathe helium and oxygen.

PS: I've heard this term "rapture of the deep." Did you ever have any experience with that?

CB: Well, "rapture of the deep" is just like nitrogen narcosis. Every individual experiences that at four atmospheres or more; some are more severe than others. Now, on your initial training, they'll take you down to 287 feet in the chamber so the instructors can watch you. Everybody had a task to do at that 287 feet, to see which of those divers they had to be concerned [about] the most because of possible nitrogen narcosis.

While I was under that pressure, I figured my base pay for a year, and I wrote on the lines on the paper. Some people couldn't write on the lines. Some people couldn't take those pages and punch in the holes after a period of time. That was just how it affected them. I figured my base pay for a year and sat there and waited for those people to bring me back to the surface. Some guys would start laughing and couldn't stop. Nitrogen narcosis or "rapture of the deep" has different effects. Physiology has quite a bit to do with it.

I noticed that my lips would feel like they had a little oil or something on them. But as far as I'm thinking, I don't notice it.

PS: What kind of a compartment or a chamber were you in when they did this test?

CB: Decompression chamber or recompression chamber. Now they call it the hyperbaric chamber. Of course, you have viewing ports, and you have the inner lock and the outer lock. So when they run this test, they open both locks and put enough people in there that they can watch through three ports on this side and three ports on the other side.

PS: What sort of duty did you have after you passed the first-class diver's test?

CB: I went to first-class school and graduated number three. They didn't have a job on an ARS, so I went to an ATF[19], the USS *Shakori*. You cannot get the proper

[19]A designation for a fleet ocean tug.

qualification on an ATF to groom you for master, so I stayed on the *Shakori* for only one year, and requested to go aboard the *Hoist*.

Well, I got aboard the *Hoist* and was working and studying and preparing myself to be a master diver. This was when the accident happened and I tore my leg off.

PS: Please describe that.

CB: Well, in 1966, the Air Force lost a nuclear bomb off the coast of Palomares, Spain. The Air Force asked the Navy to recover that bomb, and of course, the Navy said yes. Admiral Guest formed the task force, and we started searching for that bomb in January of 1966.

The reason the bomb dropped in the water [was that] two airplanes were maneuvering; a fuel plane was fueling a B-52. According to what people said, it gained on the B-52 too fast, and they collided in midair. Three of the bombs' parachutes opened and landed in Spain. [But] one of the parachutes didn't open, and it fell in the water. So we searched for the bomb close to the shoreline for about two and a half months, and all we were getting was pings on beer cans, coral heads, and other contacts. So they made a replica of the bomb on the tender and then dropped it to see how it would [fall]. Then we went out six miles, and [on] the first pass, there the [real] bomb was, six miles in 2,600 feet of water.

The CURV[20] was going down to hook this thing up. I rigged up what I call a spider. It was a three-legged contraption that I was going to drop for this bomb to be hooked up to. I had my grapnel hooks and everything. We dropped that equipment in 2,600 feet of water, and

[20]Controlled Underwater Recovery Vehicle.

it landed fifteen feet from the bomb. The crew of *Alvin*[21] said it was amazing. The parachute on the bomb hadn't opened, so the *Alvin* went down and put the parachute shrouds in the grapnel hooks that I had on each leg of the spider. But the *Alvin* ran out of batteries and had to surface.

So we picked it up to a certain depth. Then we brought a boat alongside to [deliver a] crate and set it on the deck [so that when] I picked that bomb up I'd put it in this crate. I got the crate, [began] picking it up, and the boat broke loose. It was a Mike-8[22]. The engineer was revving up the engines, and it parted the line. I was trying to get my sailors out of the way, and I ran back down to grab a sailor, just manhandling him out of the way. Just as I started to leave, the boat pulled on the pipe that had the mooring line tied to it. That pipe came loose, flew across the deck, and it struck my leg below the knee. They said I was way up in the air just turning flips. I landed about two feet inside of that freeboard. They said if I'd been two feet farther over, I'd have gone over the side. I jumped up and started to run and fell over. That's when I knew how bad my leg was.

So there I was on the ship with my leg torn off[23]—no doctor, no morphine, six and a half miles from the [cruiser] *Albany*. So the corpsmen placed two tourniquets on my leg. He was interviewed for a program in the *Comeback* TV series, and he said that the reason he couldn't stop the bleeding with two tourniquets was because I was in such good physical condition and my leg was such a mass of muscle.

[21]A Navy deep-submergence vessel.
[22]An LCM-8 mechanized landing craft.
[23]Brashear suffered a comminuted fracture of the left tibia, in which the bones are splintered into small pieces at the site of the break.

Finally, we got to the *Albany,* which was just sitting there, this little old ARS was just going up and down, up and down. So they just literally pitched me up onto the *Albany,* and I hit the deck. *Boom!* I said, "Doggone, you didn't have to drop me that far." [Laughter]

PS: You were conscious this long?

CB: Yes, I was still conscious. I thought I was going to the sick bay on the *Albany,* but they put me in a helicopter toward Torrejon Air Force Base in Spain. They got the doctor off of the doggone cruiser. But they got in too big of a hurry. They didn't fuel the helicopter and couldn't make it. So they set me down on a dilapidated runway somewhere in Spain, waiting for a small two-engine plane to come and get me and take me to Torrejon.

Well, the accident happened at five o'clock in the afternoon, and at nine o'clock I was on the runway there. I lost so much blood that I went into shock. I don't remember the plane coming to get me, or getting into the hospital at Torrejon.

Now, I'm going to tell you some stuff that my doctor told me later in Torrejon. He said that when I was rolled into the emergency room at Torrejon Air Force Base, he said I didn't have any pulse whatsoever, no heartbeat, couldn't feel a thing. He said he told the medics to do something, but the medics were slow about doing it, and he said he thought he'd feel on me one more time. I had a very, very faint heartbeat, and that's when he found out I was alive. He said I was almost in the morgue. Right away, he started making arrangements to get some blood, and they pumped eighteen pints of blood in me, and I came to.

Then they were going to piece my leg back on and do

plastic surgery. Well, they were going to make my leg three inches shorter than the other leg. When they took the bandage off, my foot fell off. So they tried again, and it would fall off. It got gangrene and got infected. Well, I was slowly dying from that. So they transferred me up to Wiesbaden, Germany. There the doctor said that he could fix me, but it would take three years and could have me walking on a brace. So I raised all sorts of hell in that hospital.

So he said, "Well, do you want to be air-mailed out to the States?" That's the term he used.

I said, "Yes, sir! Air-mail me out of here!"

So he air-mailed me to the States, and I arrived in McGuire Air Force Base. Three days later, I came down to Portsmouth Naval Hospital. Here again, Dr. O'Neill said he could have me fixed in thirty months, have me walking on a brace. He told me all the different types of pins he could put on there. So I said, "Well, I can't stay here that long." I said, "I've got to get out of here. Go ahead and amputate."

So he said, "Geez, Chief! Anybody could amputate. It takes a good doctor to fix it."

I said, "Yeah, but I can't stay here three years. I can't be tied up that long. I've got to go back to diving." They just laughed. "The fool's crazy! He doesn't have the chance of a snowball in hell of staying in the Navy. And a diver? No way! Impossible!"

So they messed around with my leg so much and got it infected so bad I convinced them to go ahead and amputate. So they did a guillotine-type of operation, just chopped it off, cleared up the infection. A while later he said, "We didn't go high enough. We need to cut off another inch and a half." So they cut off an inch and a half to make sure they got it. This was in May 1966.

After that I kept saying, "I'm going to be a deep-sea

diver, doggone it!" By this time, I was reading some
books about a Canadian Air Force pilot that flew airplanes with no legs. I had also read books that said a
prosthesis can support any amount of weight. I also read
that you've got to develop an attitude that "Hey, look,
I'm going to accept this. I'm gong to make it work." I
worked toward it.

So they got me good enough to go to Philadelphia to
a prosthetic center. I got up there, and they told me it
would be about two months before they could fit me
with a temporary cast to shrink my stump. And so I
talked to them a little bit. About the next week after
that I had a cast on my leg to shrink my stump, and I
could walk with a cane. Then I said, "Well, I've got to
start working out." I was feeling bad. So I was working
out outside the hospital and broke my doggone leg off.
So I went over to the brace and limb shop and got me
another one.

They said, "How'd you do it?"

I said, "I was shadow boxing." [Laughter]

So they fixed me up another one, and they were telling
me how long it would take to make a leg. I got in good
with them. I'd go over there and work. I mean, I'd do
everything around the hospital. I didn't want anybody
doing anything for me. So I started working in the brace
and limb shop, helping them out. I'd go sweep the shop,
just do things.

About the third or second of December, they gave me
a leg. "Doctor," I said, "once I get a leg, I'm going to
give you back this crutch, and I'll never use it again. I'm
going to walk back to the hospital."

"No way! No way you can do that! Impossible!"

The day they strapped that leg on me, I gave those
crutches back to those people, and I don't have one
today, never used one, don't have one in the house.

Well, then I had to say, "Now, how am I going to get out of Philadelphia back down to Virginia to be around that diving school?" So I called to try to get a tango number.[24] They wouldn't give me one. So I said, "Well, I'm just gong to let it all hang out." So I caught a bus, came down to Portsmouth, [and] tried to turn in at the naval hospital; they wouldn't let me in. So they ran me back to Philadelphia. So [once] I got up there, I raised so much hell, they got me a tango number and sent me to the hospital over here in Portsmouth.

Chief Warrant Officer Axtell was the officer in charge of the diving school. I sneaked off from the hospital and went over and saw him. He knew me from salvage school, and I said, "Ax, I've got to dive. I've got to get some pictures. I've got to prove to the people that I'm going to be a diver."

He said, "You son of a bitch, if something happens to you, you'll ruin my career!"

I said, "I know that, Ax. I've got to dive."

So he said, "I'm going to take a chance."

He took a chance, and I got me a photographer. I dove in a deep-sea rig, dove in a shallow-water rig, dove in scuba gear. So I got the pictures, and then they held my medical board at the naval hospital. [Though] the nurse put me on report for not being at the hospital, Admiral Yon talked to me about returning to diving.

In the meantime, they were getting tired of me at the naval hospital, so they sent me to the naval station for medical hold. [Finally] they called me to Washington, D.C., and I had to spend a week at the deep-sea diving school diving with a captain and a commander. Quite a few people from BuMed[25] came over and watched me.

[24]The Navy uses tango numbers to authorize transportation.
[25]Bureau of Medicine and Surgery.

They watched me dive for a week as an amputee and run around the building, do physical fitness every morning, lead the calisthenics. I said, "Pretty good, a captain watching a chief work." I'd just wise off at them, you know.

So at the end of that week, they called me over to BuMed, had me stand outside of a door there like a dummy, and they were all sitting around a table. Captain Jacks was policy control, and he told me, "Most of the people in your position want to get a medical disability, get out of the Navy, and do the least they can and draw as much pay as they can. [But] you're asking for full duty. I don't know how to handle it." He said, "Suppose you would be diving and tear your leg off?"

I said, "Well, Captain, it wouldn't bleed."

I reported back to the diving school. They wrote a letter telling [them] what to do to me. They wanted to evaluate me for one year, and at the end of that write [a] report back to BuMed. You know, [they] dove me every day, every cotton-picking day—weekends and all. At the end of that year [they] wrote the most beautiful letter. Boy, that was something. I was returned to full duty and full diving—the first time in naval history for an amputee.

PS: That's quite an inspiring story, Master Chief.

CB: That was an accomplishment. Sometimes I would come back from a run, and my artificial leg would have a puddle of blood from my stump. I wouldn't go to sick bay. In that year, if I had gone to sick bay, they would have written me up. I'd go somewhere and hide and soak my leg in a bucket of hot water with salt in it—an old remedy. Then I'd get up the next morning and run. I was to lead the calisthenics every morning with the students. I was a chief. All the other students were white hats.[26] But I could hear them say, "That old chief—he's going to kill us. He gets out there, he ain't got no quitting sense on those calisthenics. He does this. He does that." They didn't know I was an amputee.

[In] the third week [of] second-class school you go to the swimming pool. When I went to the swimming pool, I came out with my other leg under my arm. Those kids down there almost had a heart attack. [Laughter] The same guy that was leading them had only one leg and was swimming them to death. But that would build those kids up, make them mad. That was sure a good motivational period for those kids.

At the end of that year, I was restored to full diving on full duty. I went to the boathouse at Norfolk Naval Air Station, where I served two years. At the end of those two years, I attended saturation diving training at the Experimental Diving Unit in Washington, D.C. While I was at the boathouse, I was division officer and also in charge of the divers. The boathouse had four divers, and our primary duties were search and rescue, recovery of downed aircraft, and whatever other underwater work that we might have to do.

During the period I was there, we had the opportunity to pick up a crashed helicopter off of the high-rise bridge near the Chesapeake Bay Bridge-Tunnel. We also picked up a helicopter that crashed at the end of the runway, right off of the boathouse, plus underwater work on boats, ships, and aircraft. We would be called upon from time to time to go and assist the civilian divers in underwater work on the ships that were in the Norfolk Naval Shipyard. That included plugging up sea suctions, main

[26]"White hat" is slang for an enlisted person below the rate of chief petty officer.

circulation valves, taking off and putting on prop guards for the screws.

PS: Could you describe some of the work on those helicopters and recovering those?

CB: Well, while I was there, we had to attend a school that they call "aircraft and helicopter salvage methods." If a helicopter or a plane wasn't damaged severely, you'd go down and find the lifting points and place slings on it. We used the YD, which is a yard derrick that has a crane on it. We would make a moor and use the crane to pick up the helicopter or the plane. You just have to use your own experience and ingenuity and salvage the aircraft without damaging it further. You always try to bring it up as intact as possible, where the people can investigate and make a determination of what caused the crash.

PS: How many men did you have working for you in that job?

CB: We had four divers, but the total crew at the boathouse ranged between forty-eight to fifty-two with three civilians. We had fourteen boats. That included a diving boat, which was an LCM,[27] and that was equipped with scuba diving equipment, which is a self-contained underwater breathing apparatus and, of course, the Mark V deep air equipment. When we had to use a crane, we would get it from public works.

PS: Handling that many men was a pretty good-sized administrative workload.

[27]Landing Craft Mechanized.

CB: Yes, it was. It was a challenging job. I was the division officer. I had a lot of paperwork. Plus, you had your civilians there with PDs—position descriptions. Of course, you got into a different situation when you were evaluating civilians rather than military people. So it was a challenging job, and a lot of responsibility for an enlisted man.

PS: Did you contemplate becoming either a warrant officer or an LDO[28]?

CB: Well, I thought about it from time to time. But, see, my primary goal was to make master diver, and if you accept a commission, then you cannot be a master diver. The requirement to be a master diver is E-7 [chief petty officer], E-8 [senior chief petty officer], or an E-9 [master chief petty officer]. If you become an officer, then you can only be a diving officer, and you can't also have the responsibility of being a master. My primary goal was to be the first black master.

PS: Well, you worked so hard for it, you didn't want to get promoted out of it.

CB: That's for sure. After I made master, I thought about going from E-9 to W-3 [mid-grade warrant officer], but I was a little too old. And then I enjoyed being a master chief. There's an old saying in the Navy, you know: "The master chief knows everything. Then when you go to the wardroom being junior, you don't know anything."

[28]Limited Duty Officer.

PS: How much training did you do in that job?

CB: Oh, it was a tremendous amount of training. We would get at least four or five drills in a week just on rescue. We would simulate a crash and monitor how long it would take to get a full crew on our crash boat. It was a sixty-three-foot crash boat that was equipped with gasoline Hall-Scott engines. From the time we'd sound the warning, we would try to get that boat out of the slip in thirty seconds.

Plus, there was a lot of training [by] showing films and slides and talking [about] aircraft salvage. Or if an individual set his plane down, and he still had a few minutes to breathe on his oxygen, how you go about getting him out of there and not get involved with the ejection seat. We had to train on the ejection seat, because if you dive on an aircraft, you have to know not to hit the ejection lever, because it will blow you away, too.

PS: Did you have any actual crashes during that time?

CB: Yes. One of the jets crashed over near Newport News. The pilot ejected, and all we had to salvage was the aircraft.

PS: Did you get any first-aid training?

CB: Yes. You'd get your regular first-aid training, and we went through all types of artificial respiration when we started diving. It was arm-lift, back-pressure method, and mouth-to-mouth resuscitation. It was quite extensive in medical and first aid.

PS: This was a far cry from the segregated Navy you had come into. Did you have any problem with people working for you who were uncomfortable with a black division officer?

CB: Not at the boathouse, I didn't. They were all very comfortable at this point. I recall my department head gave me a letter of outstanding commendation for the improvements and for the morale and the overall appearance of the boats and the boathouse itself. I tried to maintain high standards, and I think that's part of my nature. I've always had that "can-do" spirit, and I think that stuck with me even until today.

PS: Then you went from [Norfolk] up to Washington.

CB: Yes, I went from the boathouse to Washington, D.C., in 1970 and attended saturation diving school at the Experimental Diving Unit. Saturation diving is diving at deep depths and remaining [there for] long periods of time. A couple of purposes for this are to measure the reaction of the body and to see how a body would adapt to deep depths. We dove there at 600 and 1,000 feet. It was simulated in an igloo and a recompression chamber. The igloos have about twelve feet of water in them, and then you can pressurize them to any depth you like. You would work in the water for eight hours, and then at night you'd come back into the recompression chamber and eat, sleep, watch movies, make telephone calls to your wife. I completed that phase of training, and then I phased right on into master diver's training.

PS: What kind of gear were you wearing at those simulated depths?

CB: We would be wearing what we call a Titan II. It's a helium mask that fits right over your face, and you strap it to your head. It's on an umbilical, [so] you could swim the simulated distance. We were breathing a helium-and-oxygen mix. I believe it was ninety-four percent helium and six percent oxygen.

PS: Do you have anything else on your body—a wet suit or just swimming trunks?

CB: See, you can do that just in swimming trunks, because you can make the temperature of the water whatever is comfortable for the subjects that are down there. But now if you were diving off someplace like San Clemente, California, you may have to use a wet suit.

PS: What kind of sensations do you remember from being under that kind of pressure?

CB: Well, it slows you down tremendously. You will be thinking you are doing a job, but you haven't gotten to it yet. Or you will be telling someone up at the surface, "I'm getting ready to hook up this down-haul cable." Or "I'm getting ready to ride my bicycle." But you wouldn't be doing it.

PS: Is it hard to move your arms and legs physically?

CB: No, it's not hard. Just a mental thing. And a lot of times nitrogen narcosis will build up, even though you are breathing that mixture of gas. You'll [feel] like you're drunk or dizzy. You might get some joint pains, or you won't be able to equalize your ears. You have to stop and come back a few feet to be able to equalize and then start down again. And you have different descent rates going down, whatever the mixture is, but you're not supposed to exceed sixty-five feet a minute.

PS: Could that be cured if they had more oxygen in the mixture?

CB: No, that wouldn't solve it because you get too much oxygen, then you'll get into oxygen toxicity. And it affects individuals differently, whatever the individual's tolerance is. That's why we use four subjects, and we monitor the actions of each one of them.

PS: What kind of conclusions did the experiments come up with?

CB: We can put a man down to the continental shelf and get him back. See, that was one of the purposes of it, to see how you get an individual back from that depth, how you're gong to decompress him up here to get him back here to 14.7.[29] We hurt a couple of people, too, with this type of training. Decompression sickness can affect you in various ways. We have people who cannot control their urine, cannot control their bowels, they don't have the articulation of their limbs, their arms, their vision. When a guy gets a serious case of decompression sickness, they call it a central nervous system problem, and it cannot repair itself.

That's why at the Experimental Diving Unit we like to say that we [were] the guinea pigs. We learned a lot. From the time I started diving until the time I finished my diving career, it was amazing how some of us survived. We just learned a lot, and we were lucky [with] some of the things that were putting our lives in jeopardy.

PS: What's the greatest actual depth you've been to?

[29]The atmospheric level of air pressure at sea level is 14.7 psi.

CB: The greatest depth that I've been to in open sea was 380 feet. That was in a deep-sea suit.

So I had a two-week period from the time I graduated from saturation school until I went to master school, if [I] was approved. So I wrote my paper to attend master diver school, and everybody approved it except three masters. Three master divers gave me thumbs-down because I was an amputee. But they were overruled by the rest of the staff, and so I stared master diver school in 1970.

PS: You use this term "master diver." What does that mean?

CB: Master diver is a man that's proficient in all phases of diving. The highest position that you could hold in the diving community is master. The first prerequisite to being a master diver is that you've got to be an E-7, E-8, or E-9. You have to have a well-rounded background in diving, and then you request to be evaluated to be a master. Then you go to the school, which is now in Panama City, Florida. You go before a board, and the board will talk to you while you are there, what's expected out of you, and what they intend to do with you. There is no flunking or failing or passing or anything of that nature in a master diver's evaluation. You make it or you don't.

So you start five weeks of evaluation with four people watching you every day in all of the drills you can run. The people that are evaluating you are officers that are ex-master divers or master divers or the CO or the XO[30].

They put a lot of emphasis on emergency procedures: what you do if you hurt somebody, how you treat some-

---

[30]Commanding Officer; Executive Officer.

body for the bends, air embolism, spontaneous pneumo-thorax. All the diving diseases and accidents that you can encounter, that's what they will evaluate you on, because those things can happen. You could make 4.0 marks on all of your exams and blow a drill or emergency and you would not make master. And they will try to get to you any possible way they can. They rattle your cage any way [they can], because this is what can happen out in the real world.

Like you were bringing a diver up and you shift him to pure oxygen. Well, then they'll get a senior officer on the rack, and you might say "Stand by to shift to $O_2$." A lot of times he won't answer you or acknowledge, but you've got to get him to do what you want him to do. They'd see how you handle those situations.

PS: When did you make it?

CB: Tenth of June, 1970. There were six people in my class. Four of us made master and two didn't. The first guy went in, he made master. The second guy, he didn't make it. The third guy called in, he made it. Fourth guy didn't make it. The fifth guy made it. So I'm last. They called me in [and] said, "Senior Chief Brashear, the master diver's course does not give marks. Either you make it or you don't." They went on and on about what I'd been doing and where I'd been and all. And they would talk about my physical stamina, what kind of shape I was in.

I said, "Please don't talk to me, if you don't mind! Get to the point!" Then the CO said, "Let me tell you something. If there was a mark that we give, you [would have] made the highest mark of any man [to] ever come through this school to be evaluated for master." He said, "You did not make a mistake. We vote you master."

All the black chiefs that were in that area knew that I was at the school. They were just sweating it out—was I gong to make master? Had about eight black chiefs standing outside the school, and they found out I made master diver, they carried me to the club bodily. So I was the first black master diver in the Navy.

PS: Did you have competition from anyone else in this quest to become the first black master diver?

CB: Yes, a man named John Davis almost caught me. As a matter of fact, when I lost my leg, he said, "I got you now." [Laughter] But I made it. I lost my leg and came back up that ladder again and made it. I made it about a year and a half, two years before Davis did. He made it in '72.

PS: What qualities does a master diver need that those at a lower level don't need?

CB: A master diver is required to treat all types of diving accidents. He's to supervise and manage all types of diving, submarine rescue, salvage, [and] all phases of diving; helium and oxygen, air, pure oxygen and scuba. One prerequisite for a master is that he's required to have served a certain amount of time on an ASR, which is a submarine rescue vessel, and a certain amount of time on a ARS, which is a salvage vessel. You can be a deep-sea diver for years and years [as] a tender. It does not qualify you to be a master. And your quarterly marks have to be at a certain level.

Once you become a master, the only person on a ship that can relieve you of your duties is the captain. You have a tremendous amount of responsibility, too, because the welfare and lives of all those divers are in your hands.

You're supposed to have the expertise that you can look at a man, and know if there's something on his mind that would [reveal if] he's not supposed to dive. If he's not acting himself, you're supposed to question him and see if he's in a frame of mind to dive. In other words, they're your children. You have to look out for them because they belong to you.

I used to take them home—I call it "taking them home"—with me. I would think about each one of my divers, his personality, how he responds to different situations, how he acts under pressure. See, you have to know all of this.

PS: If a guy doesn't pass that course, is there ever a second chance?

CB: They can give you a second chance if it's not too big of a flunk, and they will put in your record whatever they recommend for you to do. "Beef up on this and return in such and such a time frame." Or they could put in your record, "Not recommended to return." That's left up to the board.

PS: Where did you go from there?

CB: From there I went aboard the USS *Hunley* down in Charleston, which was a tender for nuclear-powered submarines, and served one year. That was an exciting year for me. I was the R-7 division officer, which consisted of the divers, sail-makers, and the riggers. That was my first experience diving on nuclear-powered submarines and just regular old submarines; fast attacks and the boomers. Quite an experience diving around the cottonmouth snakes and alligators.

I spent a lot of time in the tech library learning about

the nuclear-powered submarines. That was a good education hooking up the TDU[31] that pumps the residue of the nuclear-power waste into the ship. We had to hook that up from time to time to pump it into our tanks. And we had to hydrostatically test it to make sure it wasn't leaking.

Plus, I had to go through radcon school to be able to be a radioactive worker. I dove around the submarines so much during that time as a master. I dove with each one of my divers. I had seventeen of them. And my film badge read too high, so they had to take me out of the water for a while, because I was getting too much radiation.

PS: Is there that much radiation just external to the submarine?

CB: Yes, especially when you're hooking up the TDU. And it has a tendency to leak during the hydrostatic test, so you have to be down there watching it or feeling around it. You have to dive on the nuclear-powered submarines when the reactors are critical.

There's a tremendous amount of diving on submarines. When a submarine comes in to the tender, you have to dive and make a security check. And then every other day you have to dive and make an underwater security check. Then you've got your ballast tanks you have to go inside and work on. You've got your missile doors. You've got your chain compressors.

PS: What sort of things were you looking for in these security checks?

[31]Trash Disposal Unit.

CB: Well, you were looking for foreign objects, somebody placing bombs on these submarines, and just giving the underwater body a thorough check. Then you have that call at three o'clock in the morning that somebody's placed a bomb, and you have to swim at three o'clock and show there's no bomb on your submarine. Well, diving on those submarines was just repetitive, and I wanted to get out and work on wrecks. That's the type of diver I was. I wanted to go to sea and make things happen instead of sitting at the pier.

We had one job while I was at Charleston. A submarine had returned from deployment, and this first class thought his wife had been messing around on him. So he went to beat her up. As a matter of fact, he stabbed her. Then he [went] up in back of a housing area called MenRiv Housing. I guess they named that after Mendel Rivers. And up there in back of that housing, we found his clothes, his shoes, everything was on the bank. So we determined that he had drowned himself. You could see the cottonmouths swimming on the surface. Big snakes!

So the security officer asked me if I would dive to search for the body. And I said, "Yeah."

So my divers told me, "You ain't getting me to dive in that water!"

So I told the security officer, "Well, my divers said that they wouldn't dive, and I can't dive in there by myself." I said, "My divers refused, and I can't order them." That's one thing: diving is strictly volunteer. I can't order them to dive.

So we went back to the ship. About two o'clock in the afternoon, a man named Steve Larson knocked on the CPO quarters door. He said, "Senior Chief, I'll go with you."

So we dressed up in wet suits, gloves, and everything, and we started swimming in that water around those snakes—you could feel the snakes bumping against you—and we found that body. The only reason that body didn't come to the surface was because he was hung up in the seaweed. Oh, man, he'd been in the water about three or four days. We found him buck naked, but there wasn't a snake bite on him.

PS: Then did you get an assignment of the kind you really wanted?

CB: Yes. In 1971, I reported aboard the USS *Recovery*, ARS-43. That was my home for the next four years. I was the master diver aboard there. We completed some good diving and salvage jobs.

PS: What kind of an atmosphere prevails in chiefs' quarters? I mean, you've got a whole space there full of experts in one thing or another.

CB: Well, the atmosphere in my chiefs' quarters was great. We had good working relations. I more or less had control. And that was something I didn't work at; it just came naturally. I was the president of the chiefs' quarters and the chiefs' mess.

PS: Did you have a special status with the CO because you were the master diver?

CB: That, and I was master chief of the command. Well, I had an open-door policy to the exec or the captain. But I always performed my duty in a different manner from a lot of the master chiefs of commands.

When you're master chief of a command, if a young man wants to come and talk to you, it's a policy he doesn't have to go see his division officer or his leading

PO[32]. He can come and talk to you. But if I thought it was something that the captain or the exec should know, then I'd go back to the division officer and tell him what I was going to do in case he wanted to defend himself. I just didn't run to the captain and exec and talk about somebody without first informing him.

PS: There may be another side to the story.

CB: Right. During the four years and eight months I was on the ship, with all the complaints I had, I only had two complaints during that whole tour of duty that had any validity for me to look into. There again, I went to the division officer. When we looked at the situation, the division officer said, "Damn, I made a mistake, didn't I?"

And I'd like to share those with you. We had a black guy on the ship who was a second class. Well, when he would put in for a standby, the petty officers above him would put on his chit, "This man is not qualified." But another second class would put in for a nonrated man to stand by for him, and they would approve it. So the second class came to me and told me about what was happening. I said, "Man, we've got to look into this!"

So I went and talked to the chief first. He said, "Doggone it, Master Chief, we made a boo-boo."

I said, "Yes, you did!" I said, "I've got to go talk to the division officer before I go up and talk to the exec."

So we met—the chief, the division officer, and I—and discussed what could we do to please the second class. We wanted to handle it on our level and not take it to the exec and the captain. So I went to the second class and met with him, just the two of us, and I told him,

"Well, they agreed that they made a boo-boo. What would it take to please you now to get this thing squashed?"

He said, "I don't know. I think the captain and the exec should know about it."

I said, "Okay. Think about it a couple of days." I said, "Now, this is what they will do. They'll call you and apologize to you. You know, that's a lot for somebody to come and apologize to you, especially one of those officers."

So he thought about it a couple of days and said, "Okay, Master Chief, let them come and apologize, and I'll forget about it," They did, and that was the end of that.

PS: What sorts of other complaints did you get?

CB: At the human relations committee meeting the whites brought a complaint that I would look after the blacks before I would look after the whites. And then I had to get myself in a corner and really look and see now, "How have I handled these things toward a black that I didn't handle them toward a white?" I had to do some soul-searching. Well, what I came up with was that I had a tendency to talk to a black in a different way than I did the whites, and this was unconscious. If somebody hadn't brought it to my attention, I guess I would have kept on. So when they brought it to my attention, I just apologized and said, "I'm sorry. I will try to correct it." And I appreciated the man that brought it to my attention. You know, I went back and I said, "Thank you, partner. I appreciate that."

PS: Now, to what extent does the master chief serve as kind of a "sea daddy" for the junior sailors?

CB: Well, he is the liaison between the enlisted and the chain of command. He's supposed to be there when they need him. If he can't solve the problem, he's supposed to be there to listen. Sometimes I found if you're just a good, effective listener and let somebody talk, they'll talk their problems out. That's the type of role that a master chief of a command plays. My secret is being [as] fair as I possibly can. I like to say that I was a leader by example. I wasn't too proud to get out and lend a hand on any job we had at hand, whether it was diving or rigging or whatever, and I was always available when they needed me.

PS: When you've got some kind of a potentially hazardous evolution up on deck, how did you, in your own mind, avoid being overly cautious after what you had been through with your leg?

CB: Well, I don't know. That's a hard question to answer. But I haven't been overly cautious. You know, I'm always looking out for safety, but I don't go to an extreme because I lost my leg. I just look back at that and say, "Hey, it happened." And it was for a good cause, because none of my sailors got hurt. Each time you go on a salvage job in one of those ARSs, it's dangerous. But I don't go overboard with it.

Before I [go] on a diving job, I like to have what I call a rap session. I'd always tell my divers, "I'm not perfect. If you see me make a mistake and you don't stop me, I'm going to punch you in the nose." [Laughter] You know, that was my attitude. I said, "We're all divers. We all go through these schools. Don't you let me make a mistake." I had a sign on my diving locker. "There's no one of us smarter than all of us." And I believe that.

PS: Well, from that ship you went to the safety center in Norfolk. What kind of jobs did you do?

CB: My primary job there was to investigate diving accidents. I would do an analysis to determine what caused the accident and write recommendations how to prevent more accidents in the future. I was [also] required to conduct safety presentations.

One job I did at the safety center saved the government thousands and thousands of dollars. During my tour of duty there, we had the Mark I dive system, and people had had some accidents with it. So I headed up a tiger team and conducted a field change on the Mark I dive system band mask throughout Europe—that was civilians and all—and got a letter of commendation for that. I did a field change on the breathing mechanism, and on the bail-out bottle connection. Then I bench-tested it, it proved satisfactory, and NavSea[33] approved it.

I lived out of a suitcase. I was always on airplanes going to the Med, Europe, [the] Pacific. I was all over the place in those two years I was there at the safety center. One year I investigated eighty-six accidents, and that's quite a job, plus answer all the "safety grams" that you get and look into different situations, plus giving presentations.

PS: Could you take a couple of accidents, for example, and just describe what you went through during your investigations?

CB: All of them are written in blood. I investigated an accident in California. It involved a lieutenant (j.g.) who

[33]Naval Systems Command.

wasn't experienced in scuba diving. Well, he was about ninety feet below the surface, and he started breathing hard. Well, when he started breathing hard, he thought his tanks were empty. So he went to his buddy to get some gas—or get some air, we call it gas—but he was too far from his buddy to make it. So he started to the surface. Well, he held his breath too long, and he caused himself to have an air embolism. So when he got to the surface, he was passed out, and the people on the surface didn't treat him properly, and he had permanent damage.

PS: Did you do any diving yourself during this period?

CB: I only made one dive during this period, and this was at the escape training tank in Hawaii. I went out there to dive and to reevaluate the Stenke hood. The Stenke hood was a buoyancy compensator, or a life vest so that if you made a free ascent out of a submarine, you could breathe normally all the way to the surface. I think that was about the only time I was in the water other than at the safety center. While I was there, they made the short movie called *Comeback* with James Whitmore. I had to go swimming for the underwater photographers to take pictures of me to make that movie. I [also] made my regular requalification dives—four every six months.

PS: Did you miss not diving as much as you had before?

CB: Yes, I did. I'd get sick when I'd go see somebody in the water and couldn't get there myself.

PS: At what point did you get remarried?

CB: I was single when I went to the safety center. While I was at the safety center, we would take tours around different clubs. I went to the chiefs' club here on the naval station, and I met this lieutenant. So we fined her for being in the chiefs' club during initiation according to how many stripes she had, and she didn't want to pay. Well, since she didn't want to pay, we were going to put her in leg irons and handcuffs and arrest her. But we decided, well, we'd give her a break, and all we had [her] do was put a white hat [filled with eggs] on the head of one of the new chiefs and then hit it with her fist and break the eggs. So that's where I met my second wife.

PS: She was the lieutenant?

CB: Yes. We started dating. Then we got married, and my domestic life was pretty good up until I retired out of the Navy. After that I went to college, and I think I was around her too much. We didn't get along after that, and we got divorced after she made captain. She's still on active duty.

PS: What's her name?

CB: Hattie Elam. She went back to her maiden name after we got divorced. Right now she's the chief nurse and director of nursing at the naval hospital in Charleston, South Carolina.

I was married to my first wife for twenty-one years. She and I had four sons together. And alcohol fouled me up in that marriage. I got to be an alcoholic. Well, I'm still an alcoholic, just recovering. But I got to the place [where] I'd drink too much and sort of fouled up my first marriage. So I turned myself in at the naval hospital in '78 and went through the alcoholic rehab program. It was there that I made the decision to retire.

PS: I'd be interested in your talking about that program for the benefit of others. What ways did that help you?

CB: Well, if you work your program effectively and do your inventory every day and do your psychodramas, as they call them, the psychiatrists and staff can almost determine why you drink. When you do your collage, the collage tells you a lot about yourself. I worked my program the best that I possibly could. I put all of my heart into working my program.

PS: Were they able to cure you?

CB: No, they weren't able to cure me. They weren't able to write in my record at the end of my six weeks that I was going to recover. They wrote in there, "It's a doubtful case that he will recover."

PS: Well, have you since put the kind of effort into that that you've put into everything else?

CB: Sure, I'm sober as a judge. They were wrong. I haven't had an alcohol-related incident since 1978. I can't say I haven't had a drink. But I can from this day forward. I may not ever have another one, but I've had a drink since '78.

PS: What sorts of withdrawal symptoms did you have getting out of the Navy? This had been your life for thirty years.

CB: Well, when it came time to get out of the Navy, I'd wake up some mornings and I would be so afraid, [with] butterflies in my stomach. What am I going to do when I get out? What kind of job am I going to get? It was frightening, knowing that I grew up in the Navy from the time I was seventeen years old. Now I was forty-nine years old and had to face that outside world.

I retired on the first of April, 1979. And what a retirement! I was going to retire aboard the *Hoist*. That's the ship I lost my leg on. But it got too big, so they had to move it to the gymnasium at the Little Creek Amphibious Base. They had it on the news about three days prior to my retirement, had [it] posted all over the amphibious base that I was retiring. They had a big banner across the gate. They had two TV stations there. Just a gymnasium full of people. They had the reception at the Wheel House; people were outside lined up.

We were living on Hialeah Street in Virginia Beach. So I went to QED[34] one day to see Norm Chalmers. He was a captain I used to work for [and] was the vice president of QED. So I just went over to see him. I had no mind of going to work. I just went over to see Norm Chalmers.

Norm said, "I've got a job for you."

I said, "No, you don't." I'd only been out of the Navy nineteen days.

He said, "We just got a contract to do a diving study for the Royal Saudi Navy. It won't take but six months."

I said, "Norm, I don't think I want to do it." I was thinking about the fact that my wife was getting transferred to Pax River, Maryland.

He said, "Well, what would it take? How many dollars could we pay you to do this study?"

So I told him what it would take. He said, "Well, let me go see the president." Bob Jones was the president

---

[34]QED Systems, Inc. The name is taken from the Latin phrase *quod erat demonstrandum* ("thus it has been proven").

of QED. So they came back and said, "We can't pay you that [but] we can pay you this figure."

So I thought about it. I said, "I'll tell you what. I'll do that for you for six months."

I conducted a $6 million diver study for the Royal Saudi Navy; there was $12 million in two sites. They just wanted to do one site and tailor the other site for Jubail and Jidda. When I got the diver study completed, OP-40-something in Washington, D.C., approved it.

At that time the *Forrestal* was down in Florida going through the first steps of the SLEP program. So [Norm] said, "If we give you a certain amount of dollars, will you go down there and do the electronics dry air system, the LP air system, and the HP air system for the SLEP program?"[35]

I said, "Well I guess I will."

Hattie was getting mad then, see. She was up in Maryland. So I went to Florida, and I did the SLEP inspection on the electronics dry air system and HP and LP air systems. So now I'd been with QED for about eighteen months. I was making a lot of money. So I did that, came back to Virginia, and then I said, "Norm, I've got to quit," and went to Maryland and went to college for the next two years.

PS: What did you get your degree in?

CB: I didn't. I got right up to graduating in environmental science and didn't finish.

PS: Why not?

CB: Hattie went to Puerto Rico. By that time, we were having trouble. I came to Norfolk. In Maryland I would

[35]High Pressure; Low Pressure; Service Life Extension Program.

have gotten my associate degree in eighty-some hours. But when I transferred my credits down to here, they didn't honor some [of the] credits. So I was going to have to go longer, and I just got hardheaded. I said, "Well, I won't go at all. I'll quit."

Then I went to work for CDI Marine in selective records. My job there was updating ship's information books, books of general plans. In the meantime, I put in my application to the area personnel to be evaluated as an engineer and technician, and it was approved with GS-5 through GS-9. Well, I'd been at CDI Marine about eight months until they needed someone for a job here at CAMSLant[36]. The department head had heard about me so he seemed to think that I was the guy to kick this thing off.

Here at CAMSLant they had this position because the environmental program and the energy program had gotten too big for LantDiv[37] to take care of as a collateral type of duty. Paul Rutkowsky, an environmental engineer, was doing CAMSLant environmental work. So they created this position here and brought me here as a GS-5 in November of '82, and the job has gotten so big it's qualified for a GS-11. That's what I am now.

PS: Could you talk some about the work you've done here?

CB: My title is environmental protection specialist and energy conservation specialist. I think since I've been here I've reduced the energy consumption here by thirty percent, not only here but in my component activities at

[36]Communication Area Master Station Atlantic.
[37]Atlantic Division of the Naval Facilities Engineering Command.

Sugar Grove, West Virginia, Annapolis, Maryland, and Driver, Virginia[38].

PS: How did you go about doing that?

CB: By good energy management without using dollars. That means watching the systems, keeping the boilers working at eighty-five percent to ninety percent of capacity—and that's good for a boiler—turning out unnecessary lights, turning off unnecessary equipment. Just good energy management without any capital investment in my procedure. I go out and talk and show slides and talk energy.

Since I've been here, I have never had to spend dollars on an ETAP project, which is an energy technology application program. Yet we've reduced energy by thirty percent—forty percent in Sugar Grove—just by good management. I don't talk BTUs[39] when I go out to give my briefs. I talk dollars. Because you can talk BTUs all day and people don't know what you're talking about. But you start mentioning dollars, and then you'll raise some eyebrows. I emphasize how we can take these dollars and spend them somewhere else.

As far as the environmental side of the house, I'm PCB[40]-free at Driver, Virginia. In Annapolis, Maryland, I have four PCB transformers left, but those transformers are well in compliance with the Environmental Protection Agency, because I've gone out and conducted my own dielectric strength test, analyzed my samples. I'm well in compliance with the exception of the concrete

---

[38]The Sugar Grove facility is a naval radio receiving site. Annapolis and Driver are radio transmitting facilities.
[39]British Thermal Unit.
[40]Polychlorinated Bipheny's, a toxic compound.

itself, and I'll never get in compliance with that. Sugar Grove, West Virginia, I'm well in compliance with the EPA. Our underground storage tanks are on track to be updated, taken out of the ground, or properly abandoned in place.

My major claimant is TelCom in Washington, D.C., and from the $140,000 I saved TelCom last year, I got another cash award. Every time someone goes up there, they will say how good our programs are in energy and environmental.

PS: It sounds like the studying that you did at college in Maryland paid off even if you didn't get the degree.

CB: Yes. I have put it to very good use. I'm the liaison for energy and environmental issues between NavCAM-SLant, the Naval Environmental Support Activity in Port Hueneme, California, the Chesapeake Division of the Naval Facilities Engineering Command in Washington, and the Atlantic Division of Naval Facilities Engineering Command.

PS: What sort of plans do you have for the future, Master Chief?

CB: Well, my plan for the future is quit working here maybe the end of this year and go back to one of the engineering firms and get a part-time job. My goal is to get up and be happy every morning. That's my plan for the future.

PS: Why are you leaving here?

CB: Well, there's a time you have to step down, I think, and I promised myself when I turned sixty that I would go out and get a part-time job and try to live the rest of my life on my retirement pay. Now, that was my plan until we got some projects in the mill that they asked me to stay and see through, and since CAMSLant had been so good to me, I agreed to stay.

PS: Any overall thoughts to sum up on your Navy career and your life as a whole?

CB: Well, to sum it up, I can honestly say that I reached my goal in the Navy. It was an exciting, rewarding career, but then it wasn't a bed of roses, either. I had my ups and downs in the Navy, but I would do it over if I could. I enjoyed the excitement of being a deep-sea diver. I grew a lot in the Navy. I don't think I could have made it in civilian life with the limited education I had and my attitude. I think the Navy was the best place for me to grow up and find myself.

I came here to CAMSLant with the old "can-do" spirit. And I've enjoyed it. I've learned a lot. I feel comfortable being in workshops with the professional engineers. I feel comfortable talking to senators, congressmen, admirals, [and] captains on the environmental program. I've had the occasion to meet, correspond with congressmen, senators concerning SARA—the Superfund Amendment and Reauthorization Act. I've set up workshops with them, briefed them. I've learned a lot here. And a lot of this stuff I'm doing now was foreign to me when I started here. But I set myself up a good library, and I know where to find it, and I make it work.

PS: What sort of progress have you seen in racial relations in your lifetime and in your career in the Navy?

CB: Well, I saw a lot of racial tension in my early stages of the Navy as far as down in Key West, Florida. When I first went there, blacks could only go swimming on Saturday mornings from ten to twelve in the swimming pool. You had certain places you could sit in the movie. That created a lot of tension. Aboard ships I have actually seen a couple of different standards for blacks compared to whites. That created a lot of tension, a lot of hate, a lot of discontent. I've seen a lot of people promoted, [leaving] blacks by the wayside, just on how you document their quarterly marks, what kind of write-up you give them. This will create a lot of tension.

I believe now that we've got programs for opportunity. People may not like you—they may hate your guts—but I don't think they can keep you down if you qualify and you have a desire to excel. Now, I'm going to use myself as an example. When I was on the *Opportune,* it was the first diving ship I went aboard. The boatswain on that ship told me he didn't like me because I was colored. But that didn't bother me. See, I didn't retaliate in not doing my job or trying to shirk my duty. He didn't like me [but] I wasn't working only for him. I was working for the captain, the United States Navy, and working for myself.

After a while, I had the highest quarterly marks of any boatswain's mate on the ship. [The boatswain] would invite people over to his house, but he wouldn't invite me. But I didn't let it bother me like some of the kids did in the Navy. I used to see guys in the Navy, blacks in particular—if they thought they were getting mistreated, they wouldn't want to work. I used to try to tell them, "You're not hurting them. You're hurting yourself." So I never developed that attitude. But I've seen a lot of tension build up, a lot of hate just by things like this going on.

PS: Do you think that true equal opportunity does exist in the Navy now?

CB: No, it doesn't. We've made a lot of progress, but it's not equal yet. There are some areas that we're lacking. For instance, look at the admirals. See, we've got a whole bunch of white admirals, but we don't have that many blacks. Well, now, a couple of them kept themselves down, because they didn't want to get out and take the responsibility of having a command. They wanted to stay at these universities. But in my opinion, there is something lacking as far as equality in that area. In the lower ranks, I believe that we are equal. But I don't believe we are in flag ranks and in the upper echelon.

PS: Well, you yourself are an example of somebody who's judged on the quality of his work, and obviously you've been judged as a success time after time.

CB: Yes, but I just have a different attitude. You know, "Hey, I can work with you whether you like me or not. I'm just here to do my job."

# Personal History of
# Master Chief Boatswain's
# Mate Carl Maxie Brashear
# United States Navy (Retired)

**Personal Data**

| | |
|---|---|
| Born: | January 19, 1931, Tonieville, Larue County, Kentucky |
| Parents: | McDonald and Gonzella Brashear |
| Married: | Junetta Wilcoxson in 1952; divorced in 1978 |
| | Hattie R. Elam in 1980; divorced in 1983 |
| | Jeanette A. Brundage in 1985; divorced in 1987 |
| Children: | Shazanta Brashear, born on May 17, 1955; died 13 July 1996 |
| | DaWayne Brashear, born on January 16, 1957 |
| | Phillip M. Brashear, born on July 4, 1962 |
| | Patrick S. Brashear, born on July 31, 1964 |
| Education: | Sonora Grade School, Sonora, Kentucky, 1937–46 |
| | Passed GED test in U.S. Navy, 1960 |
| | Charles County Community College, Great Mills, Maryland, 1980–82 |
| | Tidewater Community College, Virginia Beach, Virginia, 1983 |

## Dates of Rates

Seaman Recruit (E-1) through Boatswain's Mate First
    Class (E-6), 1948–55
Chief Boatswain's Mate (E-7) 1960–66
Senior Chief Boatswain's Mate (E-8), 1966–71
Master Chief Boatswain's Mate(E-9), 1971–79

## Dates of Diving Specialties

Salvage Diver, 1953–60
Second-Class Diver, 1960–64
First-Class Diver, 1964–70
Saturation Diver, 1970–79
Master Diver, 1970–79

## Decorations and Medals

Good Conduct Medal (eight awards)
Navy Commendation Medal
Navy Achievement Medal
National Defense Service Medal
China Service Medal
Korean Service Medal
United Nations Medal
Navy and Marine Corps Medal
Armed Forces Expeditionary Medal
Presidential Unit Citation
Navy Occupation Service Medal

## Chronological Transcript of Service

February 25, 1948: Enlisted in the U.S. Navy

February–May 1948: Naval Training Center, Great Lakes, Illinois—Recruit Training

May 1948–June 1950: Squadron VX-1, Key West, Florida—Officers' Mess; PBM Beachmaster Unit

June 1950–November 1951: USS *Palau* (CVE-122)—Deck Division; Motor Whaleboat Coxswain

November 1951–March 1955: USS *Tripoli* (CVE-64)—Second Division Petty Officer; Master-at-Arms; Temporary Additional Duty at Salvage Diving School

March 1955–June 1956: USS *Opportune* (ARS-41)—Deck Division; Salvage Diver; Section Leader; Repair Party Leader

June 1956–June 1958: Naval Air Station, Quonset Point, Rhode Island—Leading Petty Officer; Salvage Diver; Escort for President Dwight D. Eisenhower

June 1958–July 1960: Ship Repair Facility, Guam, Marianas Islands—Salvage Diver; Skipper of Yard Salvage Derrick

July–September 1960: Deep-Sea Diving School, Washington, D.C.—Student, failed the course

September 1960–March 1961: USS *Nereus* (AS-17)—Deck Division Chief Boatswain's Mate

March 1961–April 1962: Fleet Training Center, Pearl Harbor, Hawaii—Chief Master-at-Arms; Requalified as Second-Class Diver; Temporary Additional Duty with Joint Task Force Eight

April 1962–October 1963: USS *Coucal* (ASR-8)—Ship's Chief Boatswain's Mate; Second-Class Diver; Underway Officer of the Deck; In-Port Duty Chief

October 1963–June 1964: Deep-Sea Diving School, Washington, D.C.—Student, graduated as First-Class Diver

June 1964–September 1965: USS *Shakori* (ATF-162)—Ship's Chief Boatswain's Mate; Leading Diver; Underway Officer of the Deck

September 1965–March 1966: USS *Hoist* (ARS-40)—Ship's Chief Boatswain's Mate; Acting Master Diver; Underway Officer of the Deck; Repair Party Leader; In-Port Duty Chief

May 1966–March 1967: Naval Regional Medical Center, Portsmouth, Virginia—Treatment following the amputation of left leg below the knee

March 1967–March 1968: Harbor Clearance Unit Two—Under Evaluation at Diving School for return to full active duty and diving

March 1968–December 1969: Naval Air Station, Norfolk, Virginia—Leading Chief Petty Officer; Leading Diver

December 1969–June 1970: Experimental Diving Unit, Deep-Sea Diving School, Washington, D.C.—Saturation Diver; Master Diver Evaluation

June 1970–May 1971: USS *Hunley* (AS-31)—Master Diver; R-7 Division Officer; In-Port Officer of the Deck; Minority Affairs Officer

May 1971–June 1975: USS *Recovery* (ARS-43)—Master Diver; Work Center Supervisor; Command Master Chief; Repair Party Leader; Underway Officer of the Deck; In-Port Command Duty Officer

June 1975–June 1977: Naval Safety Center, Norfolk, Virginia—Master Diver

June 1977–October 1978: USS *Recovery* (ARS-43)—Master Diver; Work Center Supervisor; Command Master Chief; Enlisted Watch Officer; Repair Party Leader; Underway Officer of the Deck; In-Port Command Duty Officer

October 1978–March 1979: Shore Intermediate Maintenance Activity, Norfolk, Virginia—Master Diver

April 1, 1979: Retired from the U.S. Navy as a master chief petty officer and master diver

**Civilian Employment**

April 1979–August 1980: QED Systems, Inc., Virginia Beach, Virginia—Diving Study for the Royal Saudi Navy; USS *Forrestal* (CV-59) Service Life Extension Program

February–November 1982: CDI Marine Company, Chesapeake, Virginia—Engineering Technician

November 1982–January 1993: Naval Communication Area Master Station Atlantic, Norfolk, Virginia—Envi-

ronmental Protection Specialist; Energy Conservation
Specialist

January 1993: Retired from government service in the
grade of GS-11